D1007349
the
BOOKWORM
box

BB Easton

Published by Art by Easton

ISBN: 978-1-7327007-1-0

Cover Design by BB Easton
Cover Photography by BB Easton and stock photo
Content Editing by Traci Finlay
Copyediting by Jovana Shirley of Unforeseen Editing and Ellie McLove of My Brother's Editor
Formatting by Jovana Shirley of Unforeseen Editing

SUIT is a work of creative nonfiction based on characters and events introduced in BB Easton's memoir, *44 Chapters About 4 Men*. While the settings and many of the situations portrayed in this book are true to life, the names and identifying characteristics of all characters have been altered to protect the identities of everyone involved.

For that motherfucker Ken.

Full disclosure: I don't know what the hell I was thinking when I decided that giving all four guys from my memoir, *44 Chapters About 4 Men*, their own books was a good idea. The first three novels end in breakups, and the last one, this one, is about the most boring man in America.

He knows it, too. When I told Ken I needed help coming up with ideas for his book, he fucking laughed at me—*he laughed!*—and said, "Good luck with that. I'm boring as shit."

Yeah, I'm aware, asshole.

So, now what do I do?

I have to write *something*.

Marriage and babies? Is that what you guys came here for? The happily ever after? The story of how crazy-ass, pink-haired, spoiled-brat BB fell in love with an infuriatingly emotionless, living Ken doll? *Ugh.* Fine. I'll tell you how it happened, but don't blame me if it's boring.

Blame Ken.

That's what I do anyway.

PART

January 26, 2003

My ass might have been parked on Jason's swanky leather sofa, but my mind was on the empty apartment across the parking lot. The one I used to call home. The one I'd shared with my rock-star boyfriend, Hans, until I found him in bed with one of my best friends. The one I'd trashed on my way out the door, taking everything that wasn't nailed down with me.

Okay, I might have taken some of the nailed down stuff, too.

It had been six weeks since the breakup from hell, and even though I wasn't quite ready to revisit the scene of one of the worst days of my life, my friend and former neighbor, Jason, was having a Super Bowl party, and I needed a fucking drink.

Jason lived in the newest, tallest, fanciest building in the Midtown Village apartment complex. His unit had stainless steel appliances. Mine had Formica countertops and an apocalyptic ant infestation. During the months I'd spent pacing my vinyl floor and wondering where the fuck my live-in boyfriend was, Jason's place had become my home away from home. His friends had become my friends. And his plush Italian leather sofa—frequented by beer-drinking boys, double-malt scotch–drinking men, and a certain Gatorade-drinking guy—was a far more comfortable place to pout than my empty apartment.

Jason plopped down next to me on his sofa and threw his arm around my shoulders. He smelled like designer aftershave, and his crisp khakis barely creased when he rested his left ankle on his right knee.

"I missed you, girl."

Jason was only three years older than me, but he was already pulling down six figures a year at an IT firm and dealing recreational drugs on the weekend "to raise capital for his start-up." I, on the other hand, was an impoverished college student who still wore wifebeaters and combat boots like the '90s hadn't ended three years ago, worked a part-time job at Macy's, and couldn't even get my shit together enough to maintain a hairstyle. While I'd been busy trying not to have a nervous breakdown those last few weeks, my once-fierce platinum-blonde pixie cut had grown into something resembling a fluffy two-tone mushroom.

"I know, man. I missed you, too. Thanks for inviting me."

"Thanks for coming. I thought it was gonna take a goddamn miracle to get you back here."

I giggled. "You can't say *goddamn* and *miracle* in the same sentence. It makes no fuckin' sense."

"*You* make no fuckin' sense," Jason sassed back, shaking his head from side to side.

"Ooooh…burrrrn." I rolled my eyes as he downed the contents of his glass in one swallow.

"I'ma go get a refill. You need anything?"

"Nah, I'm good." I smiled, sipping my Johnnie Walker Red or Blue or Black or whatever the hell color he'd given me.

I had just settled in for a long night of staring at the TV, fighting off his yuppie friends' blatant sexual advances, and pretending like I knew jack shit about football when something by the door caught my eye.

No, not something.

Someone.

Time slowed down.

An invisible wind machine roared to life.

And Jason's newest arrival waltzed in with the grace of a Grecian god.

Or perhaps a fallen angel, considering his wardrobe.

Jason's mystery guest was tall and lean and dressed in black from head to toe.

He shrugged off his black wool coat and draped it over an armless chair in the entryway. He shoved the rolled-up sleeves of his black button-up shirt a little higher above his elbows, exposing two well-defined forearms. His shirt was tucked into a pair of black slacks that looked soft, not starched, and hung casually low on his hips. And, as he turned and glided toward the living room, he reached up and loosened the knot on a stylish, skinny black tie. Above that tie, I was pleased to discover a jawline that rivaled Captain America's, cheekbones for days, and short light-brown hair that flipped up in the front effortlessly.

He looked like a bad boy with a good job and a great body, and I was definitely in the market for one of those.

I canceled my pity party, slurped the drool back into my face, and formulated a plan. I was either going to fall onto the floor at his feet and fake a seizure or pretend to be choking so that maybe he'd give me the Heimlich maneuver. Either way, I was positive that it would end with him thinking he'd saved my life and us forming an instant, unbreakable bond.

I was about to make a dive for it when I heard Allen, one of the regulars at Jason's apartment, shout, "Ken!"

I looked around.

Ken?

Ken wasn't at the party. I would know. Ken was my Gatorade-drinking, athletic-wear-wearing, smart-ass-comment-making, kind-of-cute-if-you're-into-clean-cut-jocks—which I most definitely was not—sometimes study buddy. He wasn't—

My mouth fell open as Allen bounded into the living room, his bowl cut and big glasses bouncing on his head as he charged toward Jason's newest arrival with his arms outstretched. "Bring it in, bro!"

With a last-minute duck and lean, Mark McGrath-in-a-tie completely evaded Allen's attempt to tackle-hug him, smirking as his stocky four-eyed friend nearly crashed into the coffee table.

Oh my fucking God. It's Ken.

I suddenly had no idea how to act, what to do. Ken was my pal. I should have at least been able to say, *What's up?*, but I just sat there, hiding in plain sight, waiting for more signs of Ken-ness.

He'd already avoided human contact like a ninja.

Very Ken.

He walked into the kitchen and pulled a Gatorade out of Jason's fridge.

Super Ken.

And when that GQ-looking motherfucker turned and looked out over the living room, he smirked…at me.

Sooooo Ken.

I leaned forward and sighed with dreamy hearts in my eyes before I remembered that I was supposed to smile or…something.

There was nowhere on the couch for him to sit, so my first instinct was to get up. I was going to go over there and talk to him. I could do that, right? We were friends.

I stood and took three steps across the living room before I panicked and made a sudden right-hand turn, bolting out the back door onto the balcony. In January. With no jacket.

Like a fucking moron.

The vibe outside was totally different. White party lights hung from the ceiling, and the local alternative rock radio station was playing on Jason's outdoor speakers. Whereas inside, it was loud and bright and warm and chaotic, outside, it was dark and cold and still and melodic. A brooding song by Linkin Park was just ending, so I curled up on Jason's cushy outdoor love seat, lit a cigarette from the pack in my pocket, and enjoyed the moment as much as I could while slowly dying of hypothermia.

The moment didn't last long. Within the first three seconds of hearing the next song, I was already considering throwing myself off the balcony. As if it wasn't bad enough that I'd committed to sitting outside in the freezing cold, staring at the apartment across the parking lot where my entire life had gone to shit, the universe thought it would be absolutely hilarious to make me listen to "Falling Star" by Phantom Limb—the song Hans had written for me when we first started dating.

It had been their first and only radio single. Phantom Limb had been dropped from their record label soon after we broke up due to low album sales, but that didn't stop the local radio stations from playing "Falling Star" every fucking hour on the hour.

With nowhere else to go, I sighed and surrendered to my fate.

As I listened to the lyrics, really listened to them, it was as if I were hearing the song for the first time. It didn't make me sad. In fact, it made me giggle. And then laugh. And then cover my own mouth to shut myself up so that I could listen some more.

"Falling Star" wasn't some epic tale of fated destinies and true love, like I'd made it out to be in my mind. It was about a girl who was meant for bigger things than her lover. He'd tried to keep her small, but in the end, she exploded into a supernova, leaving him in the dust.

"You like this song?"

I jumped, my hand still clasped over my mouth, and turned to see Mark McKen closing the door behind him. He was wearing his coat and carrying mine.

A smile split my face wide open. I didn't know who I was happier to see—Ken or my coat.

Handing over my shiny maroon flight jacket, Ken said, "It's kinda whiny, don't you think?"

I burst out laughing as I pulled my coat on like a blanket. "It's whiny as shit!" I cackled.

I scooted over to make room for Ken on the love seat, but he retreated to the opposite side of the balcony, just like always.

Never too close.

"So, what's your favorite band?" I asked, taking a drag from my cigarette as if I wasn't in danger of losing my fingers to frostbite.

"Sublime," Ken answered without missing a beat.

Snort. "Sublime? Shut the fuck up."

"What's wrong with Sublime?"

He was serious?

"Nothing!" I backpedaled. "They're awesome."

"Then, what is it?" Ken arched a brow and leaned against the balcony railing, enjoying watching me squirm.

I enjoyed watching him watching me squirm.

"Um, *literally* all they sing about is drinkin' forties and smokin' weed."

"And child prostitution," Ken deadpanned.

"Oh, right." I giggled. "How could I forget about 'Wrong Way'?"

"I don't know. It's basically the greatest song ever."

"Hey," I said, distracted yet again by his appearance, "I like your outfit. Why're you so dressed up?"

God, I hope that didn't sound as creepy as it felt.

"I had to work. I'm usually off on Sundays, but a buncha assholes called out because of the Super Bowl, so I had to go in for a while."

"Guess that's the problem with being the boss, huh?"

Ken was the general manager of a movie theater, but he refused to let me come see any movies for free because I'd called him an asshole *one time.*

"Yeah, especially when all your employees are fucking teenagers." Ken smirked. "No offense."

"Whatever," I scoffed, throwing a pillow at him from Jason's love seat. "I haven't been a teenager in *months*."

I had terrible aim, but Ken reached out and caught the projectile before it flew over the railing. The movement was so effortless I think he could have done it in his sleep. Ken smiled and cocked his arm back as if he were about to bean me with it, but as soon as I squealed and covered my face, he gently tossed the pillow onto my lap.

Asshole.

Lowering my hands, I tried to give him an *eat shit and die* look, but one corner of my mouth wouldn't quite cooperate. It kept pulling up instead of down.

"You should try out for Cirque du Soleil with those skills." I rolled my eyes, pretending not to be as impressed with his former football-star reflexes as I was. "Then, you wouldn't have to work with *teenagers* anymore."

"Yeah, just carnies who don't speak English," Ken quipped.

"Excuse me? Those people are *performance artists*, sir."

Ken regarded me for a minute with a semi-smile and then asked, "Have you been?"

"What? To Cirque du Soleil?" I could hear the pitch of my voice already beginning to rise. "Oh my God, it's, like, my favorite thing ever. I leave there, and I just feel so…I don't know…stupid? Or uncreative or something. The stuff they do, the things they imagine, it's just…gah. Have you been?"

Ken watched my fangirling in amusement, then shook his head.

I gasped. I audibly gasped. "Oh my God, Ken! You would love it! You love art and music and Europe—I mean, you don't *love* them, obviously, because you love nothing, but—" Ken grinned at my usual jab. It was a joke but a truthful one. That fucker didn't feel strongly about anything, except for avoiding fun. "It's all of those things but better! They come every spring! You should go!"

"Maybe I'll check it out." Ken's face suggested that he was *not* going to check it out.

"Oh my God," I groaned, the Johnnie Walker in my bloodstream making itself heard. I pointed the red-hot tip of my cigarette right at his smirking face. "You're not gonna go because it costs money!"

Ken laughed, really laughed, and I wanted to hold the sound above my head like a trophy.

"I forgot I was talking to a future psychologist." He chuckled.

"Listen, buddy, you're gonna go even if I have to pay for it myself."

"Okay."

"Okay."

Wait. What?

Ken and I fell into a strange silence just as "With Arms Wide Open" by Creed began to play.

"Oh, Jesus. Speaking of whiny rock stars." I hopped off the love seat and took a few steps toward Ken to flick my cigarette butt into the parking lot below. "C'mon." I grabbed him by the lapel of his structured wool coat; it was the closest thing to touching him that I thought he would allow. "I can't handle this shit."

Ken came willingly as I dragged him back into the apartment, and I made a mental note.

Weird about hugs. Does not mind being dragged around like a dog on a leash. Interesting.

As soon as Jason saw us walk in, he barreled over as if there'd been a goddamn emergency. "Ken! Ken!" He stopped right in front of us, huffing and puffing. "What's your last name, bro?"

It was a bizarre question to ask someone out of the blue, but as soon as Jason had uttered it, I realized that I wanted to know the answer with the same degree of urgency. Every cell in my body leaned forward and listened as if Ken were about to tell us the winning lottery numbers. As if he'd discovered the recipe for calorie-free beer. As if whatever came out of his mouth next, no matter how unfortunate or unpronounceable or lacking in vowels it might be, would one day be my last name, too.

"Easton," he said.

Easton, I thought. *I like that.*

"So, was it weird, being back at Jason's?" Juliet, my best friend since middle school, was sitting in the salon chair next to mine. Half of her head looked like she'd stuck her finger in a light socket while the other half had already been woven into long, skinny black braids. She'd basically staged a style intervention to get me to come with her, and now that I was there, nobody knew what the fuck to do with my frizzy mop.

"What about a pixie? We could just cut all this off," the elegant, slender man standing behind me suggested with the flick of his bracelet-adorned wrist.

I looked into the mirror at the poor bastard assigned to me and sighed. "I just grew out my last pixie. I kinda want to do something different."

His face fell.

Juliet put a hand next to her mouth and whispered loud enough for the entire salon to hear, "She just went through a bad breakup."

"Say no more." He winked. "Revenge hair. I love it."

I turned back toward Juliet, remembering her initial question. "Yeah, it was super weird being back. Seeing my old apartment…but then Ken showed up, and—"

"I know! What about a Gwyneth Paltrow/*Sliding Doors* thing?" my stylist asked, gripping the hair on the back of my head in both hands. "We could take all this off"—he tugged—"and do a long, swoopy side bang in the front."

"I had that cut, too," I said with a shrug. "I was thinking I might want to *keep* some length this time."

André—I don't remember his name, but he looked like an André—grimaced at my request.

"You should go darker," Juliet's stylist suggested. She was rocking some effortlessly messy dreadlocks that had been dyed a deep reddish purple.

"Ooh, I like your color!"

"Oh my God, yes!" André exclaimed. "Burgundy. It would be perfect with your redheaded complexion. I'm seeing a sleek, angled burgundy bob. Like a sexy secret agent."

"I don't think her hair does *sleek*." Juliet snickered.

"Oh, it'll do whatever I tell it to, honey."

I glanced from stylist to stylist and then shrugged. "Okay."

André went to go mix the color, and Juliet pinned me with a knowing grin.

"What?" I snapped.

"You called him Ken."

"So? That's his name."

"You used to call him Pajama Guy."

"Well, that was back when he wore pajamas all the time."

Juliet laughed through her nose. "Those were workout clothes, dumbass."

If Jason was the brother I never had, then Juliet was definitely the bitchy, older sister.

I folded my arms across my chest. "Whatever. I have pants with drawstring waistbands, too. I got them in the pajama section at Target because they're *fucking pajamas*."

Now Juliet and her stylist were both snickering. "So, if he's not Pajama Guy anymore, what does he wear now?"

I huffed and glanced at the mirror in front of me, telepathically imploring my stylist to hurry up at the color-mixing station. "I don't know. *Not* pajamas. Like…a tie."

Juliet's face flipped from amused to confused in an instant. "A tie? Since when are you into guys in ties? You only like guys who look like they *rob* guys in ties. *At gunpoint*."

I didn't want to, but I laughed. "I know, okay? I know! But you didn't see him. It wasn't like a normal tie *ensemble*. It was...I don't know...*edgy*."

"Oh my God."

"What?"

"He could be your rebound guy!"

"No. Ken? He's *so* not my type. He doesn't drink or smoke or have tattoos or anything. He's probably never even been arrested."

Juliet's stylist chuckled. "Girrrl, you need a new type."

Juliet looked up at her. "What she *needs* is a rebound. Everybody knows the best way to get over a man is to get a new man."

"And new haaaair!" André returned with a bowl full of purple goo and abruptly swiveled my chair away from Juliet, severing our conversation.

As he worked his magic, my thoughts kept drifting to Ken. I had to admit, the only time in the last six weeks that I hadn't spent reliving every traumatic detail of my breakup with Hans were the few moments I spent with Ken the night before.

But could I actually date him? I mean, it was *Pajama Guy*. We had nothing in common. And besides, I barely knew him. Okay, so I knew most of his friends and where he worked and that he had gone to the same high school as me and that he'd quit the football team because he refused to be yelled at by the coaches. I also knew that he'd been backpacking through Europe and been to all my bucket-list museums and already knew more about Egyptian art history than I did when he offered to help me study for my midterms. And I was *very* aware of the fact that Kenneth Easton didn't drink or smoke or do drugs or eat chocolate or celebrate holidays or acknowledge birthdays or hug or do committed relationships or even say, *God bless you*, when someone sneezed because he was a stubborn, joyless atheist.

So, why couldn't I stop thinking about him?

Three hours later, Juliet had a headful of long, tight black braids; I had a sleek, angled burgundy bob; and everyone in the salon was probably dying of cancer, thanks to the number of chemicals it had taken to tame my frizz.

Juliet and I hugged goodbye in the parking lot and hopped into our separate cars—mine a ten-year-old black Mustang hatchback that I used to race for money before I was even old enough to buy cigarettes, hers a hand-me-down minivan her mom had given her when she got knocked up by her drug-dealing boyfriend at the age of sixteen.

Ah, the good old days.

Now, we were just a couple of stressed-out, single women who spent all our free time working to put ourselves through college.

But at least our hair looked amazing.

Juliet and I pulled out of the salon parking lot in unison, matching smiles on our faces and Camel Lights between our fingertips. She turned right onto the highway, heading back toward her mom's house where she lived with her four-year-old son. I turned left, heading back toward the opium den my hippie parents called home.

With every passing mile, I could feel the depression I'd been battling since my breakup with Hans beginning to gnaw at the periphery of my mind.

Look at BB, all gussied up with nowhere to go, it taunted.

I turned on the radio.

What a waste of money.

I changed the station from pop to hard rock.

Who are you trying to look pretty for, huh?

I turned up the volume.

Your parents? They're the only ones you're going to see tonight.

Just as I was debating whether to crank the volume knob all the way to the right or yank the steering wheel instead, the universe intervened.

"Cirque du Soleil has announced that its trademark blue-and-yellow Grand Chapiteau will return to Atlanta this spring with Varekai, its latest live production. Deep within a forest, at the summit of a volcano, exists an extraordinary world—a world where anything is possible. A world called…Varekai. Varekai will premiere on March 6, but tickets are on sale now."

Before I had time to formulate a plan or so much as a thought, I had my cell phone out of my purse and pressed against the side of my head.

"What's u—"

"Jason!" I squealed. "I need you to call Ken right now and give him my number and tell him that he's taking me to Cirque du Soleil!"

"Your haaaair!" my mom yelled as soon as I walked through her front door. Waving me into the kitchen, she proceeded to pet and smooth my new purplish bob with her hands. "Oh, it's so pretty and shiny and straight. Promise me you won't shave it all off again."

I laughed. "If I can keep it looking like this? Yeah, I promise."

I could hear my father playing a Jimi Hendrix song on one of his Fender Strats in the living room. The music stopped just before he shouted in agreement, "Looks good, Scooter!" He must have seen me walk by.

"Thanks, Dad!" I yelled back, dropping my purse on the kitchen island, which was really just a wobbly white particleboard nightmare my mom had purchased from Kmart. With wobbly stools to match.

"Ooh, these are pretty," I said, admiring a fresh vase of Stargazer lilies on the island. "When did you get—"

"They're from Hans." My mom's tone dropped, just like my face when I heard his name.

Giving her a look that could sear the chrome off a bumper, I picked up the entire crystal vase, walked over to the trash can, and stepped on the pedal to open the lid.

"No!" she shouted, snatching the vase out of my hands at the last second. "They're so pretty. At least let me take them to school. Maybe I'll use them for a still-life lesson before they die. The kids will love them."

I sighed and let the lid fall shut. "Fine."

"Baby…"

Doodle-oodle-oodle-oo, my cell phone sang from my purse.

My heart skipped a beat as I snatched my purse back off the table and began rummaging through it for my glittery little Nokia.

Doodle-oodle-oodle-oo!

Grasping the device, I pulled it out and read the name on the screen. For the second time in as many minutes, my face fell.

I silenced the ringer and shoved it back into my bag. Flowers from Hans, never-ending phone calls from Knight…all I needed was for Harley to get out of jail, and the Terrible Trio would be complete.

Looking up at my mom with an expression that I hoped said, *That was absolutely* not *Ronald McKnight who I just sent to voicemail,* I tried to remember what we'd been talking about.

"That was him, wasn't it?"

"Who?" I smiled innocently.

"You know who." She wouldn't even say his name. It was as if Knight was so evil that my mom was afraid he could be conjured, like a demon or a ghost. "When are you going to change your number?"

"Mom…" I scoffed. "It's fine. I don't even answer."

Anymore.

"It's not fine. I saw him parked in the cul-de-sac on his motorcycle just last week, staring at the house!" She threw her hand in the direction of the front door and street beyond. "You know, your father and I watched a *Dateline* episode about guys like this. They called them lurkers.

No…*stalkers.* They called them stalkers, and they said that they are dangerous and have no boundaries and will stop at nothing to get what they want."

I wanted to laugh so bad. If she only fucking knew. Knight had been terrorizing me for a quarter of my life. At fifteen, he'd isolated me from my friends, threatened anyone who so much as spoke to me, introduced me to a world of bondage and bloodplay, intimidated and humiliated me at every turn, then shattered my heart when he left for the Marines. I had gotten a brief reprieve during his two tours of Iraq, but both times, he'd come back more aggressive and volatile than ever.

Knight's new favorite pastime was leaving irrationally angry, obscenity-filled voicemails on my phone, but no matter how bad it got, I couldn't change my number. I just…couldn't.

Knight wasn't a stalker.

He was worse.

He was my first love.

My mom opened the kitchen junk drawer and pulled something out. "Here," she said, turning and presenting me with a small black pouch on a key ring.

I accepted the canister, my fingers grazing the word *Mace* embossed on the side of the leather carrying case.

"Your father wanted to give you one of his guns, but I think you have to be twenty-one to carry a concealed weapon. So…maybe for your birthday."

"Mom"—I rolled my eyes, dropping the poison dispenser into my bag—"I am not carrying a *gun*."

"Well, I'd feel a lot better if you did. Look at you. You couldn't fight your way out of a wet paper bag."

Here we go again.

"Welp, thanks for the mace. I'm going upstairs now." I stood up and grabbed my purse, trying to make an exit before the issue of my weight, or lack thereof, came up. That was how these conversations went. No matter how they started, they always ended with a—

"Have you eaten today?"

"Uh-huh," I lied, backing out of the kitchen.

"Good," she called after me as I turned and practically sprinted up the stairs. "And be sure to take that pepper spray to school. You know, fourteen people get mugged downtown every day!"

That night, I dreamed of circus tents and acrobats and a mysterious prince dressed all in black. He was wearing a mask, so he could go out among the commoners without being recognized, but I knew it was him. I followed him through the crowd of spectators inside the big top, popcorn kernels and peanut shells crunching under my feet.

Every time I caught a glimpse of his intense aqua eyes peering out from behind that wide swath of black fabric, he would disappear again into the crowd. I had just found him, standing in the shadows beside the sawdust-covered stage, and was about to reach for his mask when a circus clown grabbed me from behind. He covered my mouth with his sweaty palm and chuckled as he dragged me away from my prince. I struggled against him, throwing my elbows and kicking my feet, but it was no use. He was so strong, and I was so light.

Too light, the doctors had said.

As the plump clown carried me onstage over his shoulder, a parade of dancers in white lab coats and white masks pranced out in a chorus line, shaking their fingers at me.

Doodle-oodle-oodle-oo, a series of cascading digital beeps sang out, ripping me from one nightmare into another.

I'd chosen the most cheerful ringtone I could find, but it didn't matter. The sound still hit my brain like an atom bomb every time.

Opening my eyes, I squinted at the clock on my nightstand. It was after midnight.

Fuck.

Knight was the only one who ever called that late. Usually after being thrown out of a bar for almost killing someone with a broken beer bottle in a blackout fit of rage. I couldn't talk to him like that. I couldn't talk to him at all anymore. Not only because he was irrational and irate, but also because I knew why.

I was the only one who knew why.

My cell phone rang again in my hand as I carried it across my childhood bedroom, its illuminated screen lighting my way with an ominous green glow. I don't know how, but even in my semiconscious condition, I could sense his presence, smell the notes of cinnamon in his musky cologne, and feel the heat and hatred radiating off his hulking body. I knew, even before I parted my nicotine-stained blinds, what I would find parked beneath the streetlight outside.

But that didn't prepare me for the sheer terror of actually seeing it.

My fingers released the blinds, letting them fall closed as my hand flew to my gasping mouth. Even though our driveway was long and flanked by woods on both sides, I would know the shadowy figure standing at the end of it anywhere. He was the thing that went bump in the night. He was the monster under my bed. And the last time he'd shown up where I was, he'd crossed a line I swore I'd never let him get close enough to cross again.

"What's the matter, Punk?" Knight's voice was sinister as he approached. Predatory.

I always parked on a run-down side street near the concert venue where Hans's band played. But that night, after the show, my car wasn't the only familiar thing waiting for me on Mable Drive.

"You don't look very happy," he sneered.

I took a step backward and flinched when my lower back collided with the tailgate of his jacked-up monster truck.

"That is what you said, isn't it? That you're so much happier *now?" Knight threw my earlier words back in my face as he came to a stop right in front of me.*

I saw his hand shoot out, but all I had time to do was wince before he wrapped his meaty palm around my jaw.

Knight dug his thumb and fingers into the corners of my mouth and pushed them up into a forced grin. "Smile, Punk. Show me how fucking happy *he makes you."*

Hot tears slid down my mortified face as I tried to slap Knight's hand away. "Fuck you!" I mumbled through my misshapen mouth, shoving his hard chest with both hands.

Knight shook his head from side to side. "Tsk-tsk. *That's not very ladylike, princess."*

"Don't call me that!" I yelled, kicking him in the shin.

"But you like being his little princess. You said he made you happy.*" Knight's grip on my mouth tightened, pushing the corners of my mouth up even higher.*

I closed my eyes, causing more tears to spill down my cheeks, and whispered through my clenched teeth, "I hate you."

Knight leaned in and pressed his forehead against mine. He smelled like Southern Comfort and Camel Lights.

Just like me.

"Good," Knight whispered.

Without releasing my distorted smile, he slammed his mouth against the upturned seam of my lips.

I waited for the spark. The zap of electricity that coursed from my head to my feet like a lightning bolt seeking the earth whenever Knight's lips touched mine.

But it never came.

Instead, all I felt was humiliated. Violated. Powerless. I felt Knight's rough hands shove my vinyl pants down to my ankles. I felt my nipple rings snag when he yanked my bra and tank top up under my armpits. But I didn't feel him enter me. My mind went somewhere else for that part. Somewhere happier.

The phone in my hand, which had gone silent, began to ring again. My heart slammed against my protruding ribs.

Don't look, BB. Just go back to bed. Maybe it's not him. Please, don't—

Without my consent, my fingers crept forward and lifted one of the filthy plastic slats again, just a fraction of an inch. Knight's chopper was still parked beneath the streetlight outside, but he wasn't standing next to it anymore.

Doodle-oodle-oodle-oo!

In a panic, I opened the blinds a little wider, scanning the expanse of darkness between the street and my second-story window. Knight wasn't in the driveway. He wasn't at the front door. My eyes darted across the almost-pitch-black front yard, ping-ponging between the pine trees until a familiar pair of almost-colorless blue eyes emerged from the shadows.

Knight's pale skin seemed to glow in the dark. His once-baby-soft blond buzz cut was grown out and slicked back. And his camouflage cargo pants had been traded in for a pair of black Levi's and a leather cut. Knight's new biker persona was just as intimidating as his military look, but unlike his dog tags and fatigues, it didn't even give the illusion that he was a good guy.

Knight was the motherfucking boogeyman.

He shouldn't have been able to see me. My light was off, and my blinds were only cracked wide enough for one of my thoroughly dilated pupils to peek through, but Knight stared at that crack anyway. It was as if he could smell my fear.

Don't fucking move. He can't see you. You're fine. He can't see you.

I held my breath as Knight narrowed his eyes at my window and growled something into his cell phone. I couldn't read his lips in the dark, but I didn't have to. My phone dinged in my hand a second later, indicating that I had a voicemail.

With one last murderous glare, Knight spat on the ground in front of my house, tucked his phone back into his pocket, and headed back down my driveway, silent as a shadow.

As I watched him climb onto his chopper and speed away, my shaking thumb navigated to his voicemail and pressed Delete, just like it had done a hundred times before. I knew Knight was still calling in the middle of the night, still leaving me random, venomous voicemails.

I just didn't know he'd been doing it from outside my bedroom window.

The nearly full moon peeked out at me from its own hiding place behind a cluster of pine trees. Evidently, it was scared of Knight, too.

"Don't worry," I whispered to it, my voice brittle and unconvincing. "I'm gonna get us out of here."

After staring at the glow-in-the-dark stars on my bedroom ceiling for the rest of the night, I got up to the sound of my alarm and dragged my tired, bitter ass out the door.

Georgia State University prides itself on being urban as fuck. The campus is in the heart of downtown Atlanta, straddling Peachtree Street, and within walking distance of Centennial Olympic Park, Philips Arena, the CNN Center, and some of the most crime-ridden neighborhoods in the country. One of my classrooms was in a converted parking garage. Literally. Instead of stairs, you had to walk up a concrete ramp from floor to floor. You could hardly have a conversation outside due to the traffic noise, construction noise, and emergency vehicle sirens screaming by all day—not that you'd want to loiter anyway. Stand in one spot too long, and you'd get attacked by a swarm of very aggressive panhandlers.

And don't even get me started on the subway.

I had just walked into Langdale Hall and tucked my pepper spray back into my purse when my phone rang. Right on cue, my palms began to sweat, but when I pulled my phone out and didn't recognize the number calling, my blood pressure spiked, too.

Oh my God. It could be Ken!

Shut up. It's not Ken. It hasn't even been twenty-four hours since you asked Jason to give him your number. Guys usually wait, like, two days to call a girl.

But it can't be Knight. It's—I glanced above the unknown number at the time on the screen—*eleven eleven in the morning. He's never called me before noon.*

So…telemarketer?

Totally. It's totally a telemarketer.

I took a deep breath and pressed the Talk button. After saying, "Hello?" I winced and braced myself for a barrage of angry expletives or a rapid-fire spiel about timeshares.

Instead, I heard a dry, deadpan voice reply, "So, I hear I'm taking you to the circus."

A burst of nervous laughter flew out of me as my face pulled up into a grin that had every sad, serious GSU co-ed staring at me like I'd lost my mind.

I held the phone to my ear and began walking to my next class. "That's right," I said. "I set up an interview for you. They need a new pillow juggler."

"Do they offer a 401(k)? What's their policy on matching?"

I snickered. "I guarantee you, they do *not* offer a 401(k)."

"Damn. I guess I'll just have to go as a spectator then. Want to come with me?"

My face hurts. Why does my face hurt? Is this what smiling feels like? It's been so long.

"Sure," I squeaked.

"I'll pick up some tickets this afternoon. The show isn't until March. Do you know what your schedule looks like that far out?"

"Yeah. I either have school or work every day, except Sunday."

"Sundays. I can work with that."

I can work with that.

Pajama Guy was smooth; I'd give him that.

I leaned against the cinder-block wall outside my classroom to finish our conversation.

"Hey, thanks for going with me," I said in a more serious tone. "I'll pay you back for my ticket the next time I see you."

"Are you going to Jason's house on Friday?"

I smiled at the immediacy of his question. "Yeah. What about you?"

"I'll probably be there."

"Okay." I beamed.

"Okay."

We were both silent for a minute before I remembered where I was.

"Hey, I'd better let you go," I sighed. "My next class is about to start."

"Which one?"

"Egyptian Art History."

"That's funny. I think I'm taking that class, too. This girl I know makes me quiz her with flash cards before every fucking test. Now, I can name all the pharaohs by dynasty."

"You'd better watch your mouth, or I'm gonna make you help me study for statistics, too."

Ken chuckled. "I would love to help you study for statistics."

"No, you wouldn't. It's boring, and you love nothing." I smirked.

"Well, *I'm* boring, and *I* love statistics."

"Whatever, liar. I have to go."

"Okay."

"Okay."

You hang up first. No, you hang up first.

"Bye, Brooke."

I bit my lip to squelch my stupid grin. "Bye, Ken."

I might as well have just stayed on the phone with him instead of going into class because, by the end of the day, my notebook looked like one big doodle with maybe three notes, the wrong date on the top, and the word *FRIDAY* in huge, three-dimensional block letters at the bottom.

As I walked around Jason's pool table, pulling the balls out of each pocket, my eyes naturally kept drifting toward the front door.

Stop it, damnit.

What if he's not coming?

It's Friday! Of course he's coming!

Oh God, what if he does come? What do I do? Give him a hug?

What? No! You know Ken doesn't do that. He won't even let Allen hug him.

But we're, like, dating now.

You have one *date scheduled over a month from now. Calm down.*

My ears picked up the sound of the front door opening, even over the stereo and TV and crowd noise. As I racked the balls, I glanced up and watched Jason's newest guest enter. Then, I let out an exasperated sigh when I saw that it was just another one of his khaki-clad co-workers.

Plastering a fake smile on my face, I looked over at Allen and gestured to the table. "You wanna break?"

"Nah. You go ahead. I'm just gonna call Amy real quick." Allen's big, round eyes looked puffy and tired behind his glasses.

I felt bad for the guy. I didn't know what was up, but it was obvious that he was going through some shit.

Jason's pool table was in what was supposed to be his dining room, so it took some maneuvering to take a shot without punching a hole in the Sheetrock with my stick. *Again.* The balls scattered, but only one went in—a solid.

"You play?"

I spun around and found Ken standing in the entryway between the living room and dining room with a smug smile on his stubbled face. He must have come straight from work again. The sleeves of his gray-blue button-down shirt were rolled up to his elbows. His silky gray-blue tie was loose around his neck. And his soft charcoal slacks hung about an inch or two lower than what was professional. It wasn't all black, and it wasn't meant to be edgy, but there was an air of *fuck you* about the way he wore it that turned me on anyway.

"Hey." I beamed.

"Hey," Ken said with a half-smile, crossing his arms over his chest.

Okay, so no hug.

"You play pool?" He gestured toward the table with a flick of his chin.

"Not very well." I laughed. "But, yeah, my parents have a table."

"Good thing you're playing Allen then."

Ken's best friend was pacing back and forth on the other side of the table, waving his stick around with one hand and holding his cell phone to his head with the other.

Ken walked into the room and turned so that his back was toward Allen. Lowering his voice, he said, "Amy broke up with him last week and moved to Arizona to live with her sister."

My hand flew to my mouth. I looked over Ken's shoulder at the poor bastard on the phone. "Oh my God!" I whispered. "They've been together for, like, five years!"

Ken turned around. "Allen, take your shot, man."

Allen looked startled. Nodding at Ken, he held the phone with his shoulder and took the worst shot imaginable. Then, he returned to his pacing.

"How's he doing?" I asked, watching his friend wear a hole in the carpet.

Ken shrugged. "I dunno. He says he's gonna go to Arizona and get her back."

Ken walked over to his buddy and took the stick out of his hand. Allen didn't even notice. Nodding to the table, Ken gestured that it was my turn.

"Like, caveman-style?" I asked. "Like, throw her over his shoulder and bring her home?" I lined up a shot and prayed to the gods of coolness to let me sink it. I exhaled in relief when I made it. Then I missed my next shot by a mile.

"I guess so," Ken replied, leaning over the table with one eye closed. "I told him it was a bad idea." *Smack.* "If she doesn't want him"—*smack*—"she doesn't want him." *Smack.* Ken had sunk the red-, purple-, and yellow-striped balls by the time he finished his sentence.

Show-off.

"What makes you think she doesn't want him?" I asked, lining up my next shot.

"Because she moved to the other side of the country."

"Hey, can I use your ball to—"

"Nope." Ken smirked.

"No?" I pouted, but Ken just shook his head.

Asshole.

I tried to bank the orange ball off the side bumper to avoid Ken's ball, but I misjudged the angle and knocked one of his other balls in instead. "Shit."

"Thanks." Ken chuckled, chalking his cue.

"You know, she probably left because she got sick and tired of waiting for him to propose. I know he's your friend and all, but…five years and no ring? I mean, how long was she supposed to wait?"

Ken arched a brow at me, the end of his stick poised to strike. "You think she left him because she wants to marry him?" I could see the microchip in his brain lighting up, trying to compute what I'd just said. "That doesn't make sense." Ken tapped the ball a little too lightly. It stopped just short of the hole.

"Ha!" I yelled, pointing at his mistake.

I walked over to Ken's side of the pool table where I had the best shot. I expected him to move away like he usually did when someone threatened to penetrate his massive bubble of personal space, but he didn't. He stayed put. And he held my gaze as I approached.

As soon as I stepped into his invisible force field, I felt hairs on the back of my arms stand up. It was electric, being that close to him. Maybe because he was kind of a robot.

I planted the end of my stick on the ground and looked up into his chiseled face. "Let me ask you this…did Allen do anything wrong?"

Ken's angled light-brown eyebrows pulled together. "What do you mean?"

"Did he cheat? Did he hit her? Did he steal her car and sell it for drugs?"

"No."

I smiled and glanced over at Ken's BFF, who was now sitting on a barstool with his head in his hands.

"Hey, Allen," I called out, leaning around Ken's dryer-sheet-scented V-shaped torso.

The stocky guy in the Falcons jersey and glasses looked up, misery aging his youthful features.

"Your girl wants to get married."

A small, sad smile tugged at the corners of his lips. "You think so?"

"Uh, yeah." I nodded. "Ken says you're gonna go get her back."

Allen rubbed his eyes behind his glasses and glanced from me to Ken. "I'm thinkin' about it."

"If you go, you'd better take a ring with you."

Allen's smile spread the rest of the way. "You sure?"

"Yeah, you sure?" Ken's doubtful voice echoed. "What if she says no?"

I looked up at him sporting a grin as big as Allen's. "Man, you guys don't know shit about girls. It's a good thing I'm here."

Something happened during that conversation that I hadn't expected. When I'd breached Ken's impenetrable force field, I think I broke it. For the rest of the night, he stayed within arm's reach of me. I tested his limits by touching him here and there, but he never flinched. I grabbed his tie and dragged him outside when I went to smoke. He came willingly. I laughed and swatted him on the chest whenever he said something sarcastic, which was always. I clutched his veiny, muscular forearm and whispered in his ear whenever I was talking about someone at the party. And he let me, all the while smiling and making eye contact and leaning in to tell me his own stories about the people there that I didn't know.

When it was time for me to leave, Ken grabbed his empty Gatorade bottle—which I knew from previous conversations would be responsibly recycled as soon as he got home—nodded his goodbyes to his friends, and walked me down the four flights of cement stairs to the parking lot. Our elbows rubbed the whole way.

My heart was pounding—and not from the stairs. Ken Easton was letting me touch him. The man had a personal-space bubble the size of a planet, but he didn't seem to mind my intrusion at all. Which was good because I liked it inside Ken's bubble. It was quiet and warm in there, but the energy was electric.

I knew I shouldn't push my luck, but when Ken walked me to my car, stopped a mere twenty-four inches away from me, and gave me that look—the one that felt like a challenge—I said, *Fuck it.*

And with a flying leap, I wrapped my arms around his neck.

And with the reflexes of a ninja, he caught me.

My eyes shot open in surprise as Ken's strong arms clamped around my waist, as his face—rough, thanks to a dusting of evening stubble—came to rest against my neck, and as my toes dangled at least six inches above the pavement.

For possibly the first time in my life, I felt grounded, and my feet weren't even touching the ground.

Just when I was beginning to think that I might like to spend the rest of my life *on* Kenneth Easton, he slowly lowered me to my feet.

"You're working tomorrow, right?" His eyes dropped to the ground as he adjusted his coat.

"Yeah," I replied, looking around for a rock to kick. "Hey, maybe you could come have lunch with me?" My voice, my face, and my eyebrows all lifted in hopeful expectation.

But Ken did not mirror my enthusiasm. As he pulled his car keys from his jacket pocket, he cast a guarded gaze my way. "Maybe." Then, without so much as an explanation or another embrace, he turned and walked away.

"Okay, something's up," Jamal stated, appraising me from head to toe.

On Tuesdays and Thursdays, I covered the Urban Streetwear section of Macy's by myself, but on Saturdays, I had Jamal to keep me company. He was only an inch or two taller than me but weighed at least twice as much in pure muscle. I could always tell whenever there'd been a cute girl at the gym that morning because Jamal would hit the weights so hard; he'd barely be able to lift a stack of Sean John jeans above his head during his shift.

"What do you mean?" I asked, pretending like I was engrossed in the sweaters I was refolding.

Jamal held up one thick index finger. "First of all, you got your hair done. Looks sharp, by the way."

"Thanks." I smiled, refusing to look at him.

"Second"—he held up another finger—"you been over here, refolding these Coogis that ain't even need to be refolded for, like, a hour now."

"Whatever. It's been, like, five minutes."

"Uh-huh. And third"—another thick finger joined the first two—"every time I look over here, yo' ass is lookin' down there." Jamal jerked his thumb over his shoulder in the direction of the main walkway that cut through the center of the store. "So, who is it? Who you hookin' up wit'?"

"Are you serious right now?"

"Is it Freddy? It's Freddy from Men's Fragrance, isn't it? That's cool. He fly."

"Oh my God!" I turned to face Jamal, trying to act insulted but failing miserably. "I am not fucking Freddy from Men's Fr—"

My face lit up, causing Jamal to turn and glance over his shoulder.

He looked from me to the guy in the navy-blue V-neck sweater and low-slung khakis walking toward us and then back to me. "Oh, *that's* who you lookin' for, huh? I knew somethin' was up."

"Shh. Shut up," I whispered through my teeth, not taking my eyes off of Ken.

I'd never seen him walk before. At least, never more than a few feet at a time. We were always cooped up inside of Jason's apartment or walking side by side to the parking lot. Seeing Ken from a distance was a whole new experience.

He was beautiful, tall and toned and graceful, but without a shred of ego. He moved as if he was confident that no one was looking at him, which couldn't have been further from the truth.

Jamal and I were staring.

When Ken's eyes met mine and the corners of his chiseled mouth curved upward, I wanted to physically shove Jamal out of my way, bound down the main aisle, and leap into his arms all over again.

I didn't, of course. Not only because mauling people while on the clock was frowned upon by management, but also because, right before Ken got to us, he put his hands in his pockets.

No hug.

Ken smirked and glanced down at my chest. "No, thanks. I think it's a little big for me."

I looked down and realized that I was still holding a men's extra-large sweater up by the shoulders.

I blushed and dropped the sweater on the table. "Ken, this is Jamal. Jamal, Ken."

"What's up, man?" Jamal shoved his hand in Ken's direction.

I watched a glimmer of hesitation flash behind Ken's eyes before he finally accepted.

With a tense smile and a firm shake, he replied with a clipped, "Hey."

Jesus. He's even weird about handshakes?

I darted over to the checkout stand to grab my coat and purse. As I clocked out on the cash register, I watched Jamal and Ken chatting. I couldn't hear what they were saying, but whatever it was, it had Ken laughing by the time I got back to them.

I glared at Jamal, telepathically communicating to him that I would not hesitate to kick him in the nuts if he tried to embarrass me.

Ten minutes later, we were sitting on my favorite bench outside, both holding giant smoothies, as I lit my first cigarette.

"So, you hate being cold, yet you spend your entire break outside, in February, drinking a frozen beverage?" Ken took a sip of his smoothie.

"That's why I sit here." I smiled, gesturing toward the sun overhead with my lit cigarette. "It's, like, ten degrees warmer on this side of the mall. But we can walk around if you want. That's what I do when I get really cold."

Ken smiled and shook his head. "I'm just giving you shit."

That was good because, the way we were sitting, angled toward each other, my foot was touching his shin, and it was the highlight of my day.

"How's that papaya-mango treating you?" I asked, flicking my eyes down to his giant Styrofoam cup.

"It's pretty fucking amazing," he deadpanned.

"Lemme try it," I said, sticking my cigarette between my teeth so that I could hold out my empty palm.

Ken held my stare as he took another sip, shaking his head.

"No? Why not?" I snapped.

"You didn't say the magic word."

"What? Like, *please*? That magic word?"

Ken nodded, straw still in his mouth. He was so fucking cute and so fucking infuriating, all at the same time. I had to fight the urge to slap his drink to the ground and then kiss the shit out of him.

With a dramatic eye roll, I said in my best British orphan accent, "Please, Mr. Easton? May I *please* have a sip of your smoothie, sir?"

Ken's lips curled around the straw in triumph.

Asshole.

I jerked the cup out of his hand and replaced it with mine. Giving him what I hoped looked like a *fuck you* death glare, I took a sip, and my eyes instantly rolled up into the back of my head.

"Holy shit, that's good." I took another sip. "I'm keeping this one. You can have mine. There's more of it left anyway. That's, like, a better ounce-per-dollar ratio or something. You can't argue with that."

Ken smiled and tapped the side of his new cup against mine. "Only because of the ounce-per-dollar ratio."

I watched as he put the straw that had been in my mouth into his mouth. There was no sense of *ickiness*. No traces of germaphobia at all.

Weird about touching. Not weird about swapping spat. Interesting.

As we sat and talked, I realized that I could not keep my hands out of my hair. I had a ton of nervous tics. My hands and mouth were pretty much always busy—smoking, talking, chewing pen caps, gesticulating, laughing inappropriately, picking threads from my clothing, chewing my fingernails, twirling my hair. But trying to make small talk with Kenneth Easton made it worse than ever.

"Oh my God, if I don't stop playing with my hair, I'm gonna go bald." I laughed, sitting on my hand. "I'm not used to it being straight. I normally can't even get my hands through it."

Ken watched me in amusement but said nothing.

"Did you notice?" I turned my head from side to side, my burgundy bob twisting and falling back into place. "I just got it done a few days ago."

"I noticed."

That was all he said. No smile. No innuendo. Just *I noticed.*

My face fell. "You don't like it."

"It doesn't matter whether or not I like it." Ken's features were serious. As in he was seriously not going to tell me that my new fucking haircut looked pretty.

"Why not?" I snapped, heat rising to the surface of my ice-cold cheeks.

"Because you're Brooke Bradley." Ken set down his cup and faced me head-on. "The first time I ever saw you, you had a shaved head. You didn't give a shit what people thought then, and you shouldn't start now. Do *you* like it?"

I blinked. Then, I blinked again. "Uh, yeah…I love it."

"Then that's all that matters." Ken relaxed against the back of the bench and took another sip from his almost-empty smoothie, the *slurrrrrp* sound adding some much-needed levity.

No one had ever flat-out refused to compliment me before. Hans had told me I was beautiful every day of our two-year relationship. Every day that he had bothered to call or come home, that is. My parents had been showering me with praise since I was born. My friends and I were constantly feeding each other's egos. But, somehow, by not telling me what I wanted to hear, Ken made me feel even more special than if he had.

Just then, Ken shifted in his seat, pulling a vibrating phone out of his pocket.

"Hey, man." His brow furrowed. "Shit. I don't know." Looking at me, he added, "Do you want Brooke to come help?"

Brooke. Nobody called me that, except my professors during roll call on the first day of class.

Placing his fingertips over the speaker, Ken whispered, "Allen came with me. He's looking at rings, and he needs some help."

My eyes went wide. "Engagement rings?"

Ken hadn't even finished nodding before I was up and at 'em, practically running in place as I waited for Ken to point me in the right direction.

"Bales Jewelers," he whispered, flicking his chin in the direction of the mall entrance.

No more than thirty seconds later, I was tackle-hugging Allen as Ken hovered near the entrance of Bales Jewelers.

"What about this one?" Allen tapped on the glass case we were peering into.

"It's pretty"—I smiled—"but I think it might be platinum."

"So?"

"So, platinum costs way more than white gold and looks basically the same."

The saleswoman behind the counter cleared her precious-stone-adorned throat. "Actually, platinum is far more durable than gold and never loses its natural white hue."

"White gold loses its hue?" Allen sounded alarmed as he glanced from the saleswoman to me. "I don't want it to lose its hue…do I?"

Poor bastard was so clueless.

"It's fine. If it starts to look yellow, you can bring it in, and they'll make it look white again." I lifted my eyes to the woman with the big fake smile and even bigger fake boobs. "Isn't that right"—I glanced at the name tag clinging to her ample chest for dear life—"Karen?"

Karen's plastic smile widened. "Yes, *ma'am.*"

In the South, ma'am is code for bitch.

"Do you know what kind of stone she might like?" I used a very different tone with Allen. The same one you would use on a frightened animal. Or a child.

He looked like he was about to hyperventilate. Ken, who had wandered over to us, looked like he was about to take a nap.

"Uh…square? I think she likes the square ones."

I smiled sweetly at Karen. "Will you please show us what you have in a princess cut with a white gold band…" I turned back to Allen. "What's your budget, honey?"

His large eyes got even larger. "Uh…"

"How much do you make a month?"

"Shit. Like, two grand? Maybe?"

I nodded and glanced back at Karen. "Under four thousand dollars, *please.*"

As Karen began pulling rings out of the case and placing them on a little velvet-lined tray, Allen turned to me with his eyebrows hiked up even higher than the top of his thick glasses.

"How do you know all this stuff?"

"My dad used to be a jeweler…and a guitar store owner and a car salesman and a stereo salesman and a flooring salesman. I know all kinds of useless information, thanks to his inability to keep a job."

Allen smiled weakly. "It's not useless if it gets Amy back."

I beamed back at him. "It will."

Ken had wandered off again. I peered over my shoulder and found him lazily perusing a case full of expensive watches. Hand in his pocket, stubbled square jaw, navy-blue sweater clinging to his toned shoulders and biceps. If I didn't already know him, I'd be drooling. At Jason's house, he was just one of the guys, but out in the wild, where I could watch him from afar, he was breathtaking.

"Here you go," Karen announced with a fake smile as she placed a black velvet-lined tray on the glass case in front of us. "These are all of the white gold bands we have that are already fitted with princess cut diamonds in your price range. But we can always swap out—"

I snatched a ring off the tray and slipped it onto my finger, ignoring the rest of her speech. I'd never seen anything like it in my life. It was a white gold band with tiny square diamonds inlaid across the front, but unlike a traditional engagement ring, the prongs held the large center diamond so that it hovered *over* the band. You could see all four sides of the crystal-clear stone and even a sliver of space underneath, as if it were floating.

"You like that one?" Allen asked, narrowing his eyes as he inspected the rock on my left hand.

"Uh-huh," I murmured, staring at the rock on my left hand in a daze.

"Let me see…" Allen leaned over to get a better look, but I jerked my hand away and sneered at him like Gollum guarding my precious.

"Not this one," I blurted. "It's not…Amy's style. Like, at all. I'm pretty sure she'd hate it and dump you all over again."

"Jeez. Fine," Allen mumbled as I pointed at the tray of other perfectly acceptable engagement rings.

Ten minutes later and after much reassurance from Karen and me, Allen bought Amy two rings—a beautiful white gold engagement ring with a romantic filigree design and a wedding band to match.

Ken had magically appeared during the checkout process to grill Karen on the interest rate and compounding, revolving something-or-other of the store credit card she was trying to get Allen to open.

Evidently, "Twenty-one percent," was the wrong answer because Ken snatched the credit application out of Allen's hand as if it were about to self-destruct.

Then, he reached into his own wallet and handed Karen his Mastercard.

When Allen asked what the fuck he was doing, Ken said, "Saving your ass a couple grand in interest. You can just pay me when you get the money."

It was really sweet—in a Ken kind of way.

As we exited the store, Allen gave me a huge hug, little black gift bag in hand, but when he went to hug Ken, he stopped mid-lunge.

"Thanks, man," he said, dropping his arms with a sheepish smile. Then, flicking his eyes back and forth between us, he added, "I'll just meet you at the car."

I floated back to Macy's on a static-charged cloud. I was excited for Allen, but mostly, I was excited about the fact that my arm kept touching Ken's as we walked.

It didn't make any sense. He wasn't my type. He'd never once come on to me. And he was about as emotionally available as a cucumber. But there was an intoxicating current of energy surrounding him that I couldn't get enough of. I knew that electric charge was meant to keep people out, but I was a defiant little shit. I was the girl who unwrapped her presents before Christmas because her parents had told her not to. I was the girl who pushed red buttons marked *Do Not Push.* And, when we got back to my department, I was the girl who hugged Kenneth Easton even though he did *not* do hugs.

I don't know if it was because we were in public or if I'd just imagined our connection the night before, but for whatever reason, Ken was as stiff as the starched collars on the men's dress shirts just down the hall.

"Thanks for coming," I whispered into his ear, my voice low and husky.

"Yep," Ken replied, standing straight up, causing my hands to fall away from his neck.

I forced a smile despite the scalding slap of rejection and embarrassment staining my neck and cheeks pink.

"I, uh…" Ken buried his hands in his pockets. "I get off at six tomorrow…if you want to grab dinner."

Huh?

I nodded with my eyebrows pulled together. "Sure. Yeah. I'm off on Sundays, so—"

"I know," Ken interrupted.

"Oh. Right." I smiled.

"Right," Ken echoed.

I waited until he made it all the way to Men's Fragrance before I let out the dramatic, wistful sigh I'd been holding in.

"Okay, he cool, but you have *got* to work on yo' hugs. That was not even a little bit smooth."

I turned around and glared at my co-worker, who was shaking his head at me in disapproval. "Shut up, Jamal. Nobody asked you."

The next day, I pulled into the Showtime Movie Theater parking lot, prepared for our dinner date to begin just like every other encounter with Ken had begun—with some smart-ass comment and zero physical contact.

As I parked my Mustang and checked my appearance in the rearview mirror, I gave myself a little pep talk to make sure that my expectations were nice and low.

Listen, homie. This is so not a big deal. You're gonna go in there, Ken is gonna give you some shit about being five minutes late, and then you guys are gonna ride in an awkward silence to some chain restaurant where he'll make you order a combo because he has a Buy One, Get One Free coupon. This will not be romantic. This might not even be fun. But it will probably be better than sitting at home, screening your calls. Maybe.

Satisfied with the hair and makeup I'd spent all afternoon working on, I grabbed my purse and slammed my door.

No big deal, I repeated in my head as I crossed the parking lot with my fists shoved in the pockets of my flight jacket. *Just a little BOGO dinner between friends.*

I stepped up onto the sidewalk and marched past the box office window.

He'll probably even make me drive to save on gas.

Grabbing the freezing cold handle on the heavy glass door, I had to throw most of my ninety-eight pounds backward just to yank it open.

Warm air blasted me in the face as I stepped inside. Concession stands lined both sides of the large, open foyer, and there, in the middle, addressing a group of zit-faced teenage employees, was Ken's black-clad alter ego, Mark McKen.

He looked every bit as breathtaking as I remembered from Jason's Super Bowl party—sexily mussed sandy-brown hair, hands tucked inside the pockets of his casually loose black slacks, biceps straining against the rolled-up sleeves of his black button-up shirt, and that goddamn skinny black tie.

His expression was dead serious as he addressed his teenage minions, but as soon as his eyes landed on me, Ken's sharp eyebrows lifted along with the corners of his mouth. He said something that made the underlings scatter, then walked across the lobby to where I was trying real hard to keep my saliva inside my face.

"Hey." He smiled.

"Hey." I smiled.

"You ready to go?"

"Uh-huh." I nodded in three slow, exaggerated movements.

Opening the door like it didn't weigh five tons, Ken held it for me as I stumbled back out.

No sarcastic comment.

No gibe about me being late.

But also, no hug.

Two outta three ain't bad.

"So, where do you want to go?" Ken asked as he led the way to his little maroon Eclipse convertible parked in the primo front spot.

I wanted to be easygoing and relaxed like the cool girls I knew or coy and demure like the pretty ones, but it simply wasn't in my nature. I was a headstrong, spoiled only-child with no filter, and when presented with the opportunity to get my way, I took it. Every. Single. Time.

"I love Italian," I blurted out.

"Really?" Ken asked, meeting my gaze over the roof of his car. "Italian is my favorite."

Much to my surprise, we didn't end up at a chain restaurant. We went to some mom-and-pop Italian place that neither of us had ever been to before. And the ride wasn't an awkward cringe-fest. It was…easy. Fun even. I flipped through Ken's CD case as he drove—no more than five miles over the speed limit—and squealed in delight over every single album in his collection. He had underground punk, pop punk, ska punk, ska ska, power pop, pop rock, grunge rock, classic rock, alternative rock, and emo for days. Our musical tastes were so similar; I think we could have switched CD cases without ever realizing it.

"No fucking way," I gasped, clapping a hand over my mouth.

"What?" Ken glanced at me in amusement.

I stared at him with wide, astonished eyes.

"What?"

"This is what!" I held the heavy black canvas CD case up, open to the last sleeve. "You have *Marvin the Album* by Frente!?"

Ken chuckled. "I had to, man. They did that cover of—"

"'Bizarre Love Triangle'! I know! It's amazing!"

"I don't even remember where I first heard it. Probably on MTV, back when they still—"

"Played videos!" I cackled. "Now it's all goddamn *Real World* and *Road Rules* and—"

"Fucking *Cribs*," Ken added.

"Fucking *Cribs*." My giggles morphed into a gasp as the next track on the CD we were listening to began to play. "Oh my God, I love this song! It's about me and Juliet!"

Ken smirked at my enthusiasm and turned the volume knob to the right just a little. We were listening to Weezer's *Pinkerton* album, which I also didn't know anyone else on the planet owned, and "El Scorcho" had just come on. It's a silly, almost-spoken-word jaunt with a chorus like a barroom sing-along.

"*Goddamn you half-Japanese girls*," I shouted along with Rivers Cuomo.

"*Do it to me every time*," Ken quietly sang back, eyeing me sideways as he drove.

What the…

Turning toward him in shock, I grinned and belted the third line about a redhead.

And, right on cue, Ken took the fourth, singing quietly and with *much* better pitch. His stern mouth curled upward just a little, but when the chorus kicked in, it spread into a full-blown smile as we sang the rest of the song together, Ken watching me out of the corner of his eye the whole time.

Holy shit! Ken, the enemy of fun, is actually having fun!

"Dude! You should come do karaoke with me sometime!" I blurted once the song was over. It seemed like a great idea. I liked to sing. Ken could *actually* sing. "We could do a duet!"

Ken's face fell as he pulled into the parking lot of Gusto's Trattoria. "I don't do karaoke."

"Aw, why not? You're so good!"

I could see him shutting down before my eyes. His face paled under my stare, and he seemed agitated as he threw the car in park and cut the engine.

"It's fun!" I pushed.

Ken jerked up on the emergency brake.

"And, if you're too embarrassed to sing, you can just rap. That's what I do. Nobody deserves to hear me sing into an actual microphone."

Ken opened his car door without a word, so I followed suit, hopping out and scurrying to catch up with him.

"Man, you *really* don't want to do karaoke, do you?"

"No," he snapped.

I looked at him as though he'd sprouted a second head as he held the wooden door open for me. His features softened a bit under my glare.

"I don't like attention," he offered as I walked past him.

Who doesn't like attention? It's basically my favorite thing ever.

"Welcome to Gusto's. Table for two?" the young brunette at the hostess stand asked, her eyes bouncing from me to Ken.

I paused, waiting for Ken to be a typical guy and speak for us, but he said nothing. When I glanced up at him, he flicked his chin toward the hostess, gesturing for me to answer her question.

"Uh, yes?" I said, not meaning for it to come out as a question. Turning toward her, I clarified, "Table for two."

Gusto's was dark, dripping in Old World charm, and smelled like they'd soaked every board and plank in garlic butter before building the place.

I didn't make a habit of eating—in fact, I actively abstained from it unless I felt like I was about to pass out—but Italian food was my weakness.

My mouth watered, and my palms began to sweat in anticipation of what was about to happen. Of the damage I was about to do. Of the guilt I was going to be racked with later.

"This is my new favorite restaurant," I murmured, watching our server set a plate of baseball-sized garlic knots dusted with Parmesan cheese on the table.

With far more class than I could ever hope to possess, Ken nodded in approval as he pinched a piece off of his fluffy hunk of heaven and popped it into his mouth.

Resisting the urge to shove mine into my mouth all at once, I took a bite out of the side like an apple and immediately felt a shot of dopamine explode through my body. My eyes rolled up in the back of my head as I partook in my guiltiest pleasure—carbs.

After the first bite, I was triggered. I wanted to binge. I wanted to eat my roll, Ken's roll, and every beautiful golden-brown ball of sin in the building, but I had to pretend to be normal. I had to smile and breathe and make small talk with my cute, quiet date.

"So"—I set the doughy crack rock onto my plate and looked up—"how did somebody so…shy end up being the manager of a movie theater? It seems like you would have to be *the center of attention* a lot with that job." I'd chosen my words carefully, not wanting to accidentally insult him.

"Not really." Ken shrugged, taking a sip from his glass of water. "I mostly stay in the office, doing paperwork, all day. If there's a problem with a customer, I have one of the assistant managers deal with it."

"Nice." I laughed.

"It's a job." Ken lifted an impassive shoulder and let it fall. "But I get to see every movie that comes out for free, so that's cool."

"What would your dream job be?" I asked, taking another unladylike chomp out of my roll.

"I dunno," Ken deadpanned. "To watch movies all day *without* having to work."

"Dude, are you telling me, you have zero ambition to do anything but watch movies?"

"Yes," Ken answered without a shred of sarcasm.

"Okay, so what if you had to work? Movies no longer exist, and you have to find a new job. What would you want to do?"

Ken stared at me like he was trying real hard not to roll his eyes. Then, he sighed. "I don't know. Financial planning maybe? Or accounting?"

"Oh, man! You should do that! I'd hire you…if I had any money." I giggled.

That earned a tiny half-smile from Ken. "What about you?" he asked over the rim of his water glass. "Is psychology your dream job?"

"I guess so," I answered. "I mean, I love it, but I also love making art and writing poetry. I guess I just chose the thing I love that will pay the bills." I shrugged. "Maybe, in my next life, I'll come back as a *National Geographic* photographer. Wouldn't that be amazing? To travel the world, taking pictures, and get paid for it?"

"I don't think that's how reincarnation works," Ken teased.

"You don't think reincarnation works at all." I wiggled my head back and forth like a taunting child.

"Exactly." Ken smiled, tipping his glass toward me like the smug, atheistic bastard he was.

While we teasingly debated what happens after you die, our server returned to take our orders. I got the eggplant Parmesan. Ken got the chicken Parmesan. It was the perfect metaphor for us. We had the same taste, but below the surface, we weren't even the same species.

After what was hands down the best meal of my life, our server bagged up our leftovers and placed the check on a little silver tray in front of Ken. I giggled to myself as I watched him pore over the itemized bill, waiting to see if he would flat-out ask me to pay for my half or if his head would explode from the awkwardness first. As soon as our server left with his Mastercard, I reached into my purse and tossed a handful of twenty-dollar bills onto the table.

Ken's face shot up immediately, his eyebrows stitched together.

"That's for my Cirque ticket, my dinner, and half of the tip…unless you have a Buy One, Get One Free coupon I don't know about."

I would have paid sixty bucks just to see that expression. Ken's lips parted, his shoulders relaxed, and his bright blue eyes sparkled like twin flames.

"No coupon"—Ken smiled, swiping the cash off the table—"but the chicken Parm was tonight's special. I saw it on the chalkboard when we walked in."

I laughed and shook my head. Ken might have been a cheap-ass bastard, but considering the fact that my last boyfriend had blown all his rent money on nose candy—and strippers named Candy—a grown-ass man with good credit was suddenly ranking pretty damn high on my list of turn-ons.

"And I get double cash back when I use my Mastercard at restaurants this month."

"Oh my God!" I laughed, kicking his foot under the table. "I'm starting to think you owe *me* money now!"

Ken smirked at me as our server returned with his card. "How about I'll buy you dinner tomorrow?" He signed the receipt and handed it back without taking his eyes off me. "I have a coupon for a free salad bar at Ruby Tuesday."

I laughed even harder and threw my cloth napkin across the table at him. "It's not buying me dinner if it's free, asshole!"

Ken caught it effortlessly, his tilted smile spreading. "What if *I* get the salad bar?"

"Okay. Deal." I nodded once, extending my hand across the table.

Ken stared at it for a moment, the way he'd done with Jamal the day before.

Shit. I forgot he's weird about—

Standing up, Ken took my offered hand and helped me out of the booth. I felt the warm, charged hum of electricity envelop me as he gently pulled me up and into his bubble. The air shifted from flirty to focused as he shook my hand in one slow, deliberate motion.

"Deal," he breathed, letting it fall.

Ken didn't sing with me as he drove back to my car, and he only seemed to be half-listening to what I was saying, which was highly unusual for him. I didn't mind at first because, with Ken lost in thought, it allowed me to ogle him from the passenger seat. He had a beautiful profile. Striking. The way his hair flipped up in the front mirrored the subtle upturn at the tip of his nose, which curved at the same angle as his cleft chin and enviable cheekbones. But, when Ken pulled up beside my car in the movie theater parking lot and hadn't said more than five words the whole ride back, I began to worry.

Ken wasn't a chatty guy, but something was definitely off.

Shifting the car into park, he turned to face me. I couldn't quite make out his expression in the dark, but I didn't need to. Ken gave nothing away.

"What are you thinking about?" I asked, making no move to get out of the car.

Ken held my gaze and his breath as I waited for the hammer to drop. He'd changed his mind. He didn't want to go to Ruby Tuesday tomorrow after all. He'd just remembered that his coupon had expired, and he didn't know how to break it to me.

His chest expanded as his lungs finally forced him to suck in a breath. With a face as hard as stone, he asked, "Do you want to see my house?"

Do I want to see his house? That's a weird fucking question. Does he mean hang out or, like, literally drive by and look at it?

"You want me to come over?" I asked, not meaning to sound as confused as I was.

"If you want to."

"Like, now?"

Ken nodded slowly.

I couldn't get a read on his intentions. Maybe he was just nervous about asking me to come over, or maybe he wanted to dismember me and eat my brains. Either way, the vibe was intense.

"Um…" *Fuck it. He's cute.* "Okay." I shrugged and forced a smile.

Ken suggested that I follow him in my own car so that I could leave whenever I wanted. I think he was trying to make me feel more comfortable about being alone in a strange house with him, but all it did was make me question whether or not I should be alone in a strange house with him. I mean, that was on the Serial Killer 101 syllabus, right? Lure your victims to an isolated place under the guise of safety?

Ken could totally *be a serial killer*, I thought as I followed his Eclipse convertible away from the city and into the suburbs.

Think about Christian Bale in American Psycho. *He was handsome and meticulous and quiet, too…worked out a lot…wore ties! Oh my God, I'm about to be hacked up with an ax.*

Shh…calm down. Maybe not. Scope the place out. If you find a clear poncho, an exfoliating facial mask, or a tanning bed up in there, then you can freak out.

I left a voicemail on Juliet's phone, telling her where I was going, just in case.

We drove down countless twisty, tree-lined streets, past horse pastures and elementary schools, until Ken turned into an adorable little subdivision called Pinewood Lake. I don't know where I'd pictured him living, but it most certainly was not in a swim and tennis community out in the 'burbs.

He turned right, just after the clubhouse, and drove past a half-dozen single-family traditional-style houses with Toyota Camrys in the driveways and tricycles left out in the grass.

This was *not* bachelor country.

As we crept down the street, a large white two-story caught my eye up ahead. Perched at the top of a gentle hill and illuminated by a nearby streetlight, it seemed to glow in the dark compared to the other houses. Every window was bracketed with black shutters and adorned with a flower-filled window box. A covered front porch spanned the width of the first floor and ended in an octagonal gazebo on the corner of the house. And, just when I thought we were about to pass it by, Ken's taillights brightened.

Wait.

What?

Ken pulled into the home's spacious two-car garage while I parked in the driveway behind him, trying to figure out what the fuck was happening.

Ken lives here*? How? My parents don't even have a house this nice.*

Oh my God. I'm such an idiot. Parents. He must live with his parents. Duh.

Whatever. That's fine. I live with my parents.

Gasp! Is he about to introduce me to his parents?

No, dumbass. Look around. Do you see any other cars?

I didn't. Half-delighted and half-terrified by the idea of being alone with Ken, I hopped out of my Mustang—subconsciously palming my pepper spray keychain—and bounced over to where he was waiting behind his car, bathed in light from the garage door opener overhead.

"Dude!" I cried. "You live here? This place is beautiful! And that gazebo is fucking adorable." I gestured to the front of the house with my left hand, which I realized still had a lit cigarette in it.

Ken's lips curved slightly. "Thanks. I put a swing in it last summer. Want to see?" Ken walked past me, headed toward the sidewalk that led to the front porch.

I turned and watched him go, blinking. Then, I hustled to catch up.

We walked up the white front steps, onto the white wooden porch, past two white rocking chairs, and into the little white gazebo on the corner where a white bench swing was swaying gently.

I squealed as soon as I saw it. I knew I had about T-minus five minutes before my teeth started chattering, thanks to the February chill, but I wasn't leaving without sitting on that damn swing. Zipping my flight jacket up to my chin, I hopped up on the hanging bench, leaving enough room for Ken to sit next to me.

He didn't, of course. He stood three feet away, leaning against the railing with his personal-space bubble intact.

Damnit.

I was just about to start kicking my legs to get some momentum going when Ken lifted a foot and gave the bench a gentle push. I swung away from him in surprise and rocked back in anticipation, my knees grazing the edge of his magnetic field. Ken held my gaze as I advanced and retreated, but he was quiet again. I could see the wheels turning behind his shadowed eyes.

"Now what are you thinking about?" I found myself asking for the second time that night, the future psychologist in me frustrated over my inability to read him.

Are you wondering how my brains will taste?

Do you think I look pretty?

Shit. Do I have marinara sauce on my chin?

"I'm wondering how many pounds that swing will hold."

I laughed through my nose, a smile splitting my frozen face. "You're just over there, crunching numbers, huh?"

Ken's lips pulled up on one side. "Always."

"Don't worry." I smiled, trying to hide my panic. "If it breaks, we'll just sue Gusto's Trattoria for damages. I'm pretty sure I gained ten pounds tonight, thanks to those garlic knots."

As my thoughts began to spiral about my weight and what I was going to do the next day to keep from gaining more of it, it occurred to me that Ken was wondering about the weight limit—not because I was a heifer, but because he'd never sat on that swing with another person before.

The thought warmed me from the inside out.

Then Ken's body was next to mine, and it warmed me from the outside in.

Unlike mine, Ken's legs were long enough for his feet to touch the ground, but he didn't give us a push. He let us hang, just like the silences that never seemed to bother him.

Ken was content with stillness.

I, of course, was not.

As soon as my cigarette was done, I leaped off the swing, reached through the gazebo railing, and smashed the butt of my Camel Light into the soil beneath a rose bush.

"So"—I spun around to face Ken, practically jogging in place—"can I see the inside?"

Ken nodded and walked us over to the front door, which wasn't white like the house *or* black like the shutters.

"I love your red door," I chirped as Ken stuck his key into the deadbolt. "What does that symbolize? Aren't red doors supposed to, like, protect you from evil spirits or something?"

Ken chuckled as he pushed the door open. "I wondered the same thing, so I looked it up." Holding the door open for me, he said, "In Scotland, it means your mortgage is paid off."

I giggled as I stepped inside, wondering who the fuck was paying *this* mortgage, when Ken flipped on the lights.

The interior was immaculate. Tasteful. And devoid of a single personal memento or photograph.

Oh my God, this isn't even a private residence! It's a model home! Ken tricked me! This must be where he brings all his victims!

The front door opened into a sparsely decorated living room, painted a cozy shade of sage green. A staircase leading to the second floor was on the right side of the expanse. A stately stacked-stone fireplace took up most of the left wall. And, on the back wall, a plush camel-brown suede couch was flanked by two wide entryways, one into the kitchen and another into the dining room.

The light fixtures were steel. The coffee table was wooden. And the art above the couch was an eclectic collection of watercolor paintings and pen-and-ink sketches, mostly of the Eiffel Tower.

No, seriously. Who the fuck lives here?

"I, uh…love the color," I stammered, taking it all in.

"Thanks." Ken shut the door behind us, causing me to jump. "I did all the painting, but my dad helped me with the crown molding."

I knew it!

"Oh, does he live here, too?" I unzipped my coat and wandered over to admire the wall of Eiffel Towers.

"No, but my sister does. She rents the master bedroom from me."

So, a woman lives here. That explains all the Parisian art.

"That's cool. Did she help you decorate?" I asked, focusing on one particularly good watercolor of Notre Dame Cathedral after a rain shower. The wet sidewalks looked like mirrors.

"No. She just moved in a few weeks ago."

"Really?" I turned toward Ken with my mouth hanging open and my jacket half-on and half-off. "So, you bought this place and painted it and decorated it…by yourself? It's so"—*domestic, perfect, empty*—"beautiful."

Ken smiled shyly. Holding his black wool coat in one hand, he extended the other to take my jacket. I shrugged it the rest of the way off and gave it to him.

"Where did these paintings come from?" I asked as he walked over to a coat closet tucked beneath the stairs.

"I got those in Paris," he answered, placing my jacket on a wooden coat hanger. "There are these street artists there who just sit on the sidewalks, drawing and painting famous landmarks all day. Their work is amazing"—Ken closed the closet door and turned toward me with a smile—"and it's really fucking cheap."

A strange sense of déjà vu fell over me as I held his gaze. Only, instead of feeling as though I were glimpsing into the past, I felt as if I were glimpsing into the future. Ken hadn't decorated that house for himself; he'd decorated it for *me.* It didn't make sense, but I felt it. I knew it. My soul saw that house and said *home.* My heart saw those paintings and said *home.* But, when my eyes beheld that introverted, intelligent, handsome, gainfully employed, responsible, tattoo-free man, they said, *Home?*, with a very distinct question mark at the end.

Ken wasn't my type, but perhaps my type was ready for an upgrade.

The rumble of a car pulling into the garage shook me from my trance.

"Is that your sister?" I asked, feeling suddenly awkward about standing in the middle of the living room, doing nothing.

Ken walked past me toward the couch. "Probably not. She stays at her boyfriend's most of the time."

Probably not? Who the fuck is it then?

Ken sat on the couch and turned on the TV just as a door opened and closed somewhere in the kitchen. One second later, a tiny Asian girl walked through the entryway into the living room. She looked like she was around my age, maybe younger, and was no more than five feet tall. When she noticed that Ken had company, she sheepishly averted her eyes and scurried up the stairs.

I turned toward Ken with the universal expression for, *What the fuck?*, on my face.

He smirked, enjoying my confusion, and said, "That's Robin. She works at the theater and needed a place to stay, so I'm renting out one of the other bedrooms to her."

"How many bedrooms does this place have?" I asked, my tone surprisingly salty.

"Four."

"Any other renters I should know about?"

Ken's lopsided grin widened. "Not yet, but if you know anyone who's looking, let me know."

I rolled my eyes and joined him on the couch. "How old are you?" I asked, changing the subject to keep myself from volunteering to be his third roommate.

"Twenty-three." Ken kept his eyes on the channel guide on his big screen TV. "Have you seen *About a Boy*? It's finally on HBO."

I shook my head. Both in response to his question and in disbelief that he was so young to be so damn *grown*.

"You haven't? It's so fucking good." Ken selected the movie and placed the remote on the coffee table. "Hugh Grant's my favorite actor."

I snorted.

"What?" Ken gave me the side-eye.

"Hugh Grant isn't anybody's favorite actor."

Ken laughed and turned to face me, doing a worse job at hiding his smile than usual. "I thought that, too, until, one day, I realized I liked every movie Hugh Grant has ever been in. Even *Small Time Crooks*, and I fucking hate Woody Allen. So, I was like, *Holy shit. I think Hugh Grant's my favorite actor.*"

Ken's smile was infectious.

"You're telling me you liked *Bridget Jones's Diary*?" I teased.

"Yep."

"*Two Weeks Notice*?"

Ken nodded.

"*Notting Hill*?"

"Are you kidding? *Notting Hill* is the best one. We're watching it after this. I mean"—Ken's eyes darted around the room as he cleared his throat—"if you want to."

I smiled, basking in the unexpected cuteness that was Ken Easton. Desperate to soothe his sudden nerves and charmed by his adorable love of British romantic comedies, I leaned forward and planted a chaste kiss on his chiseled mouth. I didn't think about it. I just…did it.

And regretted it immediately.

The moment our lips touched, Ken froze—along with the very breath in my lungs as I waited an uncomfortable amount of time for him to do something.

One Mississippi, two Mississippi…

But Ken just sat there, suspended in time, unblinking, hardly breathing, with my lips pressed against his closed, slightly pursed mouth.

Releasing him from the awkwardness of that kiss with a loud *smack*, I tried to play it off like it was just an innocent nothing.

What the fuck was that? He just sat there! Why would he invite me here if he doesn't even want to make out?

As I played with a string on the ripped knees in my jeans and tried to come up with an airtight excuse for why I had to leave that instant, Ken turned off the lamp next to the couch and started the movie. The gesture was subtle, but thanks to my downcast stare, I definitely caught a glimpse of him adjusting the crotch of his slacks once the lights were out.

I bit the insides of my cheeks to keep from smiling.

Maybe I'll stay…just a little bit longer.

I woke up hours later in Ken's darkened living room, horizontal on his microsuede couch. As I blinked up at the glowing TV, trying to get my bearings, I realized that my fully clothed body was lying across Ken's lap. My head was on the armrest, and Julia Roberts was standing in a bookstore.

I was fucking mortified. I must have fallen asleep on him, but he didn't seem to mind the contact. In fact, as I shifted and wiggled against him, trying to find a more comfortable position, I felt an unmistakable bulge swell and lengthen against my side. My hormones roared to life, ready for the action that usually followed such an appearance, but much to my surprise, Ken didn't press it against me. Instead of feeling me up, his hands moved away, allowing me room to move.

By maintaining complete control of his body, Ken was allowing *me* to be in complete control of the situation.

It was a gift no one had ever given me before.

In my experience, boys were opportunistic assholes. Even the sweet ones. Give them an inch, and they'd take your hymen.

But, as I'd come to realize that night, in a multitude of ways, Ken was no boy. He wasn't even a man. He was a rare subspecies, commonly referred to as a *gentle*man, that I didn't even know still existed.

And he'd been hiding in plain sight.

As Julia Roberts faced Hugh Grant with tears in her eyes and a fake smile plastered on her pretty face, Ken's quiet voice recited her next line from memory.

"*I'm also just a girl, standing in front of a boy, asking him to love her.*"

I giggled and pushed myself up into a sitting position. Ken pulled his eyes away from the screen just long enough to meet my amused stare. His lids were hooded, features relaxed, lips upturned on one side.

"That was the best part." He nodded toward the glowing screen.

I smiled, maybe even bigger than Julia Roberts, and shook my head. Ken was funny. *And* charming. And he'd just let me touch him for…I don't even know how long.

"What time is it?" I asked, looking around the living room for a clock.

Ken shifted next to me, digging his cell phone out of his pocket. Glancing at the illuminated numbers, he read, "Twelve fifty-eight."

"Shit." I jumped up, the room tilting sideways from the head rush as I scrambled over to the coat closet. "I have class in the morning. I gotta go."

Ken nodded sleepily and walked me through his immaculate white kitchen, past an adorable breakfast nook nestled in front of a bay window, and out the garage door. I noticed, as he led the way past his Eclipse and Robin's little Honda Civic, that he must have kicked off his shoes while I was sleeping. I don't know why, but seeing Ken in socked feet made me happy.

Stopping next to my car, Ken turned to face me. His mask of apathy was back in place, the one that hid his thoughts from me. Our breaths were visible in the frigid black air as they collided and swirled between us.

"So..." I stalled, trying to see inside his mind. "Karaoke tomorrow, right?"

A small smile broke through his serious exterior. "Sorry." He shrugged. "I have a date with a salad bar."

"Oh, right." I laughed. "See you then."

Ken's smile faded. "See you then."

Kiss him, dumbass! Don't just stare at him.

No! I want him to kiss me first this time!

Well, I want to be the new lead singer of No Doubt now that Gwen Stefani is going solo, but it's not gonna fucking happen, so just do it already.

"Should I...meet you at the theater again?"

Oh, nice. Perfect. Drag it out. That'll make it less awkward.

"Sure. I get off at six." Ken rubbed his frozen hands together and shoved them in the pockets of his black slacks. His black tie had been loosened but was still hanging from his neck.

Great. Now, his hands are in his pockets. That's the universal sign for, Don't hug me.

He's just cold!

Which is exactly why you should kiss him and let him go back in the house, you selfish bitch!

He didn't dry-hump me or try to convince me to spend the night or anything. What if he's just not that into me?

Fine. Don't kiss him.

I can't just not *kiss him!*

"Sounds good. See you then." I reached for my car door handle in slow motion, searching Ken's face for some trace of affection, analyzing his body language for any invitations I might have missed, but the moment we'd shared on the couch was long gone. Ken was cold again, inside and out.

With a professional nod, my tie-clad crush turned and headed back through the garage and into the house.

What the fuck? Seriously? No hug?

Just as I was about to slam my car door shut loud enough to wake the neighbors, Ken called out from the doorway into the kitchen, "Hey…Brooke?"

"Yeah?" I replied from the driver's seat, hope lifting my voice to a decibel that should have made the neighborhood dogs howl.

"Call me to let me know you got home safe, okay?"

"Okay." I sighed, pulling the door closed with a gentle click.

"Haven't you seen that *Sex and the City* episode? What if he's just not that into me?" I exhaled a stream of smoke and flicked my cigarette ash in the general direction of the overflowing bowl of butts nearby.

Juliet narrowed her black-rimmed eyes and furrowed her drawn-on eyebrows at me from the other side of the bar. Her entire makeup kit consisted of one black kohl eyeliner pencil. If it wasn't for her trichotillomania—an inexplicable compulsion to pull her eyelashes and eyebrows out—she probably wouldn't wear makeup at all.

Juliet was fresh out of fucks. I guess having a baby when you were still a baby yourself would do that to you. Despite getting knocked up by a drug dealer at the age of fifteen, Juliet had still managed to graduate high school on time *and* get accepted into the College of Business at the University of Georgia. Sure, she would have fit in way better at Georgia State where everybody chain-smoked, wore black, and experimented with veganism, but I wasn't mad about her choice. UGA had way hotter guys and way better bars, especially the one she worked at.

Fuzzy's Bar & Grill was a shithole with no discernable theme other than *the place where wooden things went to die.* There was wood paneling on the walls. The most scuffed hardwoods you'd ever seen on the floor. And every table, chair, and flat surface was made from something brown and splintery.

But damn if it didn't attract some fine-ass losers.

The ten-dollar pitchers of Pabst Blue Ribbon brought in the tattooed, working class crowd who didn't give two shits about the college-town locale. They were just there to get drunk on the cheap. The regulars loved Juliet, which was hilarious, considering what a bitch she was to everyone, and nobody batted an eye whenever she let her underage purple-haired best friend drink for free.

So, basically, it was heaven disguised as the inside of an old coffin.

Juliet handed me a Coke with plenty of Jack Daniel's in it, then snatched the cigarette out of my hand.

"You're right," she said, taking a drag as I took my first sip. "He's just not that into you."

"Ugh," I scoffed, snatching my Camel Light back. "I knew you were gonna say that."

"Hey, I call 'em like I see 'em." She shrugged, completely ignoring the impatient glares from her patrons. "You've been to his house, like, five times now, and he hasn't even invited you upstairs. That's fucked up."

"It's fucked up, right?" I threw my hands in the air. "I would have just written him off by now if we didn't have these fucking Cirque du Soleil tickets. Now, I gotta deal with this awkward bullshit for three more weeks!"

A man cleared his throat from a table behind me, prompting Juliet's pencil-thin eyebrows to shoot up.

Glaring over my shoulder, she shouted above the noise from the rowdy hockey fans gathered around the TV at the opposite end of the bar, "I'll be with you in a minute, *sir*." Then, lowering her voice, she added, "Dickhead."

"Explain to me again why you get better tips than me."

I looked up as a man with a megawatt smile and a chestnut-brown faux hawk came to stand beside Juliet. He was wearing a white button-up shirt and dark gray vest, but the tattoos peeking out of his collar and sleeves negated the formality of his outfit.

And increased his hotness tenfold.

"They're called boobs, Zach."

"Oh, right." He beamed at me even though he was talking to her. "I thought it was your glowing personality."

I snickered as Juliet rolled her eyes.

"B, this is our new bartender, Zach. Zach thinks he's funny."

Zach winked at me. "Your friend thinks I'm funny, too."

Juliet turned to face him. I don't know how she could keep a straight face while looking at something that fucking cute.

"My *friend* is on her second Jack and Coke. She thinks everything's funny."

I shrugged as Zach met my gaze. "It's true."

Juliet pushed past him to go abuse some more customers, pretending not to be affected by the potent cloud of charisma he was emanating.

Propping both forearms on the bar, Zach leaned forward and asked, "Is she always that shy?"

I giggled. I actually fucking giggled.

"She's…she's a bitch, man. I can't even sugarcoat it. She pushed me into moving traffic once."

"Hey!" Juliet shouted from ten feet away where she was standing at a table full of bikers. "I pulled you right back onto the sidewalk. Don't be so dramatic."

I rolled my eyes and turned back toward the new bartender. "It's an abusive relationship."

Zach laughed. "Sounds like you've been having all kinds of relationship problems lately."

I took a sip from my drink to mask my mortification. "You heard all that, huh?"

Zach nodded at one of the hockey fanatics who was holding up two fingers in our direction. Pulling down a couple of dusty glass mugs from an overhead shelf, he turned and began filling one from the beer tap behind him.

Glancing at me over his shoulder, Zach said, "It's none of my business, but I have a theory, if you wanna hear it."

"A theory about the guy I'm seeing?"

Zach set one mug down and began filling the second. "No. Just a theory about guys in general."

"Dude, I need all the help I can get. Spill it."

Tossing me a lopsided smile, Zach delivered the beers and returned to his spot in front of me. "You ready? I'm about to drop some serious fucking science."

I grinned and nodded enthusiastically.

Casting a sideways glance in both directions, Zach leaned forward. "Dicks…are like golden retrievers."

My face screwed up in confusion. "*That's* your theory?"

"Yep." Zach smirked, crossing his arms over his chest. "Think about it. They get excited when they see something they want. They're shit at communication. And, if they like you, they'll follow you around until you finally give in and play with them."

I snorted out a laugh that sent fizzy bubbles up into my nose. "And how is that supposed to help me?"

"Well, now that you know how dicks work, all you have to do is watch. If a guy is into you, he'll find reasons to be near you."

"In case I decide I want to pet his *golden retriever*?"

"Exactly." Zach beamed. He had a dimple on his left cheek that I hadn't noticed before. "You can't pet it if you're not there, right? So, he'll want to keep you as close as possible."

It wasn't lost on me that, at that exact moment, Zach was the one who was close. Very close.

I dropped my eyes as a prickly heat scorched my neck and cheeks. Focusing on his thick, masculine fingers, which were laced together on the bar between us, I made out the words *WORK* and *PLAY* tattooed across his knuckles.

"So…" I swallowed and forced myself to meet his whiskey-colored gaze. "What if this guy finds ways to be near me, but then, when we're together, all he wants to do is watch movies until I fall asleep on the couch?"

"Ha! That's an easy one." Zach chuckled. "He's gay."

"Oh my God!" I squealed, slapping the splintery bar with both hands. "Gay! Why didn't I think of that? This whole time, I thought he was just a serial killer!"

"Hey!" Juliet barked as she rounded the corner at the end of the bar. "Gay people can be serial killers, too, asshole."

Once, back when Ken was still just Pajama Guy, I'd gotten drunk at one of Jason's parties—per my usual—and asked him why he didn't celebrate holidays or birthdays. The conversation that had followed went something like this:

"I don't believe in blindly buying things just because of a number on a calendar. Like Valentine's Day. Who says we all have to uniformly buy heart-shaped bullshit just because it's February 14? Hallmark made that shit up. It's corporate brainwashing."

I rolled my eyes. "How does your girlfriend feel about that?"

Ken shrugged. "Never had one."

"So, let me get this straight." I held up one index finger. "You don't drink, you don't smoke, you don't gamble, and you don't believe in holidays, religion, or evidently, commitment. Next, you're gonna tell me you don't eat chocolate either."

"Actually…" Ken peeked at me out of the corner of his eye.

"Oh my God!" I squealed. "No way! You really are the enemy of fun! What about caffeine?"

"Nope."

"Sex?" My eyes went wide as soon as I heard my own question. I was just about to apologize when Ken turned to face me, wearing a smirk that said he was anything but offended.

"I'm a fan."

"Oh, you're a fan." I smirked back, arching a brow.

Lifting my almost-empty beer bottle in a toast, I said, "Well then, to sex and cursing, the only two things we have in common."

Ken smiled and lifted his Gatorade bottle. "Cheers."

The plastic container met my glass bottle with an unsatisfying thud.

That ancient conversation played over and over in my head as I drove to Gusto's Trattoria to meet Ken for dinner on February 14. I told myself not to get my hopes up. I reminded myself that we'd only been hanging out for a few weeks and hadn't done more than awkwardly kiss on his couch—*once.* I replayed the audio clip of him telling me point blank that he didn't celebrate holidays, do commitment, or even eat chocolate. I made sure to keep my expectations for the night nice and low.

Or so I thought.

Dinner was fine. The food was delicious. I overindulged and hated myself for it, as usual. And, even though Ken didn't acknowledge that it was Valentine's Day, he did at least pick up the check, which I know had to be unpleasant for him.

Things were going about the way I'd expected—until I handed Ken his gift.

I'd made the card myself, remembering how he felt about Hallmark. On the front, I'd drawn a Celtic knot, my favorite thing to doodle, and if you looked closely, hiding inside the intricate design were the letters K, E, and N. I don't even remember what I'd written on the inside of the card, probably something sarcastic. Then, I'd tucked it into an envelope and taped it to a gift-wrapped All-American Rejects CD. I hadn't wanted to get him anything expensive, just a little token, and since we'd had a car sing-along to the song "Swing Swing" the week before, I'd thought it would be the perfect gift.

A gift…

That Ken…

Refused…

To fucking…

Open.

"You shouldn't have done that," he said, his tone almost punitive as he stared at my offering.

"Why not?" I snapped, thrusting the package at him again.

Because you don't like me like that? Because I'm cool enough to hang out with but not hot enough for you to invite upstairs or break your Valentine's Day rules over? Because you're a serial killer, and you don't want to own anything with my fingerprints on it?

"Because, if I wanted something, I'd buy it for myself."

"No, you wouldn't."

"Maybe I don't want anything."

"You want this."

Ken watched me pout the way an exhausted parent watches their toddler have a tantrum. His whole being seemed to say, *Can we not do this right now?* and, *Are you done yet?*

But I wasn't done. I was Brooke fucking Bradley, a spoiled only-child whose parents had inadvertently taught her that *no* simply meant I hadn't been a big enough pain in the ass yet. Ken might not want anything, but I sure as shit did.

"Listen," I snarled as soon as our server left with Ken's credit card, "either you can open this, or I can do it for you, but we are not leaving here until you've seen your fucking present."

Ken sighed, his shoulders sagging in defeat, but he made no move to reach for the gift.

"Fine," I hissed. Pulling the envelope away from the package unnecessarily hard, I tore open the flap and yanked out the homemade card. "Ooh, would you look at that?" I cried in my sweetest Southern belle voice, blinking my biggest Disney princess eyes. "Isn't that just the prettiest thing you ever did see?" I gasped and placed a hand over my heart. "Oh my goodness, I think it even says your name." I slapped the card on the table where Ken's plate had been. "And there's more!" I tore the silver gift wrap off the CD and turned it around to face him. "The All-American

Rejects. Oh, I just love them! What a nice gift you got, Ken." Tossing the CD next to the card on the table, I fell out of character and slumped back in my booth. Napalm pumped through my veins as I glared at him, imagining a thousand and one ways that I could hurt him, using only the cutlery on the table.

"Can we go now?" Ken asked, unaffected by my performance.

Pulling on my harshest resting bitch face, I grabbed my purse and Ken's gifts off the table. "Great idea."

In addition to being a holiday engineered by American greeting card companies, Valentine's Day was also Jason's birthday. He was throwing himself a birthday party that night, and we'd promised to go.

"You still going to Jason's?" Ken asked from somewhere behind me as I stomped across the dark parking lot toward my black Mustang.

I caught a hint of remorse in his voice. Or maybe it was trepidation because I was acting like such a stabby psycho.

"Yep," I replied flatly just as Ken hit the unlock button on his key fob.

The headlights on his Eclipse blinked a few spaces away, and before I had a chance to even think about it, I'd already broken into a full-on sprint. I raced to his car, yanked open the passenger door, and tossed both the CD and card inside. Slamming Ken's door, I turned and power-walked back to my Mustang, making direct eye contact with him the whole way.

They're yours now, motherfucker. Suck it.

Ken watched me with a look of absolute boredom on his beautiful face.

I peeled out of there and was back on the highway before Ken had even cranked his engine. Even though I was doing fifteen over the speed limit, the drive into Atlanta felt like it took an eternity. I spent my time alone replaying every aspect of my Valentine's date from hell and then moved on to psychoanalyzing our entire relationship. I came to two conclusions during that trip across town.

One, Ken was a stubborn, rigid, self-restrictive asshole.

And two, I'd been right all along; he just wasn't that into me.

I threw my car into a parking spot beside Jason's apartment building and marched up the four flights of cement stairs without waiting for Ken to arrive. The way he drove, I'd probably beaten him by a solid ten minutes anyway.

Jason opened the door after the fifteenth knock, reeking of brown liquor and smiling from ear to ear.

"Whasss up, buttercup?" he slurred.

I raised my arms to hug him around the neck. "Happy birth—ahh!" I squealed as Jason picked me up and spun me around.

Kicking the door shut and almost dropping me in the process, Jason turned and carried me into the living room where more people than usual were gathered in clusters, drinking and yelling over the aggressively loud electronic dance music blaring from Jason's high-tech home stereo.

"Look what I found, muhrfuckersss," Jason announced to no one in particular.

Setting me down on my feet, he steered his stumble toward the couch, snatching a half-empty glass of scotch off the coffee table along the way. Jason landed on the sofa, sending amber liquid flying.

I dived into the spot next to him and clasped my hands around his highball glass, steadying it before he dumped the rest of the caramel-colored contents on himself.

"Easy there, birthday boy. You might wanna pace yourself. You haven't even blown your candles out yet." I gave Jason a small smile that he didn't return.

"Whasss the fuckin' point?" he slurred, his glassy, droopy eyes searching for my face but landing somewhere near my shoulder. "Nobody cares."

"Hey, what are you talking about?" I asked, placing a reassuring hand on his shoulder. "Look at all these people who came to your party. Everybody cares. What's going on?"

I'd never heard Jason say anything negative before. I'd never really heard him talk about his feelings at all. Usually, I saw him happy drunk, then sloppy drunk, then passed-out drunk, but never sad drunk.

Or sober, for that matter.

Jason went to take a sip from his glass, hitting his chin instead of his mouth.

Jesus.

I took his drink—the remaining contents inside worth more than my hourly wage—and placed it on a coaster on the coffee table. Looking around for help, I locked eyes with the only other sober person in the apartment.

Ken was standing in the kitchen, talking to Allen, but his eyes were on me.

With that single desperate glance, Ken crossed Jason's living room, met my look of pity with one of his neutral aqua stares, and placed his hand on Jason's shoulder. "Hey, man. You okay?"

Jason's head slumped forward violently, a bead of drool hanging from his open mouth.

"Shit." Ken looked at me with genuine concern peeking through his facade of nonchalance. "Let's lay him down. Maybe on his side in case he pukes."

"Okay." I stood and watched as Ken guided Jason's sad, lifeless body onto its side on the sofa. "I'll get a trash can!" I ran to the hall bathroom, returning seconds later with a white plastic receptacle.

Unlike his fucking Valentine's Day present, Ken accepted the trash can from me without hesitation, placing it on the floor beside Jason's head.

I looked around, hoping to share a pitiful glance with someone over the state our birthday boy was in, but not a single pair of eyes was watching. Everyone was laughing and shouting and drinking and dancing as if nothing were wrong. Not one of them had noticed that the person they were supposed to be celebrating had already drunk himself unconscious.

Maybe Jason had been right about them.

I couldn't just stand there and watch him sleep, but I also didn't feel right about partying when my friend might or might not have alcohol poisoning.

I could smoke though. I could always smoke.

Reaching into my purse, I realized that I'd left my cigarettes on my passenger seat.

"Hey, I gotta run to my car real quick."

I hated that I felt obligated to tell Ken where I was going, and I hated even more that he felt obligated to come with me. We weren't a couple—he'd made that abundantly clear over dinner—but Ken followed me anyway, grabbing his black wool coat off the back of the chair in the foyer on our way out the front door.

We headed down the stairs without a word. I led the way around the side of the building, annoyed to see Ken's maroon Eclipse parked right next to my Mustang. He stood in between our cars as I opened my passenger door and retrieved my babies.

"Fuck, it's cold out here," I complained, fishing a Camel Light out of the flimsy cardboard box.

"You could quit smoking," Ken deadpanned with an arched brow. His arms were folded across his chest, and his shoulders were pulled up around his ears.

I knew he was freezing, too; he was just too fucking stubborn to admit it.

I popped a cigarette into my mouth and rolled my eyes before lighting it. Warm, dirty smoke filled my lungs, and I relaxed. With a long, delicious exhale, I gave him my signature response. The one I told my doctors, my parents, my employers—basically, every responsible adult in my life—when they suggested that I give up my favorite vice.

"I'll quit when I get pregnant."

Ken's other eyebrow shot up to join the first. "When you get pregnant?"

Simmer down, asshole.

"Yeah. In, like, ten years," I sassed.

Relief washed over his face.

Oh my God. Like I'd actually want to have your *apathetic babies. Puh-lease.*

"How much money do you spend on cigarettes a month?" Ken asked as I took another drag.

I wished he'd go back inside and let me enjoy my bad habit in peace. "Are you serious?"

"Yes." A flash of interest danced on the edges of Ken's always-neutral features.

I did the math in my head and cringed. "Jesus. Like, a hundred bucks."

"Damn." Ken shook his head. "If you put that money into a total market fund every month and let the interest compound over time, you could have"—he paused, his eyes looking up and to the right as he crunched the numbers—"around a million dollars by the time you retired."

"Shut the fuck up." I exhaled on a cough. "How do you know that?"

Ken shrugged. "Investing is kind of my hobby."

I snorted. "*Investing* is your hobby? I don't think you know how hobbies work."

Ken's smile made a rare appearance, softening his serious, square-jawed, all-American face. He opened his mouth, a smart-ass comeback at the ready, but I never got to hear it because, a split-second later, his body lurched forward and slammed into mine.

I yelped and dropped my cigarette as my hip crashed into the side mirror of my car.

"What the fuck?" I screamed into Ken's chest, which was crushing me against the passenger window.

Craning my neck back, I found him hovering over me with his arms stretched up over his head as if he'd just caught a fifty-yard pass. Only, instead of a brown leather football in his hands, Ken was holding a brown leather *loafer.*

Following his gaze, my eyes traveled up, up, up the side of the building until I, too, saw the source of the projectile.

Perched on the railing of his fourth-floor balcony was the birthday boy himself. Jason's head lolled forward. His feet dangled over the edge, and one of them was missing a shoe.

"Oh my God. Ken…"

Ken cupped a hand around his mouth and yelled up to Jason, "Stay there, man! We're coming up!"

Jason yelled something incoherent back, but we were already gone. Taking the stairs two at a time, Ken and I flew back up to apartment 441 and burst through the door. Techno pulsed, and people danced as Ken and I pushed our way through the oblivious assholes Jason called friends and out to the balcony.

Closing the door behind us, I sighed in relief to see that we weren't too late. Jason was still sitting on the narrow wooden railing, staring down at the parking lot below. But he wouldn't be for long. Gravity was tugging at his heels. I could almost see it beckoning him from below. One wrong move and it would steal him from us forever.

As I stood in the doorway, struggling to catch my breath and trying to figure out what the fuck to say, Ken tiptoed toward Jason.

"Stay 'way!" Jason yelled, swinging his arm out in our direction.

Ken froze and held his hands up.

"Jason!" I screeched. "Don't move like that! You're gonna fall!"

"No'm not," he slurred, dropping his hand and returning his gaze to the asphalt below.

"Honey, I don't know what you took tonight or what's going on, but this isn't like you. Come back inside. Please?"

Jason snapped his head around, his glassy eyes unable to find mine in the dark. "Thisss *me.* Fffffuckin' real. You 'on't know. You 'on't fuckin' care." Jason tried to turn around enough to point at Ken, who was almost behind him, causing his body to slip a fraction of an inch and my heart to stop. "You come-see *him*." His head lolled again as he turned back toward the parking lot. "Not me. Nobody c-c-c-come-see-muh…" Jason's words became unintelligible as his teeth began to chatter, and his body began to shake.

Do something, BB!

"Jason," I sputtered, my mind reeling as I watched my friend teetering on a tightrope between life and death, "of course I come to see you. You're one of my best friends. I moved into this apartment complex last year because of *you*. Everybody loves you. *I* love—"

Everything happened in an instant, yet it felt like I was watching it unfold in slow motion. Before those three words could even leave my mouth, Jason spun around, ready to argue. I watched his face morph from enraged to terrified as the force of his spin caused him to lose his balance. As he realized a moment too late what he'd done.

What he would never be able to undo.

I leaped forward and reached for him on instinct, my mind refusing to accept the fact that I was too far away to save him.

But Ken wasn't.

One moment, Jason's frightened brown eyes were begging me for help as his hands grasped at nothing, and the next, Ken was grabbing him by the arms and pulling him to safety. Ken yanked Jason over the railing so hard; they both tumbled backward and landed in a heap on the cement floor. I held my breath and watched in horror as Jason thrashed and kicked and fought against Ken, but Ken didn't let him go. Not until his body went limp and his face crumpled in defeat.

The second he stopped fighting, I rushed to Jason's side, cooing to him that it was okay, touching his arms, his shoulders, his face.

I watched his chin buckle as he curled up into the fetal position and buried his face in my lap. His body shivered against the freezing cold cement, and his quiet, keening sobs broke my heart.

Stroking his short brown hair and trying not to let him hear me cry, I glanced over at Ken. He had scooted as far away from us as he could get and was sitting with his back against the farthest wall of the balcony. One leg was out straight in front of him. The other was bent with his knee pulled up toward his chest. His eyes were wider than I'd ever seen them, and they were fixed on mine in the dark.

I stared at him in wonder.

Ken, the man who didn't believe in gifts, had just given me my friend back.

Because he was sober, he'd been alert. Because he was an infuriating gentleman, he'd accompanied me outside. Because he was freakishly calm, he'd kept his cool during a crisis. And, because he was a jock, he'd had the reaction speed and strength to pull a grown man to safety. All the things I'd considered turn-offs, all the qualities I'd rolled my eyes at, I suddenly saw them as assets. They were the reasons Jason's head was in my lap instead of splattered across the sidewalk.

I watched Ken watching us—so uncomfortable in the presence of emotion, so unsure of what to do now that the time for action was over—and I was overcome with appreciation. For him. As a person. For the things that made him different from everyone else. Everyone else was partying in the living room but not Ken. Ken didn't care about fun. Ken cared about shit that mattered, like art and music and his credit score.

And, evidently, his friends.

"You okay?" I asked.

"Yeah," Ken replied immediately, his voice cold, his face once again hard as stone.

"I think he's out," I said, looking down at Jason's slack-jawed face smooshed against my thigh.

"Let's get him inside." Ken's voice was all business as he stood and approached us. Leaning over so that we were almost eye-to-eye, he reached under Jason's armpits and hoisted him to a standing position.

Revealing a huge wet spot on the crotch of his khakis.

Jesus Christ.

I hustled across the balcony to a set of French doors. Trying the handles, I exhaled in relief when they swung open, revealing Jason's large, sparsely decorated bedroom. Ken dragged his unconscious body over to the bed and laid him gently on his side. I hustled to lift his legs onto the mattress and remove his one remaining shoe. Once we got him tucked into his black satin sheets and placed a trash can next to the bed, Ken and I tiptoed out of the room and into the hall.

"You saved his life." The whispered words tumbled from my mouth the second the door clicked shut behind us.

Ken shrugged, his features severe. "I've never seen him this fucked up."

He didn't take credit for his heroism. In fact, he didn't acknowledge it at all. I added that to the long list of things I was learning to appreciate about Ken Easton that night.

"Me either." The pulsing techno from the living room mimicked my heart as it pounded in my chest. "Maybe we should stay, just to keep an eye on him until he sobers up."

Ken's eyes were shrouded in shadows as we stood a foot apart in Jason's darkened hallway. "Okay."

"Okay." I looked up at him as the warm buzzing hum of his bubble enveloped me. "So, what do we do now?"

I didn't even know which question I was asking. *What do we do for the rest of the night? What do we do about Jason? What do we do about this weird thing between us that seems to be going nowhere?*

But it didn't matter because Ken's answer would be the same for all three.

Lifting a noncommittal shoulder, he said, "Whatever you want to do."

Whatever you want to do.

What if I want to kiss you?

What if I want to go home with you and make love to you and spend the night with you and wander around museums with you tomorrow, looking at French art?

What if I want more?

There was only one way to find out. Pushing up onto my tiptoes, I leaned forward slowly, making my intentions clear. I was prepared for my lips to hit the unyielding marble that Ken sometimes turned into whenever I touched him. I readied myself for the emotional blow of yet another unreciprocated advance. I had *not* readied myself for the rush of adrenaline that shot through my bloodstream when Ken actually fucking kissed me back.

Clutching the lapels of his wool coat in my fists, I backed Ken against Jason's bedroom door. Electronic dance music rattled the thin walls all around us as I pressed my chest against his, but Ken's hands barely skimmed my sides. I sucked on his bottom lip and swirled my tongue around his, but his kisses remained featherlight. I was desperate for him to make me feel better. To make me forget my fear for Jason, my breakup with Hans, my altercations with Knight, hell, my own name, but Ken wasn't cooperating. He was infuriating.

So, I bit him.

I hadn't meant to. It just kind of happened. But the second my teeth sank into his plump bottom lip, Ken moaned and pulled my hips forward against his impressive erection.

Ughn.

My pulse skyrocketed. My hands tore at his sleek coat, twisted around his silken tie. And when my teeth captured his tongue, Ken's cock jerked against my lower belly.

I was just about to rip the buttons off his oxford cloth shirt when the sound of someone puking on the other side of the door brought us both back into the present.

Jason.

Shit.

While I had been busy taking care of Jason and Ken had been busy cleaning up after his shitty friends, Friday had turned into Saturday.

And, on Saturdays, I had to work.

I cursed every single pink and orange sunbeam streaking across the sky as I kissed Ken goodbye in the parking lot the next morning. As he kissed me back. As he opened my car door and told me to, "Drive safe."

I showed up at Macy's ten minutes late, wearing the same makeup I'd applied the day before, and spent my lunch break napping on a bed of Rocawear jeans in the storage closet. I should have just called in sick, gone home, and gone to bed, but as exhausted as I was, my bed held no appeal.

I wanted to sleep in someone else's bed.

Someone handsome and mysterious and sarcastic and quiet.

Someone whose kisses tasted like artificially flavored sports drinks.

Someone whose gentlemanly manners told me *no* while his manly body told me *yes.*

I went home after work but only long enough to pack an overnight bag. Then, I headed straight to Kenneth Easton's house where I invited *myself* upstairs.

As I lay next to Ken on his queen-size bed—our backs propped up against pillows and our bodies, stiff as statues, illuminated by the menu on his bedroom TV—I thought, *This was a terrible fucking idea.*

Ken and I might have been the only people in his house, but my GSU tote bag on his bedroom floor had a presence all its own. A big one. It might as well have been a yodeling, baton-twirling drag queen swinging on a disco ball in front of a flashing neon sign that read, *BB WANTS TO BANG YOU.*

Look how tense he is. I think he's gone through all the movie channels at least three times. He's not even talking to me.

"Have you seen *10 Things I Hate About You*?" Ken asked, hopping off the bed and crossing the room. He pulled open his top dresser drawer and began rummaging through what sounded like a clearance bin at a Blockbuster Video.

See? Not only is he super fucking uncomfortable, but the first movie that came to mind has the words I, Hate, *and* You *in the title.*

"No, I haven't. Is it good?"

Why won't you touch me?

"It's amazing."

Why are you stalling?

"It must have Hugh Grant in it then."

Ken shoved a VHS tape into the VCR next to the glowing television on his dresser and turned toward me. "It's good, even without Hugh Grant. *That's* how good it is."

Ken walked back to the bed in absolutely no fucking hurry. He still had on the white button-up dress shirt and dark gray slacks he'd worn to work, his silvery-gray tie hanging loose around his neck.

Oh my God. He hasn't even taken off his fucking tie yet! Go home, BB. Just get your purse and your stupid bag of shit and go home. You're tired, and this man obviously does not want to fuck you.

"I, uh…like your room," I said with a hopeful smile as Ken returned to his designated side of the bed. It was true.

Because he rented the master bedroom to his sister, Ken was living in the bonus room above the garage. The walls and ceiling had all kinds of slanted angles, thanks to the pitch of the roof, and there was a huge arched window that took up most of the wall behind the bed.

"Thanks." Ken smiled. "This was attic space when I moved in. I had it finished to boost the resale value."

I snorted out a laugh. "Of course you did."

"Plus, it freed up more space for renters."

I rolled my eyes. "You gonna charge me if I spend the night?"

Oh God! Did I just say that out loud?

"Nah." Ken smirked. "First night's free."

Elation exploded through my veins, and hope bloomed in my belly as I scooted over and nuzzled my way under Ken's heavy right arm. He let me rest my cheek on his fabric softener–scented chest as we both gazed at the TV, pretending to watch.

He's letting me spend the night!

He's letting me touch him!

He has on so many clothes!

Since Ken was in no rush to do anything about his clothing problem, I took a deep breath, said a silent prayer, and grasped the knot on his loosened tie. With my heart thumping in my chest, I slid the binding toward me until the knot unraveled in my hand. Glancing up at Ken's face, I expected to find him stoically staring at the television, either ignoring or oblivious to my advances, but he wasn't. His guarded blue gaze was pinned on me.

There was something about the warmth of his stare, the curled corner of his mouth, the sharp angle of his eyebrow that spurred me on. It wasn't the look of a man who didn't want me.

It was the look of a man who didn't want me to stop.

Emboldened by his silent dare, I ran my hand up Ken's chest and began to free the smooth white button at the hollow of his neck. His Adam's apple bobbed against my fingertips as I opened his collar. His lungs expanded beneath my hand as I moved to the second and third buttons down. His taut stomach muscles flexed against my fist as I popped the fourth and fifth open. And when I yanked the bottom of his shirt and undershirt free from the waistband of his slacks, the bulge beneath his belt buckle betrayed his cool exterior.

Ken shrugged off his button-up and peeled his classic white undershirt off over his head, revealing a full set of flexed abs and pectoral muscles dusted with short, well-groomed chest hair. After tossing the top half of his outfit onto the floor, Ken sat back against his pillows, shirtless and sentient.

I couldn't figure him out, but the smug expression on his face and fully hard cock protruding from his slacks suggested that he liked it that way.

Does he just want me to do all the work? Is he that lazy?

He doesn't seem lazy. Look at those fucking abs.

Maybe he just wants me to service him and be on my way?

What an asshole. I should slap him.

Do not slap him.

He might like it. He lets me drag him around by his tie all the time.

Do not *slap him.*

What do I do now? I'm not just gonna strip him naked. I still have all my clothes on!

So…maybe take your clothes off, too?

Ugh!

Instead of slapping *or* stripping him further, I leaned forward and assaulted him with a punishing kiss. Just like the night before, Ken was passively letting me have my way with him, and just like the night before, my desperation took over. I chomped down on his lip and felt that motherfucker smile against my mouth. I fisted his hair and heard a low chuckle rumble in his throat. And when I straddled his waist and ground against the swollen ridge in his slacks, Ken rested his hands lightly on my denim-covered thighs.

"Why won't you touch me?" I finally growled, my face flushed with both desire and mortification.

Ken replied immediately, the husky timbre of his voice in stark contrast with his disinterested behavior, "I don't want to pressure you…"

"Ken"—I pulled back just far enough for him to see the condescending look on my face—"I didn't show up here with an overnight bag because I just want to *sleep*."

"I know." Ken narrowed his eyes. "You probably wanna have a pillow fight first."

A laugh tore out of me as I gripped his face with my right hand, smooshing his smart-ass mouth into a little heart, which I then attacked with a gnashing, exasperated kiss. Ken responded by palming my ass with both hands and guiding me to resume my previous dry-humping pace.

He was infuriating me on purpose. That was the only explanation. The angrier and more aggressive I got, the bigger he smiled, and the more he participated.

I told you this motherfucker wants to be slapped.

Shut up! We're not doing that!

Every action I made was met by Ken with an equal and opposite reaction. As I clawed at his belt buckle and tore open his zipper, he deftly unfastened my jeans. While I ripped my own T-shirt off like a professional wrestler, Ken reached behind me and skillfully unhooked my bra. When I palmed his girth through the rough cotton of his boxer briefs, he massaged my tiny breasts and pierced nipples tenderly.

He wasn't just *letting* me lead; he was *making* me.

And nobody makes me do shit.

Once we were completely naked, I grabbed Ken by the shoulders and rolled us both over, pulling his tall, athletic body on top of mine. The weight of him felt delicious—the thump of his heart, the dewy warmth of his skin. I finally had him where I wanted him—right between my legs.

Digging my heels into the mattress, I shifted my hips so that the head of his impressive cock was poised at the entrance of my impatient, thrumming body. Then, I kissed the shit out of him.

There. I consent, motherfucker. Bring it.

But Ken didn't bring it. He tortured me further by dragging the entire length of his manhood back and forth across my slippery, pierced clit. Over and over, with each successive pass, Ken would graze my entrance, causing me to lift my hopeful hips in invitation, before denying me again.

Confused and pissed and panting with need, I glared up at his face in search of an explanation.

Is he afraid to fuck me without a condom?

Should I tell him I'm clean and on the pill?

Is he waiting for that slap? Because I'm about ready to give it to him.

But Ken didn't look worried; he looked like a smug son of a bitch. He'd won, and he knew it. Never in my life had I thought I'd meet someone more stubborn than me, but there he was, in all his handsome, hard-bodied glory.

Surrendering to his impossibly strong will and my own raging hormones, I reached between us and stroked Ken's slick girth. It was solid and ready and felt so right in my hand. As I guided him forward, I accepted my defeat, inch by glorious inch.

I don't know if it was because his dick had been custom built for me, because he'd made me work so damn hard for it, or because we were both sober—which was a first for me—but the moment we were joined, I felt a powerful, euphoric shift occur between us. With that one motion, we went from being rams tangled in each other's horns to lovers tangled in each other's arms.

I just hoped he felt it, too.

As we began to move, it became clear that Ken was definitely feeling—or *not feeling*—something. His body was even tenser than before, his movements slow and cautious, and an ocean of space separated our exposed torsos as he hovered over me. Whatever his hang-up was, Ken's inhibition was driving me fucking insane. I'd lost my virginity in bondage. I'd had every erogenous zone pierced by the age of sixteen. I'd been drizzled with honey, doused with tequila, and painted with my own blood.

And I'd loved every second of it.

Ken had a freak inside of him, too; he just needed help letting it out.

Trusting my instincts, I leaned forward and sank my teeth into the straining muscle between Ken's neck and shoulder. Rather than yelping or flinching or warding me off with an outstretched crucifix, Ken melted into me, his taut tendons turning to putty between my teeth.

Interesting.

Next, I bit his earlobe, practically puncturing it with my sharp incisors. Ken responded by pulling my thighs up around his waist and filling me to my limit.

Yes.

I threaded my fingers into his hair and yanked. Hard. Ken thrust harder.

The more I hurt him, the more his self-imposed restraint melted away. But it wasn't until I sank my razor-sharp nails into his shoulder blades that Ken's pace became unhinged. He pounded into me with abandon. His mouth crashed into mine. His hands gripped my hips, my ass, my breasts.

And I finally got the high I'd been longing for.

Caught up in the moment and craving nothing but *more*, I dragged my talons, still sunk to the quick in Ken's upper back, down the entire length of his spine. It was brutal. Medieval. I probably drew blood. But Ken...fucking...loved it.

As I sliced his back to ribbons, Ken buried his face in my neck, wrapped his arms around my torso, and came so hard that *I* saw stars.

Holy shit.

I panted and clenched around him, faking a physical orgasm but having a very real one emotionally. Ken, the poster child for self-discipline, had just come inside me, no questions asked. He'd trusted me. He'd held me. He'd let me see his kink. And, above all, he'd finally given me the one thing he valued more than anything else—control.

As well as his DNA, which I was pretty sure was permanently embedded under my fingernails.

With his dick empty and his back carved up like a prized turkey, Ken was a new man.

We spent the next few hours cuddling and talking, tickling and teasing, and when I climbed on top of him for round two, the orgasm wasn't just real; it was revelatory.

The revelation being that I was totally fucked.

That night, I had a dream that I was back in the 1600s, being tried as a witch in some back-ass-ward little village. I'd been lashed to a stake in the center of town, and all of these old white men were carrying torches, shouting that I was a mistress of Satan.

"Heretic!" they cried, shaking their fists. "Heathen!"

I never did find out what I'd done wrong because, seconds before I woke up, they gathered around me, chanted a prayer, and held their flaming sticks to the brittle straw beneath my feet.

I gasped and sat up with a start. Ken's comforter was hot to the touch when I grabbed my toes through the puffy down, causing my half-conscious mind to assume that the bed was actually on fire. Looking around in a panic, I realized that I was not about to die. The bottom of the bed was simply hot because the sun was shining directly on that spot through the arched window above the bed.

Ken didn't seem to mind the whole ants-under-a-magnifying-glass effect because he was curled up in a ball on the top corner of the bed where the sunlight couldn't reach him. His back was turned toward me. His arms were clutching a pillow. And there were at least two feet of open space between us.

So much for cuddling all night.

I glanced at the clock on his bedside table. It was a little after eight thirty. Too shaken from my near-death experience to go back to sleep, I curled up behind Ken, molding myself to his warm body, and planted a kiss on his shoulder blade.

"Ken…" I whispered.

"Hmm…"

"You have to get some blinds for that window."

"Nuh-uh." Ken shook his head and curled up tighter around his spare pillow.

"Why not?" I whispered.

"Custom," he grumbled. "Expensive as fuck."

I pouted even though he couldn't see me. If I was going to spend the night there with any regularity, I'd have to get creative. A sheet over the window maybe? Or newspaper? That was what serial killers did, right? Ken would love it.

"Hey," I whispered a little louder. "Do you want to go to the museum today? They have this exhibit that's on loan from Paris…"

Ken grunted and pushed himself up into a sitting position, his back still turned toward me. The morning sunlight illuminated every red, raised laceration I'd inflicted upon him the night before, causing my hand to fly to my mouth and my heart to plummet into my stomach.

"Can't." He yawned, rubbing his face. "I have to work."

"Ken, your back!" I squealed into my palm. "Oh my God! I'm so sorry!"

Ken shrugged sleepily and stood up, revealing even more welts marring his perfectly high, tight ass.

Jesus Christ. I'm a monster.

Ken turned and looked at me for the first time that morning. His eyelids were heavy, his features relaxed. "It's fine."

I winced. "Does it hurt?"

Ken looked at me as if I'd just asked him the dumbest question ever uttered. His head tilted an inch to one side. His eyebrows rose fractionally. "You can't hurt me," he stated. As if it were obvious. As if I should have known better. Then, he walked his tall, toned, beautiful body across the room and out the door.

"You can't hurt me."

I stared at his open bedroom door, blinking away the sting from that offhanded comment.

"You can't hurt me."

His words echoed in my ears as I heard a shower turn on somewhere beyond that doorway.

YOU…can't hurt…ME.

I knew that he was probably just referring to his pain tolerance and hadn't meant anything personal by it, but that was not how it felt.

It felt like a slap to the face.

I gave Ken plenty of space that morning. I waited until he was out of the bathroom to go brush my teeth. I took my time getting ready, applying an extra-bold swipe of liquid eyeliner and going back and forth over whether I should tuck my rumpled burgundy bob behind one ear or just brush it all forward and hide behind it like Cousin Itt from *The Addams Family.*

I went with the single ear tuck and a hefty helping of false bravado. Pulling on my favorite ripped jeans and a black Ramones T-shirt, I took a deep breath, held my head high, and sauntered down the stairs like the badass punk rock princess I was always pretending to be.

Fuck Ken Easton. Who the hell is he? Just some hot, smart guy with a killer bod and a gorgeous house. Pssh. Whatever. He doesn't even have any tattoos. I refuse to get upset over a guy who has anything less than a full sleeve. And at least three piercings.

"Good morning." I beamed as I crossed the living room into the kitchen.

Ken was sitting at his sun-drenched breakfast table, eating a bowl of cereal. His hair was still damp from his shower. I could smell the Irish Spring soap on him from across the room. And he was wearing a light-blue button-up shirt that made his eyes look like a pair of tropical lagoons.

Eyes that were trained on the television in the living room where a man in a suit was announcing stock market projections.

"Cinnamon Toast Crunch, huh?" I teased, casting a judgmental look in the direction of the box on the table. "I figured you for more of a dozen-raw-eggs kinda guy."

Ken's aqua gaze lifted to mine. "Breakfast of champions," he said with a half-assed smile. "Want some?"

My stomach growled—no, *snarled* in response. I'd atoned for all the damage I'd done at Gusto's Trattoria on Valentine's Day by successfully abstaining from food the entire next day, but now, we were going on day two, and that was pushing it. Even for me.

I could feel my mouth begin to sweat and my hands begin to tremble as I stared at the box full of empty calories on the table. With that simple two-worded question, a familiar battle had begun. The one between my basic need to survive and my irrational need to be Kate Moss. Pangs of hunger clawed at the walls of my stomach, but they didn't have the desired effect on me. I liked the pain. I liked to see how long I could hold out before it became unbearable.

Maybe Ken and I weren't so different after all.

"No, thanks," I replied after swallowing a mouthful of saliva.

Ken narrowed his eyes at me. "Not a breakfast person?"

"Nope." I met his questioning gaze with one of stubborn defiance.

Shrugging, Ken stood up and carried his bowl over to the sink.

He hadn't touched me since we woke up. Hell, he'd hardly even spoken to me.

I stood in the center of the kitchen, feeling awkward and unwelcome, as Ken placed his bowl and spoon in the dishwasher. Opening a drawer next to the machine, he began removing tiny objects and putting them into the pockets of his low-slung khakis—his car keys, his wallet, a blue pen, maybe a pack of gum. Then, he paused before removing one last item from the drawer.

Turning toward me, Ken's face was all business. I didn't like his vibe. I imagined it was how he regarded his employees whenever they fucked up. Impassive. Impersonal. Impervious to their emotional bullshit.

"I gotta go," he announced, placing the last object on the kitchen counter. "Lock up when you leave, okay?" Ken pulled his hand back, revealing a single…silver…key.

My mouth fell open. My wide eyes flicked to his. And my brain screamed one long, high-pitched syllable that sounded a lot like the word, *KEEEEYYYYYYYYY!!!*

I nodded vigorously. "Okay," I squeaked.

Then, I jumped him.

After sending Ken off to work with nude lipstick smeared all over his pretty face, I locked the front door and turned to find myself in Oz. The sun warmed my pale skin. The birds sang a collective chorus. A patch of cheery yellow daffodils was beginning to bloom beneath the large Bradford pear tree in Ken's front yard. Winter, that bitch, was finally releasing its hold on me.

In December, my relationship with Hans had crashed and burned, taking with it a few close friends and my first taste of adult independence. In January, I'd retreated into the protective shell of my parents' house, becoming a streetwear-folding, term paper–writing, psychology-studying ghost girl. But, that February, as I drove home, admiring the shiny new key hanging next to the can of mace on my key ring, I felt something I hadn't in a long, long time.

Hope.

I tried to tiptoe across the threshold of my parents' house, but it was no use. I was busted.

"Brooke Bradley, come in here and sit down." My mother was standing in the kitchen with one hand on her hip and the other pointing at a barstool, a rare show of authority coming from her. Her long red hair was pulled up in a high bun, and she had on her usual Sunday attire of yoga pants and a tie-dyed T-shirt.

I hung my head and did the walk of shame down the parquet hall.

Sitting where I'd been told, I dropped my overnight bag and purse on our sad excuse for a kitchen island.

"This whole *coming in at all hours of the night* thing has got to stop," she announced. "I know you're an adult now, but when you don't come home, I can't sleep. I stay up all night, worrying about you." She began to pace across the linoleum floor, throwing her arms this way and that. "If you're gonna keep living here, we're just…I don't know…we're gonna have to go back to a curfew or something."

Just when I thought she was done, she added, "And you need to eat. You look…Biafran!"

I snorted. I couldn't help it. She was just so cute when she was mad.

"Mom," I started, holding my hands up and trying not to laugh. Looking left and right to make sure my dad wasn't in earshot, I said, "I've just been coming home in the middle of the night because I keep falling asleep on Ken's couch."

"Well, you need to just stay there if you're sleepy. It's not safe to be on the roads with all the drunks and cops out that late."

"I did. Last night."

"Well…okay then."

"Okay."

"Fine."

I braced myself for yet another lecture about condoms, but instead, my mom blew out a sigh of relief and plopped down onto the opposite barstool.

"So…" She smiled, propping her freckled chin on her hand, leathery from years spent working with clay and paint. "Ken. He's the one who was helping you study for your art history class, right? What's he like?"

I laughed. "He's…I don't know. He's not my type. Like, at all."

"That's good." My mom smiled, exhaustion weighing heavy on her eyelids. "Your type sucks."

We both cracked up, prompting my father to shout, "Keep it down in there, wenches!" from the living room. Our laughter was probably making it hard for him to fully absorb all the doom and gloom on CNN.

Muffling her giggles with her hand, my mom stood up to retrieve her coffee cup from the counter by the sink.

"You know, you can always just call me if you're worried," I said, standing, too.

My mom took a long sip from her mug. "I did."

Pulling my cell phone out of my purse, I saw that I had not one, but three missed calls. "Oh shit. I must have left my purse downstairs all night. Sorry, Mom."

She gave me a look I'd seen a thousand times before. It was a look that said, *If it were legal, I would slap the shit out of you right now.*

Slinking out of the kitchen with an apologetic grimace on my face, I turned and ran up the stairs to my childhood bedroom. My mom had redecorated it while I was living with Hans, pulling down all my posters and painting the whole thing a depressingly generic pastel blue. But worse than the color was the size. You couldn't fit a Volkswagen in there, yet I had managed to cram all of my belongings *plus* all of the shit I'd stolen from Hans when we broke up into that tiny, shoebox-esque space. Pots and pans hung from the ceiling like suncatchers. Shower curtains and regular curtains and window blinds peeked out from under my bed. Forks, spoons, and knives shared a drawer with my unmentionables. And the remote control to Hans's big screen TV sat on my bookshelf like a trophy.

If living with Hans had been hell, then living with my parents was purgatory.

Flopping onto my unmade bed, I lit a cigarette, leaned back against the headboard, and listened to my voicemails.

Saturday, February 15, 11:50 p.m.: "Beebeeee, it's your mother. I'm just wondering when you'll be home. Call me back. Love you."

Sunday, February 16, 2:06 a.m.: "Yeah, I'll leave a fuckin' message."

Knight's clear, deep voice burst out of the phone like a sucker punch. I let out a smoky cough and sat up, my heart already racing from those six little words.

"My *message* is that you're a scared little bitch who won't answer the fuckin'—" The white noise of shouting and cursing and clanking beer bottles blurred together in the background. "I *was* leaving, cocksucker." Knight's voice sounded distant, as if he was talking to someone else. "Put your hand on me, motherfucker. I dare you. Put your motherfucking hand on me and see what happens." Then, with a scuffle and grunt and a loud crunch, the line went dead.

I sat there in stunned silence, trying to convince my nervous system that I was safe when the next voicemail began to play.

Sunday, February 16, 7:42 a.m.: "BB, it's your mother again. You need to come home right now. You've been out all night, and you never called me back. I'm worried sick about you. Okay? Okay, bye."

I slowly lowered the phone to my lap, blinking at nothing as I tried to process the warring emotions inside me. My adoration for my mother gave way to my fear of Knight, which gave way to my outrage toward Knight, which circled back to remorse for the way I'd treated my mother, when a new, unexpected feeling bubbled to the surface—giddy, girlie excitement.

Punching ten numbers that I knew by heart, I held my breath and bounced in place as I waited for my BFF to pick up.

"Sup, B?"

"Jules! Oh my God, guess what."

"Just tell me."

"Ken's not gay *or* a serial killer. He's a masochist!"

I could hear Juliet rolling her eyes at me. "A masochist."

"Uh-huh." I nodded vigorously.

"So, you're in some kind of S and M relationship with Pajama Guy now?"

"Uh-huh. *And* he gave me a key to his house!" I squealed.

"Well, that all sounds perfectly normal and not at all rushed."

"Shut up." I giggled. "You're such a bitch."

"Please tell me he calls you Mistress B."

"Oh my God, why do I tell you things?"

"Mistress B, Queen of the Dark. You should dye your hair black."

"I hate you."

"And buy some nipple clamps."

"I'm not the masochist here."

"They're not for *you.*"

"I'm hanging up now."

"Bye, Mistress B! Happy flogging!"

March 2003

"Ooh, Ken. Will you buy me wine? They have wine here!"

"Hey, that lady had a program. I need a program!"

"Oh my God. Did you see those T-shirts?"

"Tank tops!"

"Coffee cups!"

My head was on a swivel as Ken guided me by the elbow through the gift shop of Cirque du Soleil's Grand Chapiteau. Outside, the tent was the size of a city block, swirled with stripes of royal blue and canary yellow, but inside, it was a wonderland of colors and sounds and smells and merchandise, and we hadn't even made it to our seats yet.

"You can get an entire bottle of wine for that price."

"Those programs cost fifteen bucks."

"No."

"You will never wear that."

"You don't even drink coffee."

By the time we made it to our seats, I had been reduced to a pouty toddler. I folded my arms across my chest and scowled as the house lights went down, and the stage lights came up. Hans would have bought me everything my little heart desired...until his credit card got declined, of course. But not Ken. Nooooo. He had to be all responsible and shit.

Nature sounds and animal noises and tribal drums and opera singing rose to a fever pitch as acrobats dressed like fantastical prehistoric reptiles slithered onto the stage and dispersed into the audience. A particularly predatory-looking bird woman pecked her way down our aisle, stopping to claw and squawk at me. A man with snowy white angel wings tumbled down from the rafters, two silken ribbons unfurling from around his almost-naked body as he spun.

And I pouted.

Contortionists twisted.

Jugglers juggled.

Tumblers flipped and cartwheeled and landed on top of one another.

And still, I pouted.

In fact, I pouted so long and so hard that I didn't even notice Ken had left his seat until a plastic wine glass full of golden nectar appeared in my periphery. Turning to my left, I found a stoic, well-dressed man sitting next to me, his hooded eyes giving nothing away. In one hand, he held a glass of chardonnay, and in the other was a plastic bag containing something large, rectangular, and flat.

My face split into a shameless grin as I reached for my goodies with grabby hands. With the grace of an acrobat, Ken moved at the last second, holding the wine just out of my reach.

"What do you say?" he asked, a hint of amused condescension in his velvety voice.

I rolled my eyes but couldn't fully retract my smile. "Thaaank yooou, Kennnnn," I drawled, elongating every syllable.

Satisfied with my groveling, Ken handed over my wine and program. Our fingers touched as I accepted them, sending a jolt of electricity up my arm and through my body. Still images of his perfect naked form hovering over me flashed behind my eyes. It had been a week since our first night together. A week of school and work and studying and scheduling difficulties, but Ken had still managed to see me every single day. If he pulled the night shift, he'd come have lunch with me at work. If I had school, he'd meet me for dinner on my way home. And on the nights that we were both off, he'd invite me to come over, knowing good and goddamn well that I was not there for a fucking pillow fight.

If I didn't know better, I'd almost think Ken was my *boyfriend.*

Except for the fact that he didn't *do* the boyfriend thing.

Staring at his now-empty hand, I felt my mouth start to water. If hugs were uncomfortable, I knew hand-holding would be a hard pass. But I wanted that jolt again. I needed it. Just a little bump to get me through the night until I could strip off his tie and lash him to the bedpost with it later.

Downing my entire glass of chardonnay for courage, I eyed Ken's right hand resting elegantly on his knee. I was going to grab the whole thing, lace my fingers through his, and stake my claim, but I chickened out at the last minute and hooked my index finger around his pinkie instead.

What the fuck are you doing?

I don't know! Shut up!

This is so weird.

Yeah! I'm aware!

I was just about to excuse myself so that I could go die of mortification when Ken slowly rolled his hand over, exposing his palm.

I stared at it in disbelief as my skin tingled with the pricks of a thousand tiny heart-shaped arrows. Placing my palm flush against his, I bit my lip and squealed on the inside as Ken slid his warm fingers between my ice-cold ones.

I remained in my own little world for the rest of the show, thumbing through the glossy, Technicolor pages of my program, drinking the tart white wine Ken had bought me whenever he noticed that my glass was empty, and pretending to focus on anything other than the place where our hands were joined.

Once the show was over, I realized that I was having trouble focusing on the ground as well. It tilted and rolled beneath my feet as I tried to walk out of the tent. Ken and I had gotten dinner before the show, but I'd only ordered a salad and managed to push enough of it around on my plate to make it look like I'd eaten something. My stomach was full of cheap wine garnished with expensive lettuce, and I was hammered.

"Ken," I whispered, leaning on him for support, "you got me drunk."

"You're welcome." He gave me a smirking side-eye as he steered me around a couple taking a selfie outside.

"Ooh! Let's take a picture!" I pulled Ken to a stop and dug my little point-and-shoot camera out of my purse.

Shoving it into the hands of the cute couple, I wrapped an arm around Ken's waist and cheesed for the flash. I didn't want to let go once our photo op was over, so I didn't. I stumbled toward the parking garage, buried as deeply in Ken's personal-space bubble as I could get. I loved it in there.

"Did you know that being next to you is like being inside of a dryer?" I hiccuped.

"A dryer, huh?" Ken pointed at the ground in front of us. "Watch the curb."

"Uh-huh." I giggled, stepping down as we crossed the street. "You're really warm and quiet, and you smell like fabric softener, and there's, like, this tingly buzz all around you."

"Like static?" Ken pulled up on my arm. "Curb."

"Mmhmm." I nodded, gripping his bicep through his coat as he guided me back onto the sidewalk. "You're all staticky. I can't even tell what you're thinking because you're so staticky. Just buzzzzzzzz. It makes the hairs on my arm stand up."

"I think you're just cold." Ken smirked down at me. "Two steps here."

We stepped up into the parking garage and made our way toward the back where Ken's little Eclipse was parked.

"Uh-uh," I argued, shaking my head with a little too much force. "You're electric." I giggled, the lyrics to "Electric Boogie" suddenly coming to mind. "*You can feel it. You're electric! Boogie woogie woogie.*"

Ken laughed a deep, echoing sound that bounced off the concrete walls and warmed my bones. "That's not even how it goes." He chuckled, hitting the unlock button on his key fob. "Are you spending the night?" he asked, opening my car door and making sure that my ass actually landed on the seat and not on the pavement next to the car.

"Uh-huh." I nodded, smiling from ear to ear.

"Good. 'Cause there is no way you're driving home like this."

I made a frowny face as he came around to the other side of the car. "I'm not *that* drunk."

Ken tried to suppress his amused smile as he cranked the engine and shifted into reverse.

I scoffed and pointed a finger at his handsome fucking face. "Hey, I saw that. You did this to me on purpose, didn't you? Are you trying to loosen me up for butt stuff later?"

Making Kenneth Easton laugh out loud would forever go down as one of my life's greatest accomplishments. With an adorable blush, a chuckle, and sparkly white grin, Ken simply shook his head as he pulled out of the parking spot.

"So, no butt stuff?" I pouted.

Ken avoided eye contact with me but kept smiling. "I like you drunk."

"I like you…"

Those three words floated into my ears, swirled around in my brain, and sprinkled down onto my heart like glittery confetti.

I like you, too.

"Hey! If you like me drunk, you should drink *with me* sometime. It'd be fun!"

Ken's smile disappeared. He was quiet for a minute, the red taillights of the cars in front of us illuminating his serious expression. I watched his Adam's apple slide up and down in his throat before he finally said, "You wouldn't like me drunk."

"Why not?"

Ken didn't look at me as he turned onto the highway. I stared shamelessly at his perfect profile, wondering what could possibly make me not like the man it belonged to.

"I get...*violent* when I'm drunk."

"Really?" The word burst from my mouth as I leaned toward him. "But you're so"—*infuriatingly gentle...freakishly self-disciplined*—"calm."

Ken's eyes flicked to mine in warning. "I am now, but in high school..." His voice trailed off as he shook away a memory. "I used to drink by myself in my parents' basement and then sneak out and break shit. I was really depressed and destructive. It wasn't until I got arrested that I realized how out of control it had gotten."

"You got arrested?"

"Yep. And if I still drank, I'd be getting arrested again...right now."

I noticed as Ken spoke the words that the red lights splashing across his face had been joined by blue ones. Looking in front of us, I found the source of the new color. The entire highway had been blocked off by police cars for a random DUI checkpoint.

"Holy shit! Ken! I'm underage! What if they smell alcohol on me?"

Ken shrugged, seemingly unconcerned. "I dunno. Maybe just pretend like you're asleep?"

It was a solid plan. As I closed my eyes and rested my head on the passenger window, it wasn't lost on me, even in my woozy condition, that if it hadn't been for Ken, *I* might be the one getting a DUI that night.

I should take him with me everywhere.

"Evenin'. License and registration, please."

I heard Ken shuffle in his seat as a bright light swept across my face.

"That your girlfriend?"

"Yes, sir."

"What's her name?"

"Brooke Bradley."

"Where y'all coming from tonight?"

The officer asked at least ten more questions before sending us on our way, but I didn't hear any of them. I was too busy clenching my fists and biting the insides of my cheeks to keep from bursting into a song and dance routine.

"Yes, sir!"

He said, "Yes, sir!"

He didn't even hesitate!

"That your girlfriend?"

"Yes, sir!"

As soon as they waved Ken through the roadblock, I sat back up, my face splitting into a massive, drunk girl grin.

"You still awake over there?" Ken asked.

"Uh-huh…" I giggled.

"What's so funny?"

"I just heard some interesting news about your relationship status."

"Oh, really?" Ken asked, his voice wavering at the end. "Was it good news?"

I nodded, enjoying watching him squirm for a change. "It was really good news."

The next morning, I woke up, feeling like roadkill. As I slowly regained consciousness, I took a mental inventory of all my ailments.

Feet? Roasting under God's magnifying glass.

Stomach? Feels like a churning acid bath.

Head? Must have been used for a kick drum last night.

Mouth? Surprisingly minty.

Pulling my knees up to my chest to escape the magnified sunrays at the bottom of the bed, I rolled onto my side and reached for Ken. Hazy memories of him helping me into the house, holding my hair back while I puked, digging my toothbrush out of my overnight bag, and taking my boots off while I covered my face and told him to, "Stop looking at me," began to surface.

Ego? Pulverized.

When my hand landed on a mattress instead of a man, I opened my eyes. Ken was gone, and the clock on his nightstand announced that it was 11:11.

Shit!

On Sundays, Ken had to be at work by eleven.

Hopping up, I tripped over a trash can someone had placed next to my side of the bed, sending a glass of water and two tiny orange pills flying off the nightstand and onto the carpet.

Shit, shit, shit!

I ran across the room as it tilted on its axis, slammed my shoulder into the doorframe on the way out, spat every curse word I knew on my way down the stairs, and stopped dead in my tracks at the bottom.

Ken was still there.

Sitting at the kitchen table.

Talking to a beautiful blonde.

The last time I'd found an unexpected woman in my house, it had *not* gone well. But, this time, it wasn't my house. And this woman wasn't in bed with my boyfriend, wearing his oversize T-shirt.

This time, I was the one in the oversize T-shirt.

And nothing else.

Yanking the hem of Ken's shirt down, I grinned awkwardly as they both turned to face the hungover, emaciated, purple-haired girl who'd just interrupted their conversation.

The mystery woman standing at the end of the counter gave me a smile that I would recognize anywhere. It was one I usually had to earn from the man sitting next to her. "You must be Brooke."

Brooke.

Wiping my sweaty palms on her brother's shirt, I took a few steps into the kitchen. "Hi. Yeah, you can just call me BB." I gave her brother a pointed stare that said, *You can just call me BB, too, ya know,* and then extended my hand. "You must be Chelsea. It's so nice to finally meet you. I was beginning to think Ken had just made you up."

Chelsea accepted my hand with a soft laugh. "I know; I'm never here anymore. I should probably stop paying rent, huh?" She glanced over her shoulder with a smirk, which Ken returned with a scowl. "My boyfriend just got stationed at the Eglin Air Force Base, so I've been spending a lot of time in Florida lately. He bought a house by the beach and is clueless when it comes to decorating." Her voice was flat and dry, like her brother's, but what was missing from her inflection came shining through in the small smile she couldn't quite contain.

"That's awesome!" I cheered. "Let me know if you need help. I haven't been to the beach in forever."

Chelsea gave her brother some telepathic sibling look, which caused Ken to clear his throat and look everywhere but at me.

"I, uh…thought you might want to go for spring break." Ken's eyes finally landed on mine. "Chelsea said we could stay with them."

"Really?" I swung my head back and forth between the two Eastons. "You're taking me to the beach?"

Probably sensing that I was about to pounce on her brother, Chelsea grabbed her purse off the kitchen counter. "Well, I gotta go. Nice to meet you, BB."

"You, too, Chelsea! Thank yoooooou!" I beamed, turning my smile on Ken as soon as the garage door shut behind her. "You're taking me to the beach?" I asked again, Ken's Sublime T-shirt suddenly feeling way too hot.

"If you want to go," he said, watching me with interested eyes as I skulked toward him.

"Why aren't you at work right now?" I asked, taking another predatory step closer.

"I took the day off," Ken replied, scooting his chair away from the table.

"Why did you take the day off?"

"Because my girlfriend wants to go to the museum, and she's probably still too drunk from last night to drive herself." Ken smirked up at me as I placed my hands on his shoulders. He was wearing a navy-blue button-up with no tie.

I missed the tie. It would have given me something to drag him upstairs with.

"Your girlfriend sounds like a real winner." I laughed, straddling his khakis with my bare legs.

"She's all right." Ken ghosted his smooth palms up my flushed thighs. They came to rest on my bare ass cheeks, giving them a gentle squeeze. "I hear she's into butt stuff, so I think I'll keep her around."

I had just scoffed and pretended to slap Ken across the face when I heard a tiny voice squeak, "Sorry!" and slam the garage door.

I froze, staring at Ken with my mouth agape. "Was that…Robin?"

Ken nodded, his features tightened into a wince.

"Oh my God." I clamped my hand over my mouth as inappropriate laughter bubbled out of me. "Ken, you're her boss."

"And her landlord."

"*And* her landlord!" I chuckled. "I'm sorry! It's not funny!"

Ken smiled as he watched me laugh. His usually cold eyes felt warm on my cheeks. "It's kind of funny."

"It's so funny!" I blurted, cracking up. "She thinks I slapped you!"

"Maybe you should." Ken's smile disappeared. "You know, so she doesn't get the wrong idea."

I smiled and shook my head at him. "I am *not* hitting you. That's abuse."

Ken's shoulders slumped in disappointment.

"Oh my God, you really want me to hit you." I sighed, looking around the kitchen. "Can I at least use a wooden spoon or something? I don't feel right about just backhanding you across the face."

Ken's smile was back tenfold. "You can use whatever you want."

"There is something seriously wrong with you." I giggled, leaning forward to plant an open-mouthed kiss on the curve of his lips.

Ken kissed me back, swirling his tongue around the tip of mine and tenderly sucking on my bottom lip. Releasing it with a quiet pop, he said, "You're the one who wants to hit me with a wooden spoon."

"Hey, if you don't watch your mouth, I'm gonna go with a plastic spatula."

Ken's angular eyebrow shot up. "Tease."

"All right, motherfucker. You asked for it." I climbed off of Ken's lap, pretending not to notice the delicious bulge there or the glistening wet spot I'd left on it. Walking across the kitchen, I opened his utensil drawer…and slid the entire thing out of the cabinet. Holding the drawer full of spoons, spatulas, whisks, and rubber scrapers, I turned and headed straight for the stairs without giving Ken a second look. I didn't need to turn around to see if he was coming.

I could feel his breath on the back of my neck.

Once we were back in his room, I set the drawer on the foot of his bed, the utensils bouncing with a metallic clang. Spinning around, I placed my fists on my hips and pinned the man before me with a vicious stare. Mistress B was reporting for duty.

"You. Strip," I ordered, biting the insides of my cheeks to keep from breaking character.

The corner of Ken's mouth curled up in amusement, but he did as he'd been told. Button by button, I watched him lazily remove his shirt, undershirt, khaki pants, and boxer briefs, laying each garment out on the floor so that they wouldn't get wrinkled.

Suddenly feeling stupid, standing there in a Sublime T-shirt, I yanked my only article of clothing off over my head and threw it on the floor as well. My pierced nipples hardened to diamonds at the sight of Ken's chiseled body and thick, heavy cock jutting out before me.

His posture was relaxed. He didn't stand before me with his shoulders back and chest puffed up, like the Adonis he was. He stood like a man who'd left his ego at the door. Open, vulnerable, ready to be wounded.

But only physically.

Emotionally, Ken was more guarded than ever. His features were taut. Expression hidden. He seemed to be watching me from somewhere far away, deep inside his bunker of invulnerability.

Nanny-nanny boo-boo. You can't get me, his heart taunted from inside its impenetrable fortress, thumbing its nose at me from behind a pane of bulletproof glass.

Challenge accepted, motherfucker, mine spat back, giving his the middle finger.

"Here's what we're going to do," I announced in my best dominatrix voice. "You choose the implement. *I* choose the location of the strike."

Ken's eyes flashed with excitement.

Taking a step to one side, I swept my hand above the wooden drawer like Vanna White.

Ken eyed me as he approached. God, he smelled good. The piney scent of Irish Spring soap wafted off of his warm muscles as he came to stand beside me. Reaching into the drawer, Ken pulled out a metal meat mallet shaped like a blunt club with spikes on the end.

"Please tell me you're kidding."

A smile broke through Ken's mask.

"Put that back. I am not murdering anyone today."

With a shrug, Ken placed the mallet back in the drawer, opting instead for a large black plastic spoon.

"Slotted?" I asked, hesitantly accepting the utensil. "You *are* sick."

Ken grinned as I pointed to a spot on the wall with it. "Assume the position, scumbag."

Ken tilted his head and arched a brow at me.

"Ugh." I rolled my eyes. "Please. Assume the position, *please*."

Satisfied with my manners, Ken willingly stood in front of his bedroom wall, loose as a goose.

"Hands," I barked, pointing at the wall with Ken's torture implement of choice. "*Please*."

Ken placed his fingertips on the wall in front of him, clearly not expecting to need it for—

WHAM! I swung the spoon with all my might, slapping the outside of his thigh and leaving three white lines behind, surrounded by flushed pink flesh.

He chuckled softly through his nose.

WHACK! That time, I got him right between his broad, smooth shoulder blades.

Bastard hadn't even flinched.

SMACK! Left butt cheek.

Ken tilted his head to the left and right, lazily stretching his neck.

CRACK! I clocked him right in the ribs, holding the spoon like a fucking baseball bat.

Ken doubled over in what I hoped was pain, but I soon realized he was laughing as he held his side.

What the fuck? That tickled?

Dropping the spoon, I reached out with both hands and jammed my fingers into Ken's ribs, wiggling them mercilessly.

"Ahh!" Ken screamed, swatting at my hands. "Stop! Stop!"

"Is somebody ticklish?" I cooed, avoiding his grasp and diving back in.

"Fuck!" he gasped between chuckles. "Stop it!"

"I thought you were tough. You can't handle some wittle tickles?"

"Rrrrah!" Ken growled, turning and pinning my arms to my sides. His sparkly blue eyes were alight with something I hadn't seen in them before. Something resembling… excitement. "Fucking. Stop," he panted, grinning from ear to ear.

"Okay." I giggled, holding his stare as he held down my arms.

"Okay?"

"If you say I won."

"You won?"

"There. See? That wasn't so hard." I smirked, turning us so that I was the one against the wall. My arms were still restrained, so I hitched my thigh over Ken's hip, inviting him to punish me in a much different way.

The words *I love you* flitted through my mind as Ken fucked me against his bedroom wall with the door wide open on a Sunday afternoon.

Too soon, I told them, letting my head fall back against the Sheetrock.

Way too fucking soon.

PART

April 2003

Amy's parents were so happy she'd moved back that they threw her a huge engagement party. The venue was a stately old manor house with acres of charming little gardens and pathways and fountains surrounding a lily pad–spotted pond. The house sat empty most of the time unless it was being rented out for a wedding.

Or an over-the-top engagement party.

"They are so fucking cute." Juliet sighed, gazing across the pond at the happiest couple on earth.

Allen and Amy were dressed in color-coordinated outfits, sitting on the edge of a fountain, holding cutesy little signs for the photographer.

"Dude." I looked down at the four-year-old in my lap and covered his little ears with my hands.

Juliet rolled her eyes. "Relax. I'm pretty sure the first word he ever heard was me screaming, 'Fuck,' as I pushed him out."

"Um, I was there, and I'm pretty sure *I* was the one screaming that word."

Juliet burst out laughing. "Yeah, right before you fainted!"

I shook my head, shell-shocked. "If you had seen what I saw…"

"What did you see, Auntie BB?" Romeo tilted his head back and blinked at me with beautiful almond-shaped eyes, just like his mama's.

"I, uh…well…"

Juliet snickered as I tried to spin the horrors of witnessing live childbirth at the age of fifteen into something sunshiny and sweet.

"I saw *you*, little boy. I saw you, even before your mommy."

And way before your loser daddy.

"What did I look like?"

A slimy, blood-smeared guinea pig.

"You looked like a tiny little angel."

Satisfied with my answer, Romeo went back to grazing from the mountain of cheese and crackers and fruit and finger sandwiches that we'd swiped from the buffet to keep him occupied.

"You scarred me for life," I whispered to his mother.

"Whatever." She rolled her eyes. "You're gonna have a million babies."

"Pssh. I'm only having one. That's it. Unless I have twins." My stomach flipped. "Oh my God. What if I have twins?"

Of all the inopportune moments to appear, Ken chose that one. He sat on the opposite side of our picnic table and set down two plastic cups—one filled with water and one filled with punch that I hoped was spiked. Sliding the red beverage toward me, he gave me a look that said he'd heard more than he wanted to.

"Relax. I'm not pregnant." I rolled my eyes and took a sip from my drink.

Damnit. Not spiked.

"Twins run in her family," Juliet offered.

Ken's eyebrow lifted fractionally. "Sucks for you."

"Sucks," Romeo blurted with a mouthful of Gouda.

"You don't want twins, Ken?" I asked in my sweetest, most sarcastic tone.

"What I *want* is a vasectomy, but the doctors around here won't give me one until I'm at least thirty."

Choking on my punch, I coughed. "You already tried to get a vasectomy?"

"Fuck yeah," Ken replied.

"Fuck yeah," Romeo echoed.

Clamping my hand over his crumb-covered mouth, I gaped at my boyfriend.

"Let me guess; you don't believe in marriage either," Juliet sassed.

"I don't," Ken said matter-of-factly, his expressionless eyes trained on Juliet. Then, with a shift, they were on me. "But I get it."

"Oh, you get it?" I took another sip from my drink to hide my defensiveness.

"Sure. People want security." Ken glanced across the pond at his best friend, who was grinning from ear to ear as he pretended to throw his fiancée into the fountain for the camera.

"When you look at them, you see two people who want *security*?" I asked with a little too much snark. "I see two people who make each other insanely happy and want to be together forever."

"What's sick-urity?" Romeo mumbled into my palm.

"Let's go to the bathroom, buddy." Juliet reached for her son while giving me a look that said, *Calm your crazy.*

Once they were gone, it was just me and my new boyfriend and the elephant in the garden.

Ken doesn't want to get married or have kids.

I should have stood up, wished him well, and walked away from his love-aversion forever. I should have listened to Maya Angelou when she said, "When someone shows you who they are, believe them the first time." I should have found myself a nice guy with a full sleeve and an entry-level job who would give me all the weddings and babies I wanted.

But do you know what I did instead? Of course you do.

I looked at Ken's beautiful, joyless face, straightened my spine, and thought, *We'll see about that, asshole.*

When the party was over, I hugged Allen and Amy goodbye, gushed over Amy's ring one more time, and turned to find Ken standing three feet behind me with his hands in the pockets of his black slacks.

He was giving the happy couple his *don't fucking hug me* stance.

When I glanced back at Allen and saw the disappointment on his face, I decided Ken needed to get the fuck over himself.

"Hey, babe. Hold still," I said, walking around behind him. "I think I saw a little piece of fuzz on your—Allen! Quick!" I grabbed Ken's arms from behind, restraining him, while Allen tackle-hugged him from the front.

Ken tore his arms out of my grasp effortlessly, but not before Allen got one good, solid second of cuddle time from his BFF.

Allen, Amy, and I laughed hysterically as Ken retreated to the other side of the manor house's foyer, fists in his pockets and scowl on his face.

"It's like bull riding." I cackled, trying to catch my breath. "Next time, we're going for two seconds."

Ken walked out the front door while we continued to laugh at his expense, but as he passed me, I swear I saw a ghost of a smile on his face.

I chased after him, wiping tears from my cheeks as I hustled across the poorly lit gravel parking area in my stilettos. I only wore heels to weddings and funerals, and it showed.

"Hey, wait up," I called, grabbing his arm for stability once I finally caught up.

Ken's bicep tensed in my grasp, but he didn't pull away. He slowed down so that I wouldn't bust my ass.

I expected him to be pissy about the forced hugging, but much to my surprise, he wasn't thinking about that at all.

"I didn't see Jason here, did you?"

Dread slithered into my veins. "No, I didn't."

Ken opened his passenger-side door and held my arm as I climbed in. "Maybe you should call him."

Yes. Call him. Duh.

I dug my phone out of my purse, picturing Jason's body in a twisted, bloody heap on the sidewalk below his balcony.

Today's Sunday. Fuck. We didn't go over there this weekend. I didn't even think about it.

I found his number in my Contacts and hit Send.

Please be okay. Please be okay. Please be o—

"Whasss up, girl?" Jason slurred over a cacophony of background noise.

"Hey, J!" I plugged my other ear to hear him better and raised my voice. "We missed you at Allen and Amy's engagement party. Everything okay?"

"I'm at Pearl Jam!" Jason yelled into the phone.

"Pearl Jam?" I made eye contact with Ken as he pulled out of the parking area. "Those tickets were like two hundred bucks a piece."

"Two-fifty!" Jason corrected.

I laughed. "Where's my ticket, asshole?"

But Jason couldn't hear me. He'd erupted into the chorus from "Jeremy" and was singing his little drunken heart out.

I was just about to hang up when he got back on the line and said, "Hey, B?"

"Yeah?"

"You gonna come over next week?"

Guilt tugged the smile right off my face. "Yeah, man. I'll be there."

Jason's off-key voice howled along with Eddie Vedder's during the last few bars of the song. The music got significantly louder, like he was holding his phone up to an amplifier or something. I winced and hung up.

"He's fine," I said, dropping my phone back into my purse. "He's at Pearl Jam."

"That fucker." Ken chuckled. "He should hire me to be his driver."

"But you're *my* driver." I batted my eyelashes at him.

"Speaking of"—Ken flashed me a sideways smile—"can you be packed and at my house by eight tomorrow? I want to beat all the spring break traffic."

I nodded with a grin. "You got it."

I screeched into Ken's driveway the next morning at 8:52 with wet hair and no makeup on.

The entire drive down, we sang along to his CD collection—including The All-American Rejects, *thank you very much*—and we only got lost, like, three times. Every time, it was my fault for not paying attention to the highway signs. And, every time, Ken would simply pull off at the next exit and turn around like it was absolutely no big deal that I'd just caused us to drive fifteen minutes out of the way—*again.*

By the time we parked in front of Bobby's adorable little bungalow, I was almost sad we had to get out of the car.

Bobby was a country boy through and through—from the deer heads on his walls to the rebel flag belt buckle on his Wranglers. He greeted us warmly and talked nonstop as he gave us a tour of his new house. Chelsea followed behind, smiling and nodding in her preppy polo shirt and crisp white shorts.

And I'd thought Ken and I were opposites.

"Welp. Y'all wanna go to the beach or what?" Bobby asked, popping the tab on a can of Budweiser. "Better go now, so we don't hafta walk back in the dark." Bobby jerked a thumb in my direction and chuckled. "This one's so tiny; the gators 'round here might snatch her up."

Redneck beach adventures always involved beer, duct tape, and improvisation.

After Bobby plopped his aluminum lawn chair into the sand and duct-taped a golf umbrella to the side of it, he pulled another can of Bud out of his rolling cooler and offered it to me.

"Thanks," I said, reaching for it with one sunscreen-covered palm.

Ken accepted it on my behalf, looking absolutely drool-worthy in his dark sunglasses and simple black board shorts.

I smiled at my own reflection in his eyewear as I spread the lotion down my spindly, freckled arm. I hoped he was watching me because he liked how I looked in my new leopard-print bikini, but when he opened his mouth and said, "You forgot the tops of your feet," I realized he was simply watching me to make sure my dumb ass hadn't missed a spot.

Rrrrrrrip! Bobby tore off another long piece of duct tape and went to work on attaching another large umbrella to a second lawn chair.

In my mind, I'd had visions of Ken and me enjoying a long, romantic, barefoot walk on the beach, hand in hand, as seagulls sang a chorus of Toni Braxton songs.

Instead, the two Eastons grabbed their boogie boards and ran straight into the water, leaving Bobby and me behind to drink lukewarm beer in the hot Florida sun.

I sat down in the chair next to Bobby in resignation, careful not to put an eye out on the umbrella attached to it, and took a long sip from my beer. "So, Chelsea's a jock, too, huh?"

"Hell yeah." Bobby spat in the sand. "If it wasn't for her, I'd fail the fucking Air Force fitness tests every time. That girl gets my ass up every morning an' makes me go joggin' with her. Joggin'! Like a couple of damn yuppies."

I giggled. "Ken runs too. I don't get it, man. The only way I'm running is if one of those gators you were talking about tries to eat me."

Bobby laughed as I watched Ken and Chelsea ride the same wave, side by side, all the way to the sand. I was vaguely aware that my mouth had fallen open at the sight of him. Ken stood up and shook the water out of his darkened, wet hair. Then, he laughed at his sister with that Hollywood smile as a second wave knocked her back into the sand. Ken didn't offer to help her up, and she didn't ask. She simply got up on her own, and the two Eastons walked back into the ocean with their boards tucked under their arms.

"Is Chelsea weird about touching, too?" I asked Bobby without taking my eyes off the pair in the water.

"What do you mean? Like, 'cause of germs and stuff?"

"No, I think it's more like a personal-space thing." I turned and looked at my new friend. "Ken doesn't touch people unless he has to. He lets *me* hug him"—*and physically abuse him in bed*—"but he never initiates human contact with anyone unless he has to. It's so weird."

"Now that you mention it, Chelsea is kinda like that. She's a sweet girl, but she ain't real cuddly. Most girls, no offense—" Bobby held his non-beer hand up. "But most girls are kinda needy. Ya know?"

I nodded with a chuckle.

Oh, I know.

"But Chelsea's cool, man. She don't need nuthin'." Bobby took a long swig from his can and gazed out at his girlfriend, who was standing waist deep in the ocean, having a conversation with her brother.

Probably about how needy I am.

"That sounds like Ken. He won't even let me buy him gifts."

"Welp, I sure hope Chelsea ain't like that 'cause I'm thinkin' 'bout givin' her a real big gift here pretty soon."

My eyes lit up. "Like a riiiiiing?" I sang.

"Shh," he scolded, turning his anxious brown eyes on me. "Not so damn loud."

I grinned and whisper-squealed, "That's so exciting!" Then, my face fell as I thought about all the similarities between her and her brother.

"What? What is it?"

I faked a smile. "Nothing. It's just…Ken doesn't want to get married. He says he doesn't *believe* in it." I rolled my eyes.

"Pssh." Bobby waved a dismissive hand at me. "All guys say that. Hell, I don't know if I even believe in it to tell you the truth. Why do I need the government to give me a piece of paper to prove that I love my woman? It ain't none of their damn business. Next thing you know, they're gonna be microchippin' us and tryin' to take our guns."

I snorted at his backwoods honesty.

Bobby's rant died down as a wistful smile tugged at his lips. "But my girl wants to do it, and I'm gonna give that woman whatever in the hell she wants." Bobby tossed back the rest of his beer and crunched the can in his fist. "Let me ask you this…did Kenny boy say he *wouldn't* get married?"

"We've only been dating, like, two months, so we haven't really talked about—"

"That don't matter. When he said he didn't believe in it, did he say he wouldn't do it?"

I thought back to our conversation at Allen's engagement party the day before. "Well…no."

Bobby popped the tab on a new beer and tipped it in my direction. "Then, there you go."

"You *sure* you don't need me to carry you?" Bobby teased as I limped back to his house in the dark.

"I'm fine," I insisted, embarrassed that I hadn't taken Ken's advice. The tops of my feet were so badly burned; I couldn't even put my flip-flops back on.

Handing his boogie board and towel to his sister, Ken stopped on the side of the road and knelt before me. There was no *I told you so*, no gloating about being right. He didn't even laugh at my pitiful condition.

Ken simply sighed and said, "Get on."

I smiled and wrapped my arms around his tan shoulders, inhaling the lingering scent of sea on his towel-dried hair. As

Ken looped his forearms under my knees and stood to carry me home, Bobby gave me a covert wink.

Do you see this shit? I squealed at him with my mind. *Ken is giving me a piggyback ride!*

As we strolled back to Bobby's house along the slow, sleepy streets of Fort Walton Beach, I smiled and pressed a little kiss into Ken's damp hair.

Fuck a walk on the beach, I thought, squeezing his waist with my legs a little tighter.

We laughed about Chelsea's wipeout and Bobby's farmer tan along the way, but only half of my attention was on the conversation. The other half was focused intently on my thighs, right where Ken's hands were resting. Okay, maybe seventy-five percent. It was enough that I didn't hear the incessant *doodle-oodle-oodle-oo*s coming from inside the house until Bobby opened the front door.

"Who in the hell's phone keeps ringin'?"

My heart thumped in my chest as I scrambled off of Ken's back, through Bobby's modest living room, and into his 1980s era kitchen. I swiped at the wall until I found the light switch, then snatched my purse off the kitchen table.

As I clawed at my belongings, elbow deep in my bag, fear gripped my spine with both hands. I was afraid it was going to be Knight. I was afraid I was going to have to explain to everyone why I didn't answer. I was afraid it was going to be awkward.

How I wish it had only been *awkward.*

The voicemail alert buzzed in my hand as I pulled my phone out of my purse. Something told me I should sit down before I listened to it. I didn't.

Monday, April 7, 6:14 p.m.: "Hey, BB."

The voice on the other end wasn't deep or sadistic. It wasn't calling me a bitch or a whore. It was feminine and familiar. Goth Girl's deadpan drawl assaulted me with unwanted memories. Images of her long black hair fanned out across my pillow, her ample breasts filling out Hans's old Nine Inch Nails T-shirt, and her milky-white skin flushed pink after I'd slapped the shit out of her flashed behind my eyes all at once.

"I know you hate me, but…" Her voice broke, taking on a high-pitched keening sound at the end. "I need you to call me back. Okay?"

Monday, April 7, 6:59 p.m.: "BB…" Goth Girl sniffled and let out a heavy, wavering sigh. "Something really bad happened, okay? Please…just call me back."

There was one more voicemail. I made eye contact with Ken from across the room as it began to play. Bobby and Chelsea were gone, but Ken had remained behind to bear witness to whatever bad news I was about to get.

Monday, April 7, 8:21 p.m.: "Fine. Don't fucking answer," Goth Girl slurred, sounding like she'd ingested half a bottle of vodka since her last voicemail. "I was just calling to let you know that Jason's fucking dead, okay? He got shitfaced at Pearl Jam and crashed his car on the way home." Her voice trailed off with a sniffle, taking some of her anger along with it. "Sorry. The funeral's on Wednesday. Maybe I'll see you there."

I didn't blink as I tried to process Victoria's tearful, drunken message. I didn't even lower the phone from my ear. I just stared, unseeing, at Ken, whose eyes were studying the carpet.

"Jason?" he asked.

My chin lifted and fell. Slowly. Mechanically.

"Is he…"

I nodded again. I think.

I continued to stare at the spot where Ken had been long after he walked into the kitchen. After he stopped three feet away from me and said nothing. After the distance between us had a chance to settle into my bones.

Three feet.

I was back outside the bubble.

The next day, Ken and I drove home from Florida in silence.

My mind, however, was anything but.

I just talked to him that night.

I knew he was drunk. We even joked about Ken being his driver.

We fucking joked *about it.*

I didn't even see him last week.

I didn't even think about him.

God, I've been such a shitty friend ever since I started seeing Ken.

I should have hosted an intervention or something.

But I didn't. I didn't do shit, and now, he's gone.

I gave Ken a sidelong glance, his features blurry behind my unshed tears. He hadn't touched me since we found out about Jason. All I wanted to do was curl up in his lap and let him comfort me while I cried, but it was clear that my messy feelings were not welcome inside his sterile little world.

Jason would have held me, I thought, bitter tears stinging my eyes. I remembered the way he used to pick me up off my feet and spin me in the air. *Jason was always so happy to see me. Did he know I was happy to see him, too? Did he know how much I would miss his big hugs?*

Orange groves dissolved into cow pastures before my eyes. Small towns grew into large shopping centers. And, as the sun slid out of the sky, the high-rises of Atlanta climbed into it. There was so much progress happening outside the car.

But the only thing progressing inside the car was the size of my hurt as I waited in vain for Ken to comfort me. To acknowledge my grief. To do fucking anything.

By the time he pulled up in front of my parents' house after dark, I was ready to explode. He held his breath as he turned to look at me, probably expecting me to freak out or burst into tears or otherwise contaminate him with my messy feelings, so I didn't. I kept them to myself. The only thing I gave Ken was my imaginary middle finger as I slammed his car door and stomped into my house.

My mother came running as a sob twenty-four hours in the making filled the foyer. "What happened, baby?"

I pressed my face into her shoulder, her long red hair soaking up my tears. "Jason *died*…in a car accident."

"Oh, honey," she cooed, smoothing a weathered hand down my bony back. "I'm so sorry. What a shame. What a damn shame." She shook her head and squeezed me tighter. "He sure did love you."

I might have been sitting next to my boyfriend at the Ivy and Sons Funeral Home, but he felt so far away; he might as well have been on another planet. From that day on, his black shirt/black tie combo would no longer hold the appeal it once had. It would just be a reminder of the day he refused to comfort me as I sat a foot away, holding back my tears.

"He sure did love you."

My mom had met Jason only once or twice, but it had been enough for her to see what I'd been blind to. Jason had had feelings for me. And I'd spent his last few months on earth chasing someone who was incapable of feeling anything.

The longer I sat there, listening to Jason's friends and family express their heartbreak behind the podium, the angrier I got. At Jason, for putting us through the pain of losing him. At myself, for not trying harder to get him help. But, mostly, at Ken, for not putting his fucking arm around me. For not loving me the way Jason had loved me. For not picking me up and twirling me around just because he was happy to see me.

As soon as the service was over, I bolted. Wearing black high heels for the second time that week, I click-clacked down the aisle, holding the bottom of my short black dress in my fist. My sunburned feet were screaming at me to slow down, but I couldn't. I wouldn't until I was finally alone and could cry all this bullshit out.

"BB!" a familiar, deep voice called from the middle of the chapel.

I managed to catch a glimpse of the bastard just before I blew past him. Hans was looking rock-star chic in a fitted black T-shirt and black jeans, but the girl sitting next to him, slouching in her baby-doll dress and hiding behind her long black hair, looked like a bitch I'd like to slap.

Again.

I tore past Amy, Allen, the Alexander brothers, and Juliet, who didn't see me because she was too busy glaring at Ethan Alexander, who'd probably had the audacity to hit on her at a funeral.

I stomped all the way out to Ken's car where I lit two cigarettes and smoked them both at the same time.

Calm down, BB. Jesus Christ.

I paced back and forth in the parking lot, tiny pieces of asphalt crunching under my stilettos.

Where the fuck is he?

My eyes and throat burned, but I refused to cry. Not until I got the fuck away from Ken. I was in enough pain as it was. The last thing I needed was to break down in the presence of somebody who couldn't even pretend to give a shit.

I glared at the front door as a slow trickle of red-eyed couples began to exit. Old couples, young couples, gay couples, straight couples. They all held hands, linked arms, clung to one another, giving and receiving the support they needed.

I hated them all.

Especially the couple I'd found asleep in my bed last December.

When Hans and Goth Girl exited the chapel, their eyes landed on me immediately. She froze on the spot, but he kept walking, heading straight toward me.

Fuck. Not now. Goddamn it.

My heart rate rivaled a jackrabbit's as I watched Hans waltz across the parking lot on long, skinny legs. He'd lost weight over the course of our relationship, thanks to a burgeoning drug habit, but since we'd broken up, it looked like he'd gone off the rails. His face was gaunt. His once-tight jeans were lashed on with a studded belt. And he'd completely buzzed off all his sexy, shaggy black hair.

The last time I'd seen Hans, I'd thrown everything we owned directly at his head. It had been four months since that day, but the urge to take off my spiked heels and chuck one at his face was still there.

So was the urge to run to him and let him hold me while I wept.

"Hey." Hans held his hands up in surrender. His dark eyebrows were drawn together over two remorseful denim-colored eyes. "I know you're still mad at me. I just wanted to come over and say I'm sorry…about Jason. I know you guys were close."

I clenched my jaw, unable to speak around the lump in my throat, but my quivering chin gave me away.

"Shit. Hey, it's okay." Hans spread his arms, and just like that, I was back in them.

His hug wasn't as good as Ken's. He was too thin and too tall. His embrace was too loose, and he smelled like cigarettes instead of clean cotton. But he let me cry. Hans had nothing left to offer me, except his sympathy, and like everything in our apartment, I took that, too.

"Shh…" He rubbed his hand down my back too lightly, causing me to jerk in his arms. "Sorry, I forgot you're ticklish."

He forgot.

My body was already a stranger to him, and his felt like a stranger to me.

Stepping away, I swiped the mascara from under my eyes and glanced at the funeral home doors where Ken was now standing. He appeared to be talking to Allen and Amy, but his eyes were fixed on me. With a curt nod to his friends, he stalked toward us, hands in his pockets, mouth set in a straight line. The taillights behind me flashed as a beep sounded from inside Ken's car.

"Thanks." I sniffled, wiping my nose on the back of my hand. "I, uh, I gotta go."

I stumbled backward, my stilettos scraping across the asphalt, until I finally found the door handle and jerked it open. Just as my ass hit the passenger seat, Ken slid behind the wheel next to me, looking utterly cool and unaffected—by the funeral, by the sight of his girlfriend in the arms of another man, by the mascara streaks under her eyes, by all of it.

"Who was that?" he asked, shifting the car into reverse.

"Hans," I mumbled, staring straight ahead with my arms folded across my chest.

As Ken pulled out of his parking space, I noticed Hans getting into his little black BMW, alone.

Guess he and Goth Girl didn't ride together.

The thought was a tiny consolation.

I waited for Ken to act jealous, grill me with questions about my tall, tattooed ex, but he didn't. I waited for him to acknowledge how upset I was, maybe ask if I was okay, but nope. All he did was keep his eyes on the road as he reached over and switched on the mother…fucking…radio.

Kaboom.

With that simple *click*, Ken had unwittingly detonated the bomb that had been ticking away in his passenger seat.

"No," I snapped, reaching over and turning it right back off. "No! We're not gonna sit here and listen to fucking Incubus and pretend like everything's fine. It's not fine!"

"Brooke—"

I turned in my seat, facing him full-on. Anger swelled in my veins and made my temples throb. "Jason's dead, and you don't care!"

Ken didn't say anything. He didn't argue with me or defend himself. He simply clenched his square jaw and stared straight ahead and placed the final imaginary brick in the wall between us, shutting me out completely.

"Oh, perfect!" I threw my hands up. "You haven't touched me since we found out about Jason, and now, you're not gonna talk to me either? That's great. *Super* supportive, Ken. Way to be there."

"Jesus Christ! What do you want from me?" he finally snapped back.

Oh, it's on.

I leaned forward, salivating over his jugular. "I want you to have a fucking feeling!" I snarled, thrusting my hand in the direction of the funeral home behind us. "I want you to put your arm around me when I'm sad and hold my hand in public and pick me up and spin me around when I come over just because you're so goddamn happy to see me!"

"I'm sorry I'm a shitty boyfriend!" Ken barked, causing me to slink back in my seat. "This is why I don't do fucking relationships!" His tone lost its edge just as quickly as it had appeared. "I don't know why I can't do all this touchy-feely bullshit you want, but I just…can't. I don't know what's wrong with me. Maybe I'm fucking autistic or something."

Now, it was my turn to be silent.

Autistic? No. Ken?

I ran through a mental list of disorders from my clinical psychology coursework. Symptoms. Ages of onset. Prognoses. Evaluation tools. I'd just assumed Ken was an asshole, but maybe there was more to it. An autism spectrum disorder? A personality disorder? Reactive attachment disorder? I was already pretty sure the stubborn asshole had oppositional defiant disorder.

"I could test you."

For the first time since our fight had begun, Ken looked at me. His brows were knotted in confusion. His eyes guarded and skeptical.

"I have to do a full case study before I graduate. I could do it on you, if you want. It would take a lot of time though. A full psychological evaluation can take weeks."

Ken flicked his eyes back to the road. "And this would help you with school?"

"Yeah, it would."

But, mostly, it would help me figure out what the fuck is going on inside your head.

Ken sighed and glanced at me again. This time, his features didn't look guarded or skeptical. They looked downright scared. "Okay."

He nodded, turning away from me again. I noticed his Adam's apple move as he swallowed.

"If it'll help."

May 2003

I placed my bare feet on Ken's lap as we worked side by side in his bunker-like office at the Showtime Movie Theater. The room had beige walls, ugly, swirly movie theater carpet, two metal desks next to one another, a few metal filing cabinets, and stacks of rolled-up movie posters in every corner. Ken obviously hadn't redecorated since his promotion to general manager.

He looked down at my feet on his thigh but said nothing, returning his attention to whatever spreadsheet he was working on at the time. I smiled to myself and continued scoring the IQ test I'd just given him. I'd been testing him in his office whenever he worked the night shift. It was Ken's idea. After he started the last movies of the night, he had a solid two hours before he had to close up the theater, which was just enough time to get an evaluation session in.

Ken was so smart.

And, as I marveled at the numbers I was getting back, I began to realize just how smart he actually was.

"Uh, Ken?"

"Yeah?" he replied, not looking up from the clunky computer on his desk.

"I think I scored this wrong. Will you look at it for me?"

I turned the assessment manual around and showed him how to find his age and the raw score on the subtests I was looking at to calculate his nonverbal IQ.

"One fifty," he said, handing the manual and test booklet back to me.

I blinked at him. "That's what I got."

Ken shrugged and went back to work as if I hadn't just told him he was a goddamn genius.

"Ken." I pulled my feet off his lap and turned toward the desk where my binder sat open. Pulling a laminated piece of paper out of the front pocket, I shoved it in his face. "Do you see what this says?"

Ken raised an eyebrow at me, refusing to read it out loud.

Stubborn asshole.

"Ugh," I grunted, pulling it away. "It says *Psychometric Conversion Table.* Do you see this column where it says *Standard Scores*? What's the top score on the chart?"

He still wouldn't budge.

"One fifty, motherfucker." I poked the page repeatedly with my finger. "You have the highest nonverbal IQ on the fucking chart. That's visual memory, spatial relations, mathematical reasoning…"

Ken lifted a shoulder and let it fall. "So, I'm good at math."

"No, you're not just 'good at math.'" I made air quotes around the words with my fingers. "You're fucking *Good Will Hunting.* Why the hell aren't you working for NASA right now?"

Ken opened his mouth to give me some smart-ass remark, but I cut him off, "And don't tell me it's because their 401(k) program is shit. I want a real answer."

Ken closed his mouth and glared at me.

"Why are you working here?" I asked, my tone softer.

"Because I didn't go to college."

"Why didn't you go to college?"

"Because I hate school."

"Why do you hate school when you're so fucking smart?"

With every successive question, I leaned another inch forward in my seat.

"I don't know. I've just always hated it."

And, with every question, Ken's impenetrable wall of mystery grew stronger and stronger.

"You were even good at sports. You could have gotten so many scholarships."

"Not everyone has to go to college." Ken folded his arms across his chest.

"Um, people with these scores do." I flicked his test booklet with two fingers. "Like, you owe it to humanity to do something with this. You could fucking cure cancer." I laughed, remembering that you had to care about people to want to cure them. "Or...you could at least come up with some breakthrough economic plan that could reverse the national deficit!"

That got Ken's attention. His eyebrow lifted, but he said nothing. The wall was built. Now, all Ken had to do was hide behind it.

I stared at him like a puzzle that was missing most of its pieces. I'd been testing him for weeks, and I still didn't feel like I was anywhere close to figuring him out.

"Ken, why didn't you go to college?" I practically whispered, speaking to him like a caged animal. "Why'd you quit the football team in high school? Why didn't you date?"

You're so smart and handsome and athletic. Why are you wasting all of it?

"That's why we're doing this, right?" Ken deadpanned, his eyes iced over. "So, you can tell me what's wrong with me?"

"Hey." I reached over and cupped the side of his beautiful face with one hand, his midnight stubble scratching my palm. "As far as I can tell, the only thing wrong with you is *you*."

Ken dropped his eyes, sending his sable-brown lashes fanning out over his enviously high cheekbones.

I relished the fact that, for once, my touch seemed more comforting than uncomfortable to him.

Rolling my chair closer, I leaned forward and dusted his lips with mine. "You need to go to college," I whispered more gently than before. "Just think about it. Okay? You might not hate it if you find a program you like."

Ken didn't respond, so I kissed him again. I kissed him until he kissed me back. I kissed him until he forgot about the invisible wall he'd built between us and pulled me onto his lap.

Then, I reached between us and unbuckled his belt.

"What are you doing?" Ken asked, alarm in his voice.

"I forgot to tell you." I blinked up at him, trying my best to look coy as I unbuttoned his gray slacks. "This evaluation includes an oral exam."

Ken immediately wrapped one arm around my back and pushed off the desk with his foot. I squealed as we rolled across the office, coming to a stop next to the door, which he reached over and locked with a smirk.

June 2003

Twenty-fucking-one.

That was how many years I'd been on the planet.

You're supposed to go out and get shitfaced on your twenty-first birthday to celebrate finally being old enough to buy alcohol, but considering that I'd started my drinking career before I started my period, the appeal of showing my ID to a waitress at Bahama Breeze was completely lost on me. Instead, I decided to drown my birthday sorrows at Fuzzy's. The dirty beer steins and splintery barstools just seemed to fit my shitty mood better.

I don't know why the big two-one felt like such a kick in the cunt. Maybe I was annoyed because drinking, one of my all-time favorite bad-girl things to do, wasn't a bad-girl thing to do anymore. It was just a regular, legal, grown-ass woman thing to do. And that made me sad. Maybe I was in a bad place because Jason wasn't there to help me celebrate. Or maybe, just maybe, I was in a shitty mood because I was dating a guy who was weird about birthdays and hadn't given me so much as a high five all day.

It felt like Valentine's Day all over again. I'd kept telling myself not to expect anything. That Ken didn't *do* birthdays, and no amount of pouting was going to change that. But, of course, that didn't stop me from pouting like a motherfucker anyway.

I looked at the people gathered around the conglomeration of wobbly wooden tables that we'd pushed together at Fuzzy's and tried to feel some sort of enthusiasm—or at least appreciation for my friends who'd come all the way out to Athens to celebrate with me—but…*meh.* Allen and Amy were making eyes at each other, the Alexanders were hitting on the waitress, Ken was vehemently trying to talk his sister out of investing in a tax-sheltered annuity—whatever the fuck that was—and Juliet was on her way back from the bar with yet another annoyingly girlie drink prepared for me by Zach.

"Sex on the Beach for the birthday bitch," Juliet slurred into my ear as she plopped down beside me. "I can't believe you're all growns up." She reached over and ruffled the angled bob I'd spent an hour straightening to perfection.

I smacked her hand away and smoothed my hair back down with my palms. "Am not."

"Are, too." Juliet lifted a hand and began counting things off on her long, slender fingers. "You're almost done with college. You're practically living with Ken. You're old enough to buy your own booze…" Juliet sniffled and pretended to wipe a tear from her black-rimmed, eyelash-free eye. "It seems like, just yesterday, I was teaching you how to inhale."

I rolled my eyes. "You're, like, six months older than me."

Juliet was just about to reply when a big ole teddy bear put his hands on my shoulders from behind.

"What's up, slim?"

That familiar voice had a genuine smile splitting my face for the first time all day. I craned my neck back to find my favorite co-worker grinning down at me.

"You came!" I squeaked, turning around backward in my chair and sitting up on my knees to hug my bodybuilding buddy.

Juliet cleared her throat.

"Jules"—I turned toward her, one arm still around Jamal's neck—"this is Jamal. Jamal, this is my best friend, Juliet."

"What the fuck, B?" Juliet snapped. For a minute, I thought she was really pissed, but the smile on her face gave her away. "You have *another* black friend? When were you gonna tell *me*?"

"Oh my God, I hate you," I muttered, releasing Jamal so that I could bury my face in my hands.

"That's what I'm sayin'." Jamal chuckled as he walked around to sit in the empty chair next to Juliet. "I thought I was special."

The two of them began joking and laughing at my expense while I nursed the disgustingly sweet concoction in my glass. Everyone at the Frankentable was now happily paired off, engrossed in their conversations, except for me.

I grabbed my purse off the back of my chair and shoved my arm in elbow deep, looking for something entertaining. I was hoping for a pack of cigarettes or maybe a set of throwing knives, but my hand pulled out a buzzing, vibrating cell phone instead.

I deduced in a tenth of a second who was calling without even looking at my caller ID. I'd already had my traditional pizza-and-lopsided-homemade-birthday-cake dinner with my parents—most of which, I'd fed to the dog—so I knew it wasn't one of them. My closest friends were all sitting within ten feet of me, so I knew it wasn't any of them. I was fairly certain that Hans had already forgotten my birthday, and Harley was still in jail.

But Knight…Knight didn't forget shit.

"I'm going to smoke," I mumbled as I pushed my chair out from the table.

Ken turned away from his sister and glanced at the phone, now silent in my hand. Lifting his eyes to mine, he said, "You can smoke in here." There was accusation in his tone. It matched his chiseled, stoic features.

"I don't want to," I snapped, pushing the creaky old thing I'd been sitting in back under the table.

God, I'm being a bitch. Ken hasn't done anything wrong.

Exactly. It's your birthday, and Ken hasn't done anything. At all. At least Knight still calls you on your birthday.

Yeah, but he only calls to scream at me.

True dat.

I pushed the front door to Fuzzy's open, which weighed more than I did, and felt my phone vibrate once in my hand, indicating that Knight had left a voicemail. I stared at it as I leaned against the brick windowsill, debating whether to press Play or Delete. I usually deleted them so fast; you would think I was deactivating a bomb. But I was feeling especially needy.

As my thumb hovered over the Play button, I heard the sound of a motorcycle engine revving across the street. I gasped and looked up, a strangled scream caught in my terror-stricken throat, as a middle-aged man with a potbelly pulled out of a parking spot on an old Harley Fat Boy. My eyes scanned the sidewalks for any signs of a psychopathic ex-Marine in biker gear, but the only guys I could see were drunken frat boys with their polo shirts tucked into their khaki shorts.

You're okay.

He's not here.

You're totally safe.

He's not here.

But, evidently, I didn't *feel* totally safe because, when I looked down at my phone, I realized I was holding my can of pepper spray in my opposite hand.

Delete.

I had just tossed everything back into my purse and gotten my breathing somewhat back to normal when the door next to me swung open.

A faux-hawked, tattooed, fruity drink–making Zach waltzed out, wearing a megawatt smile. "Happy birthday, killer."

Killer. That was appropriate, considering my mood.

"Thanks." I pulled my pack of cigarettes out of my bag.

The spark from Zach's lighter greeted me the second I placed one between my lips. Giving him a half-smile, I dipped the end of my Camel into the flame.

"So, that's the guy, huh?" Zach nodded toward the front door as I exhaled.

"What guy?"

"The gay guy who invites you over to watch movies."

I snorted the rest of the smoke out my nostrils like a dragon. "Yep. That's him. Turns out, he's not gay after all."

Zach shrugged. "You win. Serial killer it is."

I laughed, just a little. It felt good.

"Speaking of murderers, your girl in there is gonna strangle a regular any day now."

"Probably." I smirked. "Let me know if y'all need help burying the body."

"No offense, but you don't look like you'd be much help." The yellow streetlights lining the sidewalk brought out the gold flecks in Zach's eyes as they slid up and down my body.

I blushed, taking another drag from my cigarette to hide my swoon. "What I lack in brute strength, I make up for in leadership skills." I exhaled. "I can supervise like a motherfucker."

Sticking his cigarette between his teeth, he extended a thick, tattooed hand in my direction. "Fine. You're hired."

I slipped my perma-cold palm into his with a smile. "Emergency Body Burial Supervisor BB, reporting for duty."

Zach held my hand a second or two longer than a guy who was just a friend should, and I hated the thrill it gave me. I hated how desperate for attention I was. I hated that my own boyfriend didn't look at me or touch me like Zach the bartender just had.

Finally releasing my hand, Zach sighed and flicked his cigarette into the street. "Well, I better get back in there. You good?"

I nodded and held up what was left of my Camel. "Almost done."

The second the door shut behind him, I blew out a shaky breath, hoping all my guilt would blow away with it.

We should have just gone to fucking Bahama Breeze.

Taking one last drag, I dropped my cigarette to the sidewalk and smashed it with my busted, old combat boot. Mustering all my strength, I yanked on the handle of the solid oak door separating me from my friends, but this time, it flew open almost effortlessly. I stumbled backward as Ken breezed through, adding a chill to the hot, humid air.

"You okay?" he asked, eyeing me suspiciously as I righted myself.

"Yeah, I'm fine." I straightened my spine. "I was just coming back in."

"Why are you still out here? People were asking where you went."

"To keep myself from slapping you." My eyes went wide once I realized I'd actually said that out loud. I guess all those Sex on the Beaches were catching up with me.

Ken smirked and raised one eyebrow. "I wouldn't mind."

"Ugh," I groaned and rolled my eyes. "Are you just pissing me off on purpose so that I'll hit you? That's fucked up, Ken."

"Pissing you off?" His ghost of a smile disappeared. "What did I do this time?"

"Nothing!" I yelled, throwing my hands in the air. "Nothing! That's the point! It's my twenty-first birthday, and you haven't done shit! No party. No cake. No gifts—"

"I got you a gift."

I stopped mid-rant and blinked at him. "You what?"

Ken reached into the back pocket of his charcoal-gray slacks and produced a single white envelope. "I got you a gift. I was gonna wait to give it to you until we got home, but…" Ken frowned. "Here."

I accepted the paper from him with a scowl on my face. Turning it over, I noticed the word *Brooke* written on the front in Ken's teensy, tiny, chicken-scratch handwriting.

All I'd wanted was for him to acknowledge my birthday, but now that I had a gift in my hands, I was suddenly afraid to open it. I could practically see my hopes dancing above our heads. They were way too high. What if there was nothing inside but a coupon for a free salad bar at Ruby Tuesday? I'd have to kill Ken, and then I'd be stuck supervising a body burial with Zach and Juliet on my birthday, and nobody likes to work on their birthday.

Ken stood, silent and serious, as I forced myself to open the flap. Giving him a smile that I was sure looked more like a cringe, I reached inside and pulled out some kind of glossy, full-color brochure.

The fuck?

I turned it so I could read the front cover.

EUROPEAN TRAVEL MASTERS

10-DAY BRITISH ISLES TOUR

ENGLAND ~ IRELAND ~ WALES

I couldn't breathe. I didn't know what was happening, but I knew that I couldn't fucking breathe.

"You said, the next time I went to Europe, to take you with me. So…"

I lifted my eyes, which were probably bulging out of my head from oxygen deprivation, and frantically scanned Ken's face for any trace of sarcasm. He couldn't be serious, but the hard line of his mouth said that he was even more serious than the heart attack I was about to have.

I opened the brochure and felt tears stinging my eyes as I drank in pictures of the places on my vision board—the Tower of London, Buckingham Palace, Big Ben, Stonehenge, little thatched-roof cottages surrounded by fluffy white sheep, the rolling green hills and rocky beaches of Ireland, pubs lining the streets of Dublin, and the place I wanted to go more than any other, Blarney Castle.

"There is a catch." Ken's voice wavered.

I looked up with glistening eyes, begging him not to tell me it was all a sick joke.

Please don't fuck with me, I pleaded. *Not about this.*

Ken took a breath. "I know you're taking summer classes, and I don't want you to miss school, so…the trip isn't until next May. After you graduate."

I blinked.

Next May.

I swallowed.

Next May.

"Ken…" I blinked again, expelling one big, fat, overwhelmed tear from my eye. "That's almost a year from now."

"Yeah." He smiled. "We should probably go ahead and count it as your birthday present for next year, too."

I laughed. No, I fucking cackled and buried myself in his chest.

Ken wrapped his reluctant arms around my shoulders as I cried and hiccuped and giggled all over him.

"And maybe graduation and Christmas while we're at it," he mused, gradually relaxing into my embrace.

"And Valentine's Day?" I giggled, peeking up at his stubbled, square jaw.

Ken's hard mouth curled up on one side, and I knew before he even parted his lips what he was about to say.

"Fuck Valentine's Day."

I smiled.

Yeah. Fuck Valentine's Day.

"Happy birthday to you. Happy birthday to you. Happy birthday, dear Ken and Chelsea. Happy birthday to you!"

A week later, I was sitting in Mr. and Mrs. Easton's formal dining room as the lady of the house brought out a gorgeous white bakery-commissioned birthday cake. She placed it in the center of the table, careful not to wrinkle the antique lace tablecloth, and smiled at her adult children. I laughed to myself as Ken stood there with his arms crossed over his chest, stubbornly refusing to help his sister blow out their shared birthday candles.

As soon as the pomp and pageantry were over, however, Ken helped his mother cut the cake and pass the plates out to everyone.

Realizing I didn't have a fork, I walked into the kitchen where Mr. Easton was refilling his glass of sweet tea from a pitcher on the counter.

"What can I do for you, miss?" he asked in that charming *Gone with the Wind* kind of Southern accent that you just don't hear anymore.

"I just need a fork. *Please.*" I smiled.

I liked Ken's parents. They were as conservative and traditional as my parents were unconventional and eccentric, but they were kind to me despite my purple hair, lack of manners, and the fact that I was obviously sleeping with their son before marriage.

"Comin' right up." Mr. Easton opened a drawer and pulled out a polished silver utensil. "You know," he said, glancing into the dining room and lowering his voice, "when Ken was born on Chelsea's birthday, I felt so bad for them. I thought, *These little people should have their own birthdays.* But then Ken decided not to celebrate, and it was like Chelsea *did* have her own birthday. And it was kinda sad. This is the first time he's been here on his birthday in…gosh…four or five years."

"Really?" I whispered with wide eyes as I accepted the utensil. "Why doesn't he celebrate?"

Mr. Easton shrugged. "Can't say for sure, but I think it's just on account of how much he hates being the center of attention. He's shy, that one. When he was a kid, he used to hide inside his jersey anytime he scored a touchdown just 'cause he couldn't stand everybody lookin' at him."

I stuck the end of my fork in my mouth and leaned forward, hanging on his every word. "But you guys are family."

"I know. Seems silly, don't it?" Mr. Easton glanced into the dining room and nodded at someone. "Shoot," he whispered. "The missus is givin' me a look. We'd better get in there." Glancing back at me, he added, "I just wanted to tell you, thanks. I don't know what you did, but it's sure nice to have our boy home on his birthday."

I followed an older, softer, grayer version of Ken into the dining room with a smile on my face. Had I actually done something? Was I fixing him?

We made pleasant small talk over cake and then "retired to the sitting room" for coffee. When I walked into the living room, I was horrified to find not one, not two, but, like, eight perfectly upholstered armchairs. Two plaid ones over here, two leather ones over there, two facing the TV…

Where are the couches?

Why aren't there any couches?

Everyone took a seat, at least five feet away from one another, and sipped their coffee out of miniature mugs with little matching saucers.

Except for Ken and me, who drank water.

"It's a shame Bobby couldn't get off work to join us," Mrs. Easton said to Chelsea.

"It's fine. He's taking me on a surprise trip this weekend for my birthday." Chelsea blushed while Ken and I exchanged a knowing glance.

Bobby was going to propose at Disney World. Why Disney World, I had no idea. Maybe because it would take visiting "the happiest place on Earth" to make an Easton get excited about anything.

Seeing her wistful smile gave me hope though. If Ken's parents and sister could get married and have kids, maybe he could, too. They were all the same model of robot after all.

"Brooke…"

Oh shit. She's talking to me.

I sat up and attended to Mrs. Easton like a student who'd just been called on.

"Ken tells us that you're going to Georgia State to become a school psychologist. Is that right?"

"Uh-huh." *Shit.* "I mean, yes, ma'am. I start graduate school next year."

"How many years does it take to become a school psychologist?" Mr. Easton asked, looking at me over the top of his little round glasses.

"Seven." *Sir! Say sir!* "Seven years, *sir.* I've got four more to go."

"And then you'll be the most educated one in the family." Mr. Easton smiled, completely unaware of his faux pas, but all the women in the room held their breath and looked at Ken.

Especially me.

Which, of course, made Ken stand up and leave the room.

"…hates bein' the center of attention. He's shy, that one."

Ken's parents stood as well, smoothing the wrinkles from their Sunday best as they escorted us to the front door.

"It was nice to meet you, Brooke," Mrs. Easton said with a polite smile.

Like my mother, she was a schoolteacher, but unlike my mother—who taught art at an overcrowded, underfunded public school where they let her wear tie-dye and Birkenstocks to work—Mrs. Easton looked like she was probably employed by a pricey private school where they let teachers hit kids with rulers.

"Nice to meet you, too." I beamed, spreading my arms in preparation for a hug that was clearly not going to be reciprocated.

Mrs. Easton's eyes went wide in horror as she realized what I was doing, her arms glued to her sides. I dropped my hands as heat crept into my cheeks, turning to face Mr. Easton.

Furrowing his brow as if he didn't know what to do with me, Ken's dad raised a hand and patted me on the shoulder. Twice. "Welp, y'all drive safe."

"Uh…thanks for having me," I said, distracted by the sight of Ken in my periphery, turning and walking down the front steps without so much as a goodbye. "The cake was delicious," I sputtered, stepping backward onto the Welcome mat. "Happy birthday, Chelsea!" I called into the house before turning to hustle after Ken.

He had just opened his driver-side door when I dived into the passenger seat.

"What the fuck was that?" I asked as he cranked the engine and backed out of the driveway.

"What was what?"

"That!" I threw my hand out in the direction of his childhood home. "You just…left! You guys didn't hug or say *I love you* or anything!"

Ken shrugged, shifting into drive. "We don't do that."

"What do you mean, you don't *do* that?" I screeched.

Ken glanced at me in annoyance.

"You guys don't hug?"

"No."

"Never?"

Ken gave me a warning look.

"Oh my God." I sat back in my seat, flabbergasted.

All those armchairs.

My heart hurt, thinking about Ken as a little boy in that house. No couch to cuddle on. No touching. No tickles.

"Have they *ever* told you they loved you?"

Ken kept his eyes on the road, his mouth set in a straight line. "Probably."

"Probably?" I gasped. "You can't even remember?"

Ken cut his hard eyes to mine, just for a second. "It's not that big of a deal. They're good parents, okay?"

"I know; I know." I held my hands up. "They're lovely—"

"Just because something's different doesn't make it wrong," Ken cut me off. He'd never interrupted me before.

I turned in my seat, facing him head-on. "I'm sorry. I know they're your parents, and they seem like wonderful people, but you going your whole life without hearing the words *I love you*...that is absolutely fucking *wrong*."

Ken kept his eyes on the road and didn't say another word. The conversation was obviously closed for discussion.

I didn't tell him *I love you* as I stared at the side of his beautiful, impassive face, but I thought it.

I thought it as hard as I fucking could.

July 2003

I have no idea why I was home that day. I'd been avoiding my house as much as possible ever since I saw Knight outside my bedroom window, but for some reason, I was upstairs in my room, chain-smoking and sketching out a drawing of the Eiffel Tower that I wanted to paint for Ken's wall of French art, when I heard the phone ring. And not my phone—not some cute little *doodle-oodle-oodle-oo.* No, this was my parents' loud-ass home phone that made me feel the urge to duck and cover with every successive ring.

"Mom!" I yelled from my bed. "Will you get that? I'm busy!"

RIIIIIIIIIIIIIIIIIIIIIING!

"Mom!"

Goddamn it.

I set my pencil down on the edge of my easel and waded through the piles of Hans's bullshit strewed about on my tiny bedroom floor until I got to the plastic cordless phone anchored to the wall next to my bed.

"Hello?" I huffed.

"Hey, Scooter," my dad replied. "Is your mom there?"

"Yeah, hang on," I said, stepping over a guitar amp and hitting my head on a brass pot hanging from the ceiling.

Stomping out into the hallway, I cupped my hand over the receiver and yelled, "Mom!" as loud as I could.

All I heard in response was a tiny cough from somewhere downstairs.

Then, a grunt.

"Dad, hold on a second."

I flew down the stairs, phone in one hand, railing in the other.

"Mom?"

Turning the corner in the foyer, I swung my head left and right until I spotted a pair of feet lying sideways on the linoleum kitchen floor.

One Birkenstock on. One off.

"Mom!" I rushed in and found my mother splayed out across the kitchen floor.

A barstool had been turned over during her fall, and her head had landed in Ringo's bowl of dog food.

I dived for her, picking her head up and moving the plastic bowl away, as she swallowed and coughed and stared at me with wide, frightened eyes.

"Mom? What happened? Are you okay?"

Her mouth opened and closed in labored movements, but nothing came out other than frustrated gurgles and coughs.

"Can you move? Squeeze my hand." I grabbed her cold fingers and felt a gentle squeeze. "What about this hand?" I reached for the arm pinned under her side and extracted her hand.

Nothing.

"Mom, squeeze my hand!"

Nothing.

Shit!

I laid her head back on the floor and leaped up to call 911.

"Scooter?" my dad said from the cordless phone I'd abandoned on the kitchen floor. I had already forgotten that he was on hold.

I grabbed the phone. "Dad! I think Mom had a stroke!"

"Call 911, and I'll meet you at the hospital." I'd never heard him sound so authoritative. "And, Scooter, don't you dare cry. Do you hear me? You'll scare your mother."

"Okay." I nodded and felt my chin buckle as I glanced back at my favorite person on earth, paralyzed and struggling to speak on the kitchen floor. "I won't."

The paramedics arrived so fast; I was still on the phone with the 911 dispatcher when they knocked on the door.

I don't remember them loading her into the ambulance. I don't remember following it to the hospital. I don't remember how long it had taken my dad to get there.

All I remember is that the only word my mother could say as she lay, waiting for the doctors, was *Brooke.*

And *shit.* She could also say *shit.*

Thanks to my neuropsychology coursework, I knew that my mother was exhibiting Broca's aphasia. It's when a person has a blood clot—a stroke—in the part of the brain that's responsible for turning thoughts and feelings into words and sentences. The reason people with Broca's aphasia are still able to curse is because those words are stored in a different, more primitive part of the brain.

I found it fitting that my mom had stored my name in the same place as the words *cunt* and *asshole.*

The doctors told us that my mother was extremely lucky that I'd gotten her to the hospital as quickly as I had. From what they could tell, it had only been an hour or two since the stroke occurred, which meant that she could possibly make a full recovery with treatment. I should have been happy, but the revelation made me feel like the world's shittiest daughter. If it hadn't been for my dad's random lunch-break phone call, my mom would have been lying on the floor for hours, suffering irreversible brain damage, while I sat, self-absorbed, up in my room, smoking and drawing and obsessing over a boy.

My mother believed in guardian angels, so I begged hers to help her get better.

Please, I pleaded as the doctors wheeled her away to administer the treatment that would hopefully bring her back to us. *If she recovers, I'll do better. I'll spend more time with her, I promise. We'll go to the museum, we'll take yoga classes, we'll finally learn how to play beer pong—whatever she wants. Please. Just give me another chance.*

After the treatment, there was nothing left to do but wait. My dad said I should take the first shift because he had to go home and let the dog out. I knew what that was code for. My dad had to go home and get wasted because he had no coping skills, he hated hospitals, and his anxiety was through the roof.

I stayed by her side all night, semi-reclined in that godforsaken chair, watching one of the four channels on the hospital TV and staring at my mom for signs of life during every commercial break. Nurses came, and nurses went. Things were written on the whiteboard and then erased. Trays of food were brought and taken away, untouched. And, all the while, my mother slept.

When my dad showed up, long after sunrise, he was wearing dark sunglasses and nursing a black coffee.

Good, I thought. *You look the way I feel.*

I left him with his unconscious wife, unsure if she would ever be able to say his name again, and took off. There was only one place I wanted to be, and I couldn't get there fast enough.

I'd called Ken the night before from the hospital waiting room and told him what had happened. He was at work at the time, so he couldn't really talk, but he did say that he was sorry and offered to help if I needed anything.

Well, I did need something. I needed him to fucking hold me while I fell apart.

I parked in Ken's driveway and took my foot off the clutch without thinking, causing my car to shudder violently and stall out with a hiss. That was when I knew I was in bad shape. I hadn't stalled out since I was sixteen. I needed sleep.

I needed food. I needed alcohol. I needed to cry. I needed Ken. And I needed them all at once.

It took my exhausted, emotional, brain-dead ass at least three tries to get the right key in the lock before I was finally able to open Ken's red front door. When I did, I stopped in my tracks, horrified to see him sitting to the left of the couch, watching the morning news, in a brand-new motherfucking recliner.

Bile rose in my throat.

Armchairs.

Armchairs.

A room full of armchairs.

This is how it begins.

Ken doesn't want me to touch him anymore.

Look at the couch. That's my spot.

Ken has a new spot. By himself in his MOTHERFUCKING ARMCHAIR.

"Where the fuck did that come from?" I threw a hand toward his newest acquisition.

"Uh…" Ken tilted his head and raised an eyebrow at me. "La-Z-Boy was having a Fourth of July sale, so—"

"Didn't you hear me trying to get in?" I snapped, swinging my hand in the direction of the door. "You just sat there!"

Ken gave me that look. That condescending fucking look that said, *I'm going to speak to you in small words now because you're clearly emotional and beyond all reason.* "You have a key. I didn't think you—"

"Whatever!" I cut him off as I made my way into the kitchen to drop my purse on the counter. Leaning over Ken's stainless-steel sink, I alternated between drinking the water straight from the tap and splashing it on my face. When I shut off the faucet and dried myself off, I turned around to find the kitchen empty.

Stomping back into the living room, I glared at the motherfucker in the brown leather armchair. He looked fresh-faced and well rested in a Peachtree Road Race T-shirt and a pair of running shorts. He looked like a bastard who didn't give two shits that his girlfriend had been up all night, pacing hospital floors and worrying that her mother might not ever speak or walk again.

"So, this is it? We're doing this again?" I fumed, clamping my hands down onto my jutting hip bones.

"Doing what?" Ken furrowed his angular brows at me as if he had absolutely no idea what I could possibly be upset about.

"We're playing the game where I feel really fucking sad about something"—my face crumpled—"and you stay as far away from me as you can get until it goes away." My voice broke. The levees broke. The dam that had been holding back my emotions for my mother's sake broke, and there was no one there to help me put it back together.

I stood in the middle of Ken's living room and cried while he tried to figure out what the fuck to do about it.

"Brooke…"

"Shut up!" I yelled, burying my face in my hands.

Not only did Ken shut up, he stood up and walked right out of the fucking room.

My cries morphed from a silent sob to a keening wail as soon as he was gone. I curled up on the couch, pulling my knees to my chest, and hugged *myself* until I fell asleep.

I woke up to the sound of my phone ringing. It was still light outside, but Ken was nowhere to be seen.

Stumbling into the kitchen, I answered on what had to be the hundredth chime.

"Scooter! Your mom's awake, and she's talking up a storm. She sounds like a drunken pirate though." My dad chuckled as my mom slurred something inappropriate in the background. "But the doctors say she'll be back to normal in a few days."

"That's great, Dad." I meant it, but I sure as fuck didn't sound like it.

"You okay, Scooter?"

"Yeah. Sorry. You woke me up, so I'm a little out of it."

"Well, go let Ringo out, then get your ass up here with some pizza. Your mom told a nurse that their food tastes like dog shit." He chuckled again.

"Okay." I yawned. "See you soon."

Dropping my phone into my purse, I noticed a note scrawled on a pad of paper next to it on the counter.

Brooke,

I have to go to work. Sorry about your mom. I hope she's okay.

Ken

Picking up the pen lying perfectly parallel to the pad of paper, I flipped the page and wrote a note of my own.

Dear Ken,

Go fuck yourself.

And your little chair, too.

BB

Then, I ripped both pages out of the notebook, wadded them up, and threw them in the recycle bin out in the garage.

I didn't spend the night at Ken's that night. Or the next night. Or the night after that. We'd spoken on the phone a few times, but our conversations had been clipped. Ken hadn't apologized for being completely emotionally unavailable, and I hadn't apologized for yelling at him. He'd asked if I wanted to come over, maybe meet for dinner, but I'd lied and said I needed to take care of my mom. The truth was, my mom was doing fine. She wasn't back to one hundred percent yet, but she was getting there.

I, on the other hand, was not.

After Jason's funeral, I'd thought Ken had made some kind of breakthrough. He'd seemed to be opening up, letting me in. He'd seemed to be trying. But, after my mom's stroke, it felt like we were right back where we'd started.

Ken was proving that he could be there for me in every way but one. I'd thought I could fix that one flaw, but there we were, months later, and I still hadn't even isolated the cause.

So, not only was my relationship doomed, but I was shaping up to be a pretty shitty psychologist too.

Awesome.

My days reverted to the work-study-sleep-school-study-sleep cycle they'd been on back when Ken was just Pajama Guy. My hair reverted back to the same wavy/poofy/disheveled state it had been in as well, only now it was down to my shoulders. I realized that I could pull the top half into a messy bun, so I said, *Fuck it*, busted out my old clippers, and shaved the bottom half completely off.

I'd promised my mom I wouldn't shave it again if I could keep it looking sleek and straight. But I couldn't. I couldn't keep anything good for long, evidently.

On this particular night, I'd been trying to study for my Behavioral Psychology final for hours, but my brain simply wouldn't cooperate. Over and over, my eyes would scan the symbols on the page, but they were simply admiring the shapes of the letters while my mind spiraled in a million different directions.

Is this my life now?

Should I just sell all the stuff from my old apartment and accept that I'm going to live here forever?

Should I break up with Ken?

Does he even miss me?

I'm never getting married.

I should just go ahead and freeze my eggs.

How much does it cost to freeze your eggs?

A familiar, throaty rumble reached into my head and yanked me back into the present. I realized, as my eyes darted over to my window, that night had fallen while I was busy obsessing, and my blinds were still wide open. As the distinct sound of my own personal nightmare approached, I tossed my books aside, threw the covers off my bare legs, leaped out of bed, and dived for the little plastic rod hanging from the nicotine-stained blinds.

Yanking it off completely.

I stood there, in a tank top and panties, clutching a rod that went to nothing, as Knight's chopper pulled to a stop beneath the streetlight outside.

Shit!

I dropped the worthless pole and darted over to my nightstand, turning off my lamp and grabbing my purse off the floor. The strap got caught on the corner of Hans's VCR, causing me to stumble into the wall next to the window. Sliding down so that Knight couldn't see me, I dumped out the contents of my purse, looking for my phone. I wanted to shut it off so that his inevitable call would go straight to voicemail, but he was too quick. The phone lit up and vibrated against my foot.

"Ahh!" I squealed, smacking it like a cockroach.

Doodle-oodle-oodle—

I jerked my finger toward it, aiming for the End button, but it wiggled as it vibrated, causing me to hit the Talk button instead.

"Punk!" I could hear Knight's commanding voice, both through the speaker and through the glass.

I knew if I hung up he would literally keep calling until I either gave up and answered or had the police come and escort him away.

With a shaky breath and shakier hand, I lifted the phone to my head, holding it an inch away from my face. It was like I was afraid he could bite me through the phone.

"Yeah?" I cringed.

"Come the fuck outside."

I stared up at the glow-in-the-dark star stickers on my ceiling and prayed for a sinkhole. "No, thanks."

"I'm sorry, okay? Just come the fuck outside and talk to me."

There was the tiniest hint of a slur, right where his Ts met his Ss, which told me to tread lightly. To anyone else, it would have been imperceptible, but I heard it. I'd spent the last six years of my life analyzing every subtle change in Knight's posture, pitch, tone, and expression for signs of danger. And that tiny slur was one of them.

"I can't. My dad's still awake, and he'll call the cops if he knows you're here," I lied.

"At least you have a fucking dad!"

I leaned my head back against the wall. I could almost feel Knight's rage radiating through the weathered wood siding on the other side.

"Knight…" I took a deep breath as I absentmindedly rubbed the smooth leather pouch that housed my pepper spray. "I don't have to come outside for you to talk to me. You can talk to me like this. I just need you to calm—"

"He's dead!"

I sat up. "Who's dead?"

"My fucking dad!"

I reached above my head and yanked on the cord hanging there, raising the blinds with one loud swoosh. Then, I turned and knelt at the window. As I looked down on the drunk, grieving psychopath below, Knight's ghastly, colorless eyes locked onto mine in an instant. Even in the darkness, I could tell they were red-rimmed and bloodshot.

"Knight, I'm…I'm so sorry."

Knight's father had been a prominent businessman in Chicago with a picture-perfect family. An emotionally volatile bastard son wouldn't have been a good look, so he never admitted that Knight was his son. He never even met him.

And now, he never would.

Knight growled and pointed at me with his free hand, then at the ground. "Come the fuck down here!"

I pressed my fist, still wrapped around the black leather pouch, to the glass. I wanted to go to him. I wanted to hold him and comfort him as badly as I'd wanted anything, but I knew that wasn't what he wanted from me. Knight didn't want my caress. He wanted my flesh. My blood. My broken bones. He wanted to use my body as a receptacle for his pain and then leave it bleeding in the street once he realized what he'd done.

"I'm right here," I whispered, pleading with my eyes and my voice for him to calm down. "You can talk to me. See? I'm right here."

"I don't want to fucking talk!"

"I know, but it might help."

"Grrrrrrr!" Knight growled and squeezed the phone in his hand so hard I could hear the plastic cracking on the other end of the line. "Fuck you! Come down here!"

"I can't," I whispered, pressing my forehead to the glass.

Knight stomped over to the house and punched the siding with his free hand. I felt the window rattle against my face.

"Come the fuck outside, Punk!"

"Stop it!" I looked down at the top of his head. His slicked-back blond hair had fallen forward with the force of his punch. "Knight, you're gonna break your knuckles, and you're a fucking tattoo artist. Calm down."

Knight punched the wall again, and in that moment, I realized what it must feel like to be Ken.

I knew what it was like to be in a serious relationship with someone you couldn't handle. Someone who experienced things much more deeply than you did. I knew how it felt to care about someone who demanded more than you could give them, then lashed out at you for not being able to give it.

I'd been doing it for six years.

Maybe Ken wasn't the problem after all.

Maybe, like Knight, I just needed to take responsibility for my own fucking feelings.

"Knight," I said softly, doing exactly what Ken would do if I were on his front lawn, throwing a drunken tantrum in the middle of the night. I stopped cowering. I straightened my spine. And I said, "I'm sorry about your dad. I'm so, so sorry. But I can't talk to you while you're this drunk and upset, so I'm gonna hang up now and call you a cab."

September 2003

"Ken, will you hand me that teapot?" I reached across the string of card tables and metal folding tables that stretched from one side of Ken's back patio to the other with my hand out.

We'd covered them in white tablecloths to make it look like one long, elegant table, but since there was nothing we could do about the mismatched chairs, I'd just decided to make it a theme.

Ken glanced down into the box of equally mismatched teapots that I'd collected from every thrift and antique store in the county. "Which one?"

"The blue-and-white one." I flicked my fingers at him impatiently.

Ken raised an eyebrow and pursed his lips.

"Ugh! Please!"

Ken gave me a satisfied smirk and handed over the vessel.

In the two months since my altercation with Knight, Ken and I had settled into a comfortable routine. I stayed there almost every night. He packed lunches for me on the days that I had school. I gave him psychological tests when he was slow at work. He watched *Sex and the City* with me on

Sunday nights. Life was surprisingly good, and the only thing that had changed was my attitude.

Ken and I had spent the morning picking wildflowers in a nearby field and arranging them in the teapots I'd collected.

When I'd asked him if he would help me host a wedding shower for Allen and Amy, Ken hadn't hesitated to say yes. But, of course, his brand of help involved borrowing all the tables and chairs from his neighbors, trading movie passes with the manager of a local pizza place in exchange for free food and buying all of the drinks, plates, and napkins at bulk prices through the theater. All in, I think the entire party cost us less than a hundred bucks.

"I left that questionnaire on top of your backpack," Ken said, handing me another flower-filled teapot. "That one asked some fucked up questions."

I laughed. "Yeah, that one screens for *all kinds* of fun disorders."

"Bed-wetting though? Really?"

I grinned. "Bed-wetting, fire-starting, shoplifting, cruelty to animals…let's see…what else? Bloodplay…" My face fell as I thought about someone else who fit that description. "They can all be symptoms of childhood trauma or mental illness."

"I think I'm good then. The only one I answered yes to was self-flagellation, and that's only because you won't do it for me."

"Oh my God!" I cackled, swatting at him across the table. My fingertips grazed the soft cotton of his vintage Braves T-shirt. "You're such a masochist. That's what it's gonna tell me. It's gonna say, *Kenneth Easton is a stage-five masochist. Get out while you still can.*"

I watched the jovial smile slip from Ken's face just before Amy burst through the back door with a, "Haaaaay!" dragging her fiancé, best friend, and sister from Arizona behind her.

At one point, we had about twenty-five people gathered on the patio—guys on one side, shouting at the TV, which

Ken had dragged outside, every time John Smoltz struck somebody out, and girls on the other side, oohing and aahing over Amy's three-inch-thick wedding planner. Citronella torches kept the mosquitoes away as we drank pink punch—generously spiked, thank you very much—and admired her collection of fabric swatches and wedding dress photos and magazine cutouts and invitation samples.

I smiled and nodded, pretending to be happy for her, but the entire time, I was dreaming about the day that I'd have my own three-ring binder to fill. Glancing over at the opposite end of the table, I watched Ken, smiling his movie-star smile, as he laughed with his friends. *Our* friends.

We could do this every weekend, I thought.

I glanced at his deep, wooded backyard, dotted with fireflies and blooming azalea bushes, and tried to picture where the swing set would go. I glanced at my ring finger and imagined a princess cut diamond twinkling back at me.

I was happy there, with Ken. He made me laugh and he made me crazy and he made me a better version of myself. But, most of all, he made me want things that I wasn't sure he could give me. Things he didn't *believe* in.

Things like weddings and babies and magic.

I just hoped I believed in them enough for the both of us.

PART

I woke to the familiar sensation of having my feet seared off with a blowtorch.

It used to bother me, the way the sun's rays through Ken's arched window tried to burn me alive at daybreak. I'd begged him to get custom blinds made. I'd even resorted to cutting a piece of cardboard into the shape of a semicircle and shoving it into the top section of the window, but after it had come loose one night and fallen, corner first, into my forehead while I was sleeping, I'd given up.

But I didn't mind waking up with the lower half of my body on fire anymore. Because it meant that I was waking up next to Ken.

I rolled over and molded myself to his firm back. He always slept in the fetal position, so the whole flaming-hot-rays-of-death-at-the-foot-of-the-bed thing didn't impact him at all.

I wrapped my arm around his waist, snaking it between him and the pillow he was clutching, and nuzzled a kiss into his back. "You awake?"

"No."

I lifted my red-hot foot and pressed it against his calf. "What about now?"

Fucker didn't even flinch.

"You know what? I think today's our six-month anniversary." I smiled against his back. "Well, it's been six months since we went to Cirque du Soleil. I guess, technically, we were dating before that, but that was the first time you called me your girlfriend, and—oh my God, do you remember how drunk I was?" I giggled, reminiscing about how I'd pretended to be asleep when he got pulled over. "We should go out tonight to celebrate! Wait. Shit. You have to work. Can we go out tomorrow?"

Ken nodded slightly and hummed something that sounded like, "Mmhmm."

I squealed and squeezed him with my whole body. He was so cute when he was sleepy. Normally, Ken was all hard and cold and serious—or seriously sarcastic—but the man slept, curled around a pillow every night like it was a teddy bear.

And nobody knew it but me.

Ken found my hand under the blankets and covered it with his. That simple gesture made my heart sputter and my smile spread. I laced my fingers through his, psyching myself up to finally say what had been on the tip of my tongue for months. What I'd decided needed to be said the night before while I thumbed through the pages of Amy's wedding planner.

What I was terrified that Ken didn't feel in return.

With my heart in my throat, I pressed my forehead against Ken's broad, strong back and whispered the truth into his freckles, "I love you."

The second those three words left my mouth, Ken's warm, relaxed body tensed and turned to granite in my arms.

One second went by.

Then, two.

Then, two hundred.

All the while, the statue man lay there, mute and rigid, in my regretful embrace. Confirming my fears without saying a word.

Bitter, humiliated tears stung my eyes as I waited, suspended in awkward agony, for something to happen. For Ken to speak. For lightning to strike. For my fucking alarm to hurry up and go off.

With every second that ticked by, so did another hope. Another dream. Another shiny trinket from my imaginary fucking future.

Tick.

He doesn't love you.

Tock.

He doesn't believe in marriage.

Tick.

He doesn't want children.

Tock.

He said it right to your face.

Tick.

You don't actually live here.

Tock.

You just pretend like you do.

Tick.

Ken loves nothing.

Tock.

You knew it right from the start.

Beep! Beep! Beep! Beep!

I rolled over and smacked the alarm clock, wiping an angry, embarrassed tear from my cheek with the side of my hand.

And now, time's up.

I got up and sprinted for the bathroom. I couldn't get away from there fast enough. From Ken. From that house. From the lie I'd been living in.

I got ready for school in a haphazard flurry, using the few products I had in my purse and the ones I'd stashed under Ken's sink. I pulled my purplish mop with two inches of auburn roots up into a messy bun and didn't even bother with my signature wing-tip eyeliner. There was no point. It would be running down my face by the time I got to school anyway.

With my combat boots still untied, I bolted down the stairs, grabbed my backpack off the floor by the couch, and took off out the front door without so much as a good-bye.

I was pretty sure the window-rattling *slam* had said it for me.

I replayed the events of that morning on a loop as I stared, unfocused, out the grimy subway train window. I had an hour commute to Georgia State University, which I usually spent reading or studying before class. But, as the pine trees and single-family homes of suburbia gave way to the skyscrapers and gridlocked highway traffic of Atlanta, my mind was anywhere but on my studies.

It was on a beautiful man inside a beautiful house inside a beautiful life that I'd been dumb enough to think I could actually have.

I spent my school day in a state of physical and emotional hell. Burning eyes. Churning guts. Black hole in my chest. Ken-shaped hole in my life.

I spoke to no one. I ate nothing. I focused all my energy on keeping the tears at bay until I got off the subway train that afternoon. I clenched my teeth as I trudged through the MARTA parking lot, counting the steps until my ass hit the cigarette-burned driver's seat of my black Mustang hatchback.

Then, I let myself fall apart.

I cried because I felt rejected.

I cried because I felt stupid.

I cried because I'd thought I was done crying over boys.

I cried because I missed him already.

I cried because I knew he wouldn't miss me back, which reminded me how stupid I was and made me cry even harder.

I cried until I ran out of tears. Then, I took a deep breath, lit a cigarette with shaky fingers, pulled out of the parking lot, and called the one person I knew who wouldn't try to make me feel better.

"What the fuck is wrong with you?" Juliet asked, crunching on what sounded like a handful of Romeo's dinosaur crackers after I told her what had happened. "Are you seriously crying in your car about a guy with no personality and a closet full of ties?"

"Yes!" I wailed.

"Oh my God, B. You're such a dumbass. So what if he doesn't love you? You know who will? Literally any…other…guy. Fuck Ken Easton. I know, like, three cute guys I could set you up with right now."

"Really?" I sniffled.

"Um, hello? Remember Zach? He asks about you all the time."

"No, he doesn't."

"Yes, he does. It's annoying as shit. Oh my God!" Juliet exclaimed with more excitement than I'd heard out of her in a long time. "Come see me at work tonight! Zach will be there!"

I glanced in the rearview mirror at my puffy eyes and fluffy purple bun with auburn roots. "Ugh. I look like shit."

"Whatever. Just be there."

"Okay." I nodded, swiping the tears from my cheeks. "I'll come."

"Yes! I swear to God, B, I'mma find you a new man by the end of the week."

"You promise?"

"Girl, I fuckin' pinkie swear."

Just then, I pulled into Ken's driveway and had to fight back a fresh wave of tears. Seeing the white house with the red door that I'd once thought I'd get to call home made it all so real. The swing in the gazebo was even swaying a little in the breeze, as if it were waving goodbye.

"Say it."

"Huh?" I asked, blinking back the moisture in my eyes. "Say what?"

"Are you even listening? Say, *Fuck Ken.*"

"Oh. Fuck Ken."

"Now, say, *Helllllooooo, Zach.*"

"Who's Zach?"

"Jesus, B! The fucking bartender! Snap out of it!"

"Oh, sorry. Hello, Zach."

"Good girl. See you tonight. Wear something slutty. I love you!"

"I love you, too."

I ended the call and stared at the arched window above the garage.

See, Ken? Even Juliet tells me she loves me. What the fuck is your *problem?*

It only took me about two minutes to grab the few things I'd been keeping at Ken's house. A bottle of Jameson. A few cans of beer. A lighter. A toothbrush. A handful of travel-sized toiletries from under his bathroom sink. Every room held a little piece of me, but just like my presence in Ken's heart, it was a lot less than I'd realized.

The only signs I left that I'd ever been there at all were the framed pictures of us on the mantel—the ones I'd put there in the first place—and my key on the kitchen table.

Good-bye, house, I thought as I locked the front door and pulled it shut behind me. *I'll miss you.*

As I drove to my parents' house, I wondered what Ken would think when he got home from work and saw my key sitting there.

Would he even notice? Of course he would. Fucker had a photographic memory. I couldn't move a coaster without him noticing.

Would he realize that it meant I was breaking up with him? Probably not. That would require him to interpret my feelings, which would be like asking a blind man to describe the color chartreuse.

Should I go back and leave a note? Set up a time for us to talk in person?

You know what? Fuck that, I thought and reached into my purse.

I was exhausted. From school. From work. And from chipping away, day and night, at the fortress Ken had built around his heart.

But it turned out, there was no fortress.

There wasn't even a heart.

"Hey, Ken. I know you're at work. I just…wanted to let you know that I came by and got my stuff after school. Like, all of it. I know that breaking up with somebody over voicemail is considered a shitty thing to do, but I figured you, of all people, might actually appreciate it. This way, you won't have to talk about your fucking feelings, which you're obviously incapable of doing, or—I don't know—maybe you just don't have any. Either way, you made it abundantly clear this morning that you don't feel the same way about me that I feel about you, so I'm gonna stop wasting my time now. And yours. My key's on the table. Bye, Ken."

Click.

I tossed the phone back into my purse and felt a tiny glimmer of hope—just a speck, like a piece of glitter in an ocean of self-pity—but it was there. I'd survived yet another breakup, and this time, I hadn't even thrown anything or slapped anyone or gotten kidnapped at gunpoint or anything.

I was going to be okay.

No, I was going to be better than okay because I was going to get a new man, a fun one—one who drank and smoked and had more tattoos on his knuckles than ties in his closet—by the end of the week. And, if there was one thing I knew for sure, it was that the best way to get over a man was to find another man.

As quickly as fucking possible.

I stood, facing my bed, with my hands on my protruding hip bones as my mother tied the silky straps on my skimpy black halter top.

"So, let me get this straight," she said, tightening the bow. "You have a date with a bartender tonight, but Ken doesn't even know you guys are broken up yet." My easygoing hippie mom wasn't a judgmental person, but I was definitely picking up some notes of disapproval in her tone.

I spun around and gave her a death glare. "He *might* know, okay? I left him a voicemail."

She raised one orangey-red eyebrow at me.

"Don't give me that look! What am I supposed to do? Stick around for another six months just to see if he accidentally trips and falls into some feelings? Fuck that!"

My mom held her hands up. "Okay. Fine."

"Sorry." I gave her an apologetic half-smile and gestured to the clothes strewed all over my bed. Pointing between two different pairs of pants, I asked, "Tiger stripes or pleather?"

My mom glanced between the garments. Then she pointed to a pair of python-print pants on the floor by the closet. "Snakeskin. Those are my favorite."

"Good call." I snatched the tight vinyl pants off the floor and began shimmying my shapeless legs into them.

"You know"—my mom cleared her throat—"bartenders tend to be very promiscuous. If anything happens with this boy tonight, be sure to use protect—"

"Mom!" I glared at her as I zipped up my pants.

Her freckled face was bright crimson, and she was twirling the end of her long red hair in her fingers.

"I know, okay? God!"

"I just want you to be safe." She blushed.

"I will be. I am! Jeez." I shoved my feet into my unlaced combat boots and sat on the edge of my bed to tie them.

"I also don't want you giving poor, sweet Ken the clap when you guys get back together."

"Mom!" I snatched a pillow off my bed and threw it at her.

She chuckled as she turned sideways, letting it bounce off her tie-dye-covered shoulder.

"Get out!" I shouted, pointing at the door. "Get out of my room! You're banished for life!"

"Tell Ken I said hi," she teased, twiddling her fingers at me as she slipped out the door backward.

"We are NOT getting back together! Do you hear me?" I yelled after her. "Fuck Ken Easton!"

I stomped back over to my floor-length mirror to give myself one last look before heading out to Fuzzy's Bar & Grill.

What the hell is wrong with her? I thought, straightening my tank top. *She's always been there for me whenever I've gone through a breakup. Now, she's acting like I'm not even serious. Well, I am. I'm* dead *serious.*

I applied another swipe of mascara and prayed to the universe for low humidity so that the two-tone nightmare I'd just spent half an hour straightening wouldn't frizz up. Semi-satisfied with my slutty appearance, I grabbed my purse and headed out the door on a mission to secure the world's fastest rebound guy.

Fuck Ken Easton. Fuck him right in his dick hole.

As soon as I walked into Fuzzy's, the smoke hanging in the air stung my eyes, and the noise from the crowd of men shouting at the TV above the bar assaulted my ears.

From somewhere to my left, I heard Juliet yell, "Hey, skank!"

I looked over and saw her standing at a table, obviously in the process of taking someone's order. Juliet's long black braids were pulled up in a bun, and her work attire consisted of jeans, a Smashing Pumpkins T-shirt, and a pair of old Chuck Taylors.

Pointing at me with her pen, Juliet gestured to an empty booth behind me. "Sit there!" She grinned, her drawn-on eyebrows arching manically. "I'll be over in a sec!"

"Yes, ma'am." I gave her a little salute and did as I had been told.

Juliet had always been bossy, but she cranked it up whenever she was at work. You wouldn't stiff a waitress if you thought she was crazy enough to chase you to your car and shake you down for more money.

I sat down in a wooden booth that looked like it had fought alongside Ulysses S. Grant in the Civil War and began perusing the drink menu.

Which was only about ten items long, *including* the beer section.

"Long time no see."

I looked up and felt heat rush to my cheeks as Zach himself slid into the booth directly across from me. He looked exactly the way I remembered—light-brown faux hawk, smiling eyes, dark gray vest, tattoos peeking out of his open collar. He was the quintessential sexy bartender.

But what I hadn't remembered was how fucking much he looked like Ken.

Jesus.

The resemblance was uncanny. If Ken drank beer instead of Gatorade and spent his free time getting tattoos instead of hitting the gym, that was. Zach's body was a little softer, his look a lot edgier, and his personality, well…he had one, which was more than I could say for Ken.

He really was the perfect rebound.

"Hey!" I chirped, far too cheerful for a place that drab. "Zach, right?"

Oh, real smooth. Pretend like you don't already know his full name and social security number.

"Yep." He grinned. "And you are…" Zach rubbed his scruffy chin and stared at the ceiling before raising a finger in the air. "CC!"

I beamed like an idiot and rolled my eyes. It was the first time I'd smiled all day.

"So, Juliet tells me you're havin' kind of a rough day."

What? She told him!

I shot daggers at my bestie with my eyes, but that bitch acted like she didn't see me.

"Uh, yeah." I tucked my hair behind one ear and returned my gaze to Zach, who was doing a bang-up job of at least pretending to be concerned.

His dark brown eyebrows were pulled together, and the corners of his full lips were turned town.

"I broke up with my boyfriend today…but it's fine. I'm fine. It's not like the cops were involved or anything."

Zach laughed. A real belly laugh with his head tipped back and everything.

Ken didn't laugh at my jokes like that.

"Remind me never to break up with you if *getting the cops involved* is standard practice." Zach chuckled.

I could feel my nose beginning to tingle.

Oh my God, I'm blushing in my nose!

"Okay..." I said, batting my eyelashes and swinging my hair in what I hoped was a Beyoncé-esque move. "Don't ever break up with me." I smiled coyly and held his grinning gaze for approximately three seconds before I felt my armpits begin to sweat.

Zach bit his bottom lip in a classic smolder. "I *would* say we should drink to that, but you don't have a drink. What can I bring you, killer?"

I suddenly couldn't remember a single one of the ten items on the drink menu, so I shrugged and said, "Surprise me."

Oh, super smooth!

Zach winked at me—he fucking winked!—and slid out of the booth just as gracefully as he'd arrived.

Juliet's ass replaced his almost immediately and with much less grace.

"I need a cigarette and a summary, stat."

I couldn't contain my smile as I pulled two Camel Lights out of the pack in my purse and lit both. Handing one to Juliet, I said, "So, basically, we're in love, and he already promised to never break up with me, so I guess we're engaged, too. I'd say things are getting pretty serious."

Juliet exhaled through her nose as her mouth curled up into a wicked, wicked smile.

"What?" I asked, my lips mirroring hers.

"I fucking love being right."

Just then Zach showed back up, holding some hot-pink nightmare garnished with everything behind the bar. "Excuse me, *miss*. That seat's taken." Zach gave Juliet the same twinkly eyes he'd given me, and I watched her squirm in her seat.

Nobody was born with game like that. Homeboy had *honed* those skills. I remembered my mom's warning about bartenders being promiscuous, and now, I understood what she meant. I wondered how many girls he'd bedded with his flirty banter and free drinks.

Sober BB decided she was going to make Zach work a little harder. Then, sober BB drank two of Zach's mystery drinks, and an hour later, she was ready to book a flight to Las Vegas to get hitched.

"Hey, what's your last name?" I blurted randomly, too caught up in my fantasy elopement to listen to whatever Zach had been talking about.

"Brooks."

If there had been anything in my mouth at that particular moment, I would have sprayed it all over his face.

Brooks? Brooks!

I couldn't run away to Las Vegas with a guy named Brooks! If we got married, my name would be Brooke Brooks! Brooke…motherfucking…Brooks! I might as well start wearing prairie dresses, learn to play guitar, and join a folk band!

That was it. The night was ruined. Zach wasn't the one. His last name might as well have been Butthole or Baby-Eater. I couldn't do it.

"Oh, man. I'm exhausted." I stretched my arms over my head and yawned. "I better get going. I've got a long drive back. Thanks for the drinks."

I tried to ignore the surprised look on Zach's face as I got up and scanned the restaurant for Juliet. She was behind the bar, where Zach should have been, handing a beer to one of the guys yelling at the TV. She pulled her penciled-on eyebrows together when she saw me stand up and marched over to give me a hug. She didn't say anything about me leaving, but I could tell from her frown and the tightness of her embrace that I'd catch hell about it later.

Just as I was about to leave, Zach darted between me and the door, blocking my exit.

Shit.

I knew how the world worked. Slutty clothes + free drinks = expectations. Zach expected something from me now, but what? A kiss? A quick hand job in the parking lot? Sex?

"Hey," he said, giving me his smarmiest bartender smile and placing a tattooed hand over his heart. "I've been a terrible boss. I totally forgot to get your number when I hired you." I frowned for a second until he added, "Emergency Body Burial Supervisor BB."

I burst out laughing as recognition struck. And relief. All he wanted was my number! Hell, I'd give that to anybody. It wasn't like I answered unknown numbers anymore anyway, thanks to Knight.

Pulling a pen and an old receipt out of my purse, I scrawled down my number and handed it to him with a fake scowl. "Emergency body burials don't just supervise themselves, you know. I'd advise you to take my career a little more seriously."

Zach raised his hand to his forehead in a salute. "Yes, ma'am."

Along with my number, I gave Zach a grateful smile and a super-awkward side hug. Then, I bolted out the door.

The sidewalks of Athens were filled with preppy girls in mini dresses that made my halter top and python pants look about as slutty as a three-piece suit. With every step I took toward my car, the high from my flirty banter with Zach wore off a little more. The cool air of approaching autumn sank into my exposed skin a little deeper. And the reality of my situation settled around me like an unwanted blanket.

I was single.

And would be forever.

I drove home in silence, preferring the elevator music of my own self-deprecating thoughts to the stupid love songs I knew were waiting to mock me on the radio. Maybe love was a crock of shit, exploited to sell pop songs and greeting cards.

Maybe Ken had been right all along.

Just as I pulled off the highway and onto the back roads near my parents' house, an annoyingly cheerful scale of beeps breached my cone of silence.

I dug my phone out of my purse, expecting to see Knight's name flash across the screen. Or maybe it was Zach, calling to make things even more awkward than I'd already made them. But, when I pulled my phone out of my purse, the name spelled out in black digital letters belonged to someone I wanted to talk to even less.

I sighed and hit the Talk button. "Hello?"

"Hey."

Nope, not Zach. Just somebody who looked like Zach. A harder, colder, more infuriatingly stubborn Zach. With a much better last name.

"I just listened to your voicemail." His voice sounded…neutral. Like it always did. Calm, cool, and collected. That was Ken. He couldn't even show emotion in the midst of a breakup.

Probably because he doesn't love you anyway. Remember?

I sighed louder. "Can we not do this?"

"Do what?"

"You know. Have the whole fucking…breakup talk. You made it clear how you felt this morning, and that's fine. Let's just…move on."

"I don't know what the fuck you're talking about. *What* did I make clear this morning? I didn't even talk to you this morning."

"Are you really gonna make me say it out loud?" My cheeks flamed with mortification. "Fine! I know you fucking suck at relationships, so let me spell it out for you." I said the next words slowly and with ample condescension, "I told you I loved you…and you didn't say it back…so therefore…I am breaking up with you."

I turned off the heater in my car and cracked a window, suddenly far too warm.

"Brooke, I was fucking *asleep*."

Brooke. The sound of my legal name on his overly formal lips made me see red.

"Don't give me that bullshit!" I snapped. "You were so *not* asleep. You heard me, and you fucking panicked. Let me explain to you how relationships work, *Ken.* Either you fall in love or you break up. And if you don't love me after six months, then—"

"I never said that." Ken's voice was softer than usual. Remorseful even.

"Well, you never said you did either." I let my words hang in the air, a plea for Ken to remedy the situation.

I was giving him a second chance to say what he'd been unable to that morning, and for the second time in a single day, he broke my heart instead. I drove with the phone against my ear and bitter, hateful tears in my eyes as I relived Ken's wordless rejection all over again.

When the weight of his silence finally became unbearable, I said, "I'm real glad we had this talk."

Then, I hung up on him.

The next day, I managed to make it through an entire shift at Macy's without talking to anyone. The kids were all back in school, so I had zero customers in the Urban Streetwear section. Just an endless loop of 50 Cent and Jay-Z songs to keep me company.

That night, I avoided my parents, fed my dinner to Ringo, and spent the evening researching eating disorders. As I stared at the sunken faces and protruding clavicles on the pages of my psychology textbook, I was racked with pangs of jealousy.

Pinching the tiny fold of skin that had developed above my waistband since I started dating Ken, I thought, *They take laxatives to lose weight too? I'll have to try that.*

I'd engrossed myself in my studies to the point that I hadn't thought about Ken in hours. I'd felt him—or rather, his absence—but I told myself the void I felt was just my empty stomach. That was the feeling of success. I especially liked it when the edges of my vision got blurry and my hands shook. It had been too long since I felt like that. I was always having to eat to keep Ken off my back.

Well, not anymore.

Shit. I thought about him.

It was as if he'd heard me. Before I'd even pushed the image of his aqua eyes out of my mind, Ken's name was lighting up my phone screen. Just below the time—*11:11*.

"Hello?"

"Hey."

I didn't even respond. I just sat there and waited for him to get to the fucking point.

"How was your day?"

Is he fucking serious right now?

"Uh…I've had better. How was yours?" I made sure to inject an ample amount of sarcasm into the end of that question to make it clear that I didn't actually give a shit.

"It was…weird."

"Weird?"

"Yeah. I just…I don't know. It feels weird."

"Okay."

God, this is stupid. What are we even talking about right now? I hope he can hear my eyes rolling.

"So…you had work today, right? Tuesdays and Thursdays?"

What the fuck is he getting at?

"Uh-huh…"

"How was it?"

"Uh, boring as shit. The usual. I think the only customer I had all day was a shoplifter."

"Really? Did you call security?"

"No. I'm not a fucking snitch."

Ken chuckled.

I sat up in bed and reached for my pack of cigarettes.

"Are you on your way home from work?" I mumbled with a Camel Light between my teeth.

"Yeah."

I pictured him in his dress shirt and slacks, tie loosened, hair disheveled, and I kinda wanted to reach through the phone and run my fingers through it. Then, I wanted to grab it and yank as hard as I could.

"I just realized that I'm not gonna see you when I get home, so I wanted to call, and…I don't know…see how your day was."

"Well, it was shitty," I snapped.

"Yeah…" Ken said. "Mine, too."

"Uh, listen, I gotta go. I have school in the morning," I blurted, desperate to put our strange, forced conversation out of its misery.

"When's your review?"

"Huh?"

"For your case study."

"Oh. I'm meeting with my professor on Friday."

"Well...let me know if you need help preparing for it."

I wanted to scream at him. I wanted to shout, *This is not how breakups work, asshole!* into the phone and throw it across the room.

But my stupid fucking hope told me not to. It whispered that maybe he was just stalling. That maybe he was calling because he'd had a change of heart. Maybe, just maybe, Ken was about to tell me that he loved me after all.

"Night, Brooke," Ken sighed into the phone.

"Fuck this," I replied and hung up on him again.

"Okay, so Bubby is a poli-sci major. He's in my Philosophy class, and he has great hair." Juliet chalked the end of her cue and eyed the front door of Last Call, the pool hall across the street from Fuzzy's.

"I'm sorry. Did you say Bobby or Buddy?" I asked, accepting the little blue cube of chalk from her.

"Buh-bee," she over-pronounced, leaning over the pool table to rack the balls.

"What the fuck is a *Bubby*?"

Juliet snorted. "I asked him the same thing! He said his little sister used to call him Bubby, then the whole family started calling him Bubby, and then his friends started calling him Bubby, and now he's sticking with it because it sounds like a good name for a politician."

"Only in Georgia." I rolled my eyes.

Juliet looked over my shoulder as she removed the plastic triangle from the cluster of balls she'd just set up. I followed her gaze and saw a guy waltz in the door, dressed like he thought we were playing golf instead of pool. His baby-blue polo shirt matched his blue-and-white plaid shorts, and his blond hair was coifed in what I assumed hairdressers referred to as a Businessman Special.

A guy who looked like he shopped at the same store and went to the same barber glided in behind him, his dimpled chin held just as high.

I wanted to leave immediately. Not because they were preppy or overly confident, but because they smelled rich.

Rich people scared me.

The Ken dolls walked over to our table with *Vote for me* smiles plastered on their clean-shaven faces.

Ken Doll Number One fixed his blue eyes on me and said, "You must be BB."

I plastered on my best fake smile and nodded. Extending my hand, I said, "You must be Bubby."

He let out a hearty chuckle and wrapped an arm around my shoulders, completely ignoring my outstretched hand. "BB and Bubby, together at last!" he announced to the whole bar, squeezing me into his side.

The competing smells of expensive cologne and aftershave and hair products all assaulted my nostrils at once. Ken didn't use any of that shit. The only thing he ever smelled like was Irish Spring soap and fresh laundry.

Blondie's audacity and complete lack of boundaries made me want to stomp on the top of his foot with the heel of my combat boot. Or vomit. Or both. I felt gross, just being near him. His brunette friend didn't seem so bad, but *Bubby*—I shuddered, just thinking his name—had a nasty aura of scumbag oozing out of his perfectly exfoliated pores.

I sidestepped my way out of his embrace and quickly put the entire pool table between us. Standing next to Juliet, I mumbled, "One game, and I'm outta here."

Turning her back to the guys, Juliet whispered, "What's your problem? I thought you liked preppy guys now. You dated Ken for, like, six months, and he wears a fucking tie!"

Ken. He wasn't preppy; he was just…Ken. He wore a tie to work because he was the manager. He wore athletic wear when he was off work because he was usually working out. He didn't have an image, and he didn't give a shit. He didn't command attention when he entered a room because he didn't want it. And he damn sure didn't touch girls he didn't know.

He barely even touched the one he did know.

"Yeah, but Ken's not a douche bag," I whispered back.

Glancing over my shoulder, I saw Bubby and his sidekick clink beers and smile in our direction.

Bleh.

"Whatever. I can't keep up with your taste in men. You don't like Zach, you don't like—"

I swung my head back around to glare at her. "I like Zach better than this prick."

"Well, go talk to him, dumbass." Juliet pointed toward the front door with the neck of her beer. "He's working right now."

"But he never called me."

"Pssh. It's been two days. What's the rule in *Swingers*? Like, six days. Guys wait, like, six days now."

"You mind if I break, ladies?"

Juliet and I both glared at the future politician as he leaned over and lined up his shot.

Ken would have let me go first.

I played one game, repeatedly dodging Bubby's attempts to rub up against me with his seersucker-covered ass as he lined up his shots, and then made my exit. I was going to give some polite excuse about not feeling well, but Juliet took it upon herself to announce that I'd just started my period, and it was a "real gusher."

I glared at her evil, laughing face but forgave her immediately when Bubby and Bubby Jr. both took a giant step backward and let me go without so much as a hug goodbye.

As I headed toward the door, I thought, *Ken would have at least walked me to my car. It's after eleven.*

Once I was outside, I pulled my pack of cigarettes out of my purse and lit one, stalling while I tried to decide whether or not to say hi to a certain flirty bartender across the street. Exhaling slowly, I made up my mind.

Fuck it. Right? Why not? He's cute. I'm single—

I'd just taken my first step off the curb when I heard my phone begin to ring. Jogging across the two-lane road, I stopped right outside the door of Fuzzy's and pulled the damn thing out of my bag. I glanced at the phone, then the heavy wooden door, and then back at the phone.

Goddamn it.

With an audible sigh, I slumped against the weathered brick wall outside and answered. "Hi, Ken," I deadpanned.

"Hey, Brooke."

Silence.

"How was your day?" he asked. His voice soft and sincere.

"Fine. I guess." My tone was clipped but a little less venomous than the night before. "How was yours?"

God, this is so stupid.

"Uh…I don't know."

"Let me guess…was it *weird*?"

"Yeah." If I didn't know better, I'd think he sounded sad. But I *did* know better. I knew firsthand that feelings like sadness, anger, happiness, and especially love were completely beyond Ken's robotic parameters.

"Tell me, Ken"—I flicked my ash onto the sidewalk—"why was your day so *weird*?"

"Where are you? It sounds like you're outside."

Of course. Change the subject as soon as I ask about your feelings. Typical.

"In Athens."

"Athens? Jesus. Why are you all the way out there?"

"I had a date."

More silence.

"Ken?"

"Yeah."

I could hear the sound of his garage door opening and closing in the background. Ken was at home.

And I wasn't there, waiting for him.

"Who was your date with?"

His keys hit the kitchen counter with a metallic jingle. I pictured him walking around in his big, dark house all alone, and I smiled.

"Just this guy Juliet goes to school with. And this other guy who works down here. I'm meeting him now. Gotta maximize my time when I drive this far, you know?"

Silence.

"Ken?"

He coughed. "Yeah."

"You gonna talk to me, or should I go inside?"

"For your second date?"

"Yeah. I don't wanna keep him waiting."

I was being cruel, but I didn't care. I was going to yank a feeling out of that motherfucker if it was the last thing I did.

"Are you gonna be okay to drive later? Do you need me to come get you?"

Oh my God! Are you fucking serious? Why aren't you jealous, asshole? I hate you!

"No. I'll be fine!"

"Brooke, just let me come get you. I don't want you to end up like Jason."

"We're not talking about Jason right now! We're talking about the fact that you don't even care that I have a date! Two dates! I have two dates tonight, and you don't give a shit!" I blurted.

"I didn't say that."

"Just like you didn't say that you love me or that you miss me or that I'm fucking pretty or anything! Ever! That's why we broke up in the first place, Ken! Because you never…say…anything!"

I was officially yelling into my phone with large hand gestures on the sidewalk in the middle of the night. That's what Kenneth Easton did to me. He frustrated me to the point of lunacy.

"I'm sorry."

"What? What was that?" I snapped.

"I'm sorry." His voice was a faraway murmur. "I'm sorry I'm such a shitty boyfriend. I don't…I can't…" he rambled, grasping for words and feelings that were beyond his reach. "I mean, I wish I could—"

"Ugh! You know what? Why don't you figure out whatever the fuck it is you want to say to me, write that shit down, and then tomorrow night, when you call me again, for no fucking reason, maybe you'll have something to talk about?"

I mashed the End button on my phone, shoved it into my bag, and marched my needy ass right into Fuzzy's Bar & Grill.

Doodle-oodle-oodle-oo!

"Ugggggh." I whacked my alarm clock with the back of my hand, trying to silence the cheerful digital noises assaulting my brain.

Doodle-oodle-oodle-oo!

"Fuck you," I mumbled, swatting at the other assorted bullshit on my nightstand until I finally found my cell phone.

Doodle-oodle-oodle—

"Hello?" My voice sounded like I'd been up all night, smoking cigarettes and drinking whiskey, which was one hundred percent accurate.

"Scooter? Are you okay?"

"Um…" I tried to figure out how to answer his question. *Was* I okay? I had a wicked hangover and wasn't too thrilled about being woken up by the sound of my overly perky ringtone, but as far as I could tell, I wasn't bleeding out or anything. "Yeah. I think so. Why?"

"You were in a car accident!"

Okay, that got my attention.

I sat up and reached for my cigarettes on the nightstand. "No, I wasn't."

"Yes, you were! I just left for work, and the side of your car is all dented in."

"What?" I jumped up—unlit Camel Light between my teeth, Pixies T-shirt I'd worn the night before twisted around my emaciated body, one sock on and one half off—and darted over to the window.

Getting up that fast gave me the spins. I grasped the window frame to steady myself and yanked open the blinds. There, in the driveway below, was my beloved black Mustang hatchback.

With a dent the size of a trash can lid smashed into the driver's side door.

Holy shit!

My dad repeated himself, "You got in a wreck last night. Are you okay?"

"No, I didn't," I insisted, horror-stricken and racking my foggy brain for details from the night before.

Did I? I can't fucking remember! Shit! Think, BB! I don't feel like I got in a wreck. I was with Juliet. Then, I was with Zach. And now, I'm here. Not exactly sure how I got here, but—

"Scooter!"

"Huh? Dad, I didn't get in a wreck. I swear! I…I parked on the street outside of Juliet's work last night, so maybe somebody hit my car while I was inside? That has to be it. It was dark when I left, so I must not have noticed."

You mean, you were too drunk to notice.

"Well, thank God you're okay. I'm already running late for work. The last thing I need is something else to worry about."

Work! I spun around and looked at the clock. *Nine thirty-five? Fuck! I was supposed to be there five minutes ago!*

"Gotta-go-love-you-bye!" I sputtered, tossing my phone into my purse and throwing all the clothes I'd peeled off myself a few hours before back on.

I didn't pee. I didn't brush my teeth. I didn't look in a fucking mirror. I bolted out the door, untied bootlaces flapping behind me in the breeze, and dived behind the wheel of my newly busted-up car.

As I pulled onto the highway, I went to light the cigarette between my teeth, hoping it would quell my impending panic attack, and realized that I still had my retainer in my mouth. It wasn't lost on me that my priorities were officially fucked. I'd come home so drunk that I hadn't noticed a giant dent in my car door, yet I'd made sure to remove my makeup, moisturize, and wear my retainer to bed to keep from getting acne or crooked teeth.

I was a horrible, horrible human being.

That's not true. A horrible, horrible human being would have gone ahead and fucked Zach last night even though she still had feelings for Ken.

Whatever. I do not.

Then why did you turn your head away when he tried to kiss you?

I could still feel Zach's lips where they'd collided with my cheek. The spot flushed pink with residual embarrassment.

I just…I don't know. Shut up!

Is it because you're in love with someone else? Hmm…

No. It's because Zach hasn't called me. No call, no kiss.

I swapped my retainer for a piece of spearmint gum, then lit my cigarette.

You wouldn't turn your head if Ken tried to kiss you.

Well, Ken never tries to kiss me, so…I guess we'll never know.

That shut my inner bitch up. Because it was true. Ken never kissed me. I'd kissed him. I'd chased him. I had given him my number, and I'd made him date me. I'd moved my shit into his house, and I'd weaseled my way into his life, and the whole time, he'd just…let me.

And my dumb ass called that love.

Glancing down the long, wide aisle that bisected the first floor of Macy's, I hoped against hope that I'd see Ken walking toward me with his perfect posture and his perma-smirk. He used to surprise me sometimes and show up on my lunch break. He'd always appear at twelve o'clock sharp. I didn't have to look at a clock to know that noon had come and gone. My growling, gnawing, empty stomach let me and anyone within earshot know loud and clear.

With a heavy sigh, I trudged to the cash stand. Grabbing my purse, I clocked out and headed toward the parking lot. Maybe I'd buy a toothbrush while I was on break. And some Advil. And a bottle of Jameson to wash it down.

"Hey, BB!" Freddy from Men's Fragrance chirped, leaning against a display case in all his metrosexual Latin glory. "You going to lunch? You mind if I—"

"Sure, Freddy," I sighed. "Come on."

"Are you ready for your case study review tomorrow?"

"I guess so."

I shoved all of Ken's test scores and social/emotional questionnaires into my notebook and closed the cover. I'd been staring at them, all spread out on my bed, for way too long anyway.

"Does that mean you've figured out what's wrong with me?" Ken laughed flatly. He was trying to sound sarcastic, but I could hear an echo of worry behind his words.

"No," I admitted. "As far as I can tell, you're just a really smart asshole."

Ken didn't respond.

"Who was raised in a house without couches."

Ken chuckled.

"And never had anyone try to cuddle with him or tell him they loved him until he was in his mid-twenties."

Silence. As usual.

"But I could be wrong," I continued, swallowing the lump in my throat for the sake of civility.

Ken was trying to be friends. Maybe I could try, too.

"My professor's gonna go over your scores and give me his official diagnosis when we're done."

"So, I'm not even a little bit autistic?"

"Nope, just an asshole," I teased.

Ken didn't laugh. "Hey, I'm off tomorrow, so if you guys have any questions during your meeting, you can just call me."

"Why are you off? You always work on Fridays."

"I'm gonna help somebody move."

"God, you're so nice. I'd be trying to work as an excuse *not* to help somebody move."

"So…"

I could tell just from his tone what was coming next.

"I swear to God, if you ask me how my day was, I'm gonna fucking scream."

I heard Ken's soft laughter on the other end of the line, followed by the sound of his keys hitting the kitchen counter.

"It's not funny! This is the fourth day in a row you've called just to ask how my day was. What the fuck are we even doing, Ken?"

"We're talking."

"So…you're just gonna call me every day for the rest of your life to ask me how my day was?"

"It's looking that way."

An unexpected laugh burst out of me. "Ugh!" I groaned, mad at myself for letting him wear me down. "I hate you!"

I heard rustling sounds that I knew were from him changing out of his work clothes, and a pang of longing sliced through my heart. I could almost feel the heat radiating off his hard body. Notes of soap hung in the air just beyond my grasp. I knew, in a few minutes, he would climb into bed and curl up around his pillow, and I wanted nothing more than to climb in and curl up around him.

"Ken?"

"Yeah?"

"I didn't mean that. I don't hate you."

"I don't hate you either."

The roar of a motorcycle outside vibrated my chest just before the beep of an incoming call interrupted my thoughts.

"Shit." I reached over and switched off my lamp. "I gotta go."

I tiptoed over to the window and peeked out of a gap between the slats. Knight's laser-scope eyes found mine the second he climbed off his bike. Without breaking eye contact, Knight abandoned his chopper on the street and began walking toward me. He had the same imposing posture he always had. The same muscle-bound body. The same focused scowl.

But his limp was very, very new.

I'd never seen Knight hurt before. Ever. Knight was fucking indestructible. He was the goddamn Terminator. He'd done two tours in Iraq and come back without so much as a scratch on him. If Ronald McKnight was limping, that meant his whole damn leg was probably about to fall off right there in my parents' driveway.

Still clutching my cell, I dialed his number for the first time in years and watched as he lifted his phone to the side of his head. His movements were slow, and so was his breathing when he answered on the second ring. He didn't speak. He simply breathed into the receiver as he slumped against a tree in front of my window.

"Knight…what happened?" I pried the blinds open a little wider to get a better look at him, but it was so dark.

I watched as he dug a pack of cigarettes out of the pocket of his jeans with his free hand, wincing as a hiss of pain sliced through the phone.

"Knight, talk to me."

A tiny flame illuminated his sharp features and deep frown lines. Knight shook his head slightly as he exhaled, causing his smoke to trail away in a zigzag pattern. "Laid my bike down on Moreland."

"Oh my God!" My eyes darted over to his motorcycle, which looked intact despite a crooked kickstand.

"Fucker came down on my leg. Dragged me a good fifty 'fore it came to a stop."

"Jesus Christ, Knight," I whispered, touching the glass with my fingertips through the blinds. "Are you okay?"

"You know that coat of arms I had on my back?"

"Yeah." I nodded, remembering the giant back piece Knight had gotten when he first started apprenticing at the tattoo shop.

"It's gone."

I gasped. My fingers flew from the glass to my lips.

Knight's cold, hard eyes lifted to mine. He was wearing a black Terminus City Tattoo T-shirt that fit looser than what he usually wore. It must have been a double XL. I tried to imagine what his back must look like under there.

"Does it hurt to wear a shirt?"

"It hurts to fuckin' breathe."

"You need to go to a hospital, honey."

"Fuck that." Knight shook his head, causing him to sway on his feet. "Just come the fuck down here."

There it was. The real reason he'd come.

Just come down. Just let me fuck you and hurt you and belittle you until I feel better.

My sympathy, the emotion he preyed on, morphed into anger.

"Knight, have you ever called or come over just to see how *my* day was? To see how I'm doing?"

"Probably not. I'm a fuckin' dick." Knight spat in the grass. "Why? Does your little *suit* do that?"

My suit.

Knight had never mentioned Ken before—not that I'd listened to the majority of his voicemails. It pissed me off even more.

"Yeah, he does."

"Good. He's better than me." Knight's body seemed to relax into the tree. His words hurt almost as much as seeing him in pain. He took another drag from his cigarette. "Tell me how else he's better than me."

"Knight…" I felt my chin quiver.

"Just fuckin' tell me, Punk."

I looked down at my first love—bitter, broken, beyond repair—and tried to think of all the ways I would fix him if I could. All the ways Ken had already fixed himself.

"He doesn't drink," I blurted.

Knight coughed out a laugh, and for a split second, I swear I saw him smile. It was the first time I'd seen him smile since I could remember. And not a sneer, not a smirk, a real smile.

The kind he only did for me.

"That's good," he said, slurring slightly where the T met the S. "He's way fuckin' better than me then. What else?"

"Knight, we don't have to do this."

"Tell me, Punk. Please. I need to know—" Knight took a deep breath, followed by a sharp, pained one. "I need to know I did something right."

"Okay," I whispered, unable to talk around the tightness in my throat. "He's calm. And quiet. And gentle. He doesn't ever yell at me or try to scare me." Knight became blurry as a wall of tears filled my eyes. "And he likes to help. It's really sweet." My voice broke as the wall came tumbling down my cheeks. "He just wants to help me with everything."

I reached up and wiped the tears from my face as Knight tipped his head back and looked up at my window. I couldn't make out his features in the shadow of the tree, but when he spoke, I could almost taste his tears.

"Then, it was worth it," he rasped, pushing himself to stand.

As I watched Knight drag himself away from me, like he'd been doing ever since he left for the Marines the first time, I didn't have the heart to tell him that he was wrong.

It had all been for nothing.

Because that guy I'd told him about, he was just a lie.

"This report is impressive, Ms. Bradley," Dr. Raines said over his bifocals as he closed the case study I'd prepared on one Mr. Kenneth Easton. "Very thorough. It appears as though you administered every assessment in our vault."

I let out a jittery laugh and picked at my chipped black nail polish. "Yeah…I wasn't finding anything, so I kinda just kept digging."

"Ms. Bradley, we call that a fishing expedition. It's when you go into an evaluation, looking for something, and you keep testing until you find it. Did you *want* to find something?"

A guilty blush crept up my neck. "Not really. I just…wanted answers. Ken—my client—expressed concerns about his inability to connect with people emotionally. He has difficulties with expressing himself, dislikes being touched, shuts down in emotional situations, and…prefers physical pain over tenderness…sexually." My eyes landed on a stain on the carpet in front of Dr. Raines's desk.

"And your conclusion was that he is a mathematical genius whose emotional limitations stem from his family history. Is that correct?"

I nodded. "Basically."

"Ms. Bradley, I think that is an accurate assessment of his *current* functioning. However…"

My heart sank into my gnawing, empty stomach.

Fuck. I missed something. I knew it.

"There was one glaring area of deficit that I think might help answer your question. Do you remember one particular area in which your client performed significantly below average?"

"Yes, sir. He bombed the phonological processing test I gave him. In all areas."

"I must say, Ms. Bradley, I was surprised that you chose to administer a phonics test, given that the primary concern was emotional, but after seeing your client's performance, I believe it holds the key to his primary concern."

"I'm sorry. I don't understand," I sighed and shook my head. "People who score poorly in phonics typically exhibit a learning disability, but Ken—*my client*—scored in the average range in reading and writing. Based on his scores, there doesn't seem to be an impact on his learning."

"Not *now*," Dr. Raines said, his eyes lighting up. "But how do you think a five- or six-year-old with those phonics scores would perform?"

"I would expect him to exhibit classic dyslexia with related deficits in reading, writing, spelling, and probably school interest." As soon as the words left my mouth, my eyes lit up, too. "He said he always hated school, but I couldn't figure out why."

"Ms. Bradley, for students with dyslexia, how do they typically compensate for their weak phonological processing abilities?"

"Um…visual processing, memorization…"

"And what are your client's strongest cognitive areas?"

My mouth opened to match my eyes. "Visual-spatial processing, visual memory, quantitative reasoning…Dr. Raines, are you saying that my client has undiagnosed dyslexia?"

"*Had.* I believe he *had* dyslexia, but because of his superior intellect, he was able to teach himself to read and write through memorization and context clues."

"Oh my God."

"So, you were correct in your surface-level diagnosis. Because he can read and write, he no longer meets criteria for a learning disability, but those language-based deficits are still there."

"Could that explain why he has difficulties expressing himself verbally as well?"

Dr. Raines winked at me. "Bingo. Reasoning with pictures and numbers is significantly easier for your client than reasoning with language or emotions. Therefore, I would expect him to find nonverbal ways to express himself whenever possible."

"Like what? He doesn't draw or write music. He's not even affectionate."

"Ms. Bradley, haven't you ever heard the expression, *Actions speak louder than words*?"

I leaned back in my seat, stunned silent by my advisor's revelation.

Actions.

It made perfect sense. Ken *did* have a hard time expressing himself with words and an even harder time accepting physical touch, so that whole time he'd been *showing* me he cared instead.

"Based on your client's profile, he appears to be a highly left-brained individual—a man of action and reason."

"He is." I nodded, fighting back tears. "Very much, sir."

"Then, my recommendation would be for Mr. Easton to select a life partner who is free-spirited and highly verbal, someone right-brained to help balance him out. Like a poet or a painter or perhaps"—he offered me a small, sympathetic smile—"a psychology student with purple hair."

"How'd your case study thingy go?" Juliet asked.

I held the phone up to my ear with my shoulder as I downshifted and pulled into my parents' neighborhood. "Good, I guess. How was Philosophy class?"

Juliet snorted. "Bubby asked about you."

I rolled my eyes, driving past a dozen houses in disrepair before turning onto my parents' street. "Did you tell *Bubby* to eat a dick?"

Juliet's dry laugh made me smile. "I told him you were dating Zach now."

My smile flipped upside down at the mention of his name. "Uh, I think you have to go on a date to be dating someone. Or at least fucking talk to them on the phone." My tone was so bitter; I could almost taste the salt in my voice.

"BB, it's only been—"

"Four days! I know; I know. Cool guys wait six days now. I get it."

"Then why are you pouting? He's totally into you, girl. He even said he tried to kiss you Wednesday night! What's wrong with you?"

"I don't know!" My shout filled the car. "Maybe I don't want a cool guy anymore! Maybe I want a guy who will *fucking* call me just because he wants to *fucking* call me! Maybe I want a guy who's more concerned with finding out how my day was than protecting his stupid fucking ego!"

I drove down a long, skinny driveway into the woods where our little square house sat, visualizing the smug smile on Juliet's pretty face.

"Just say it," I spat.

"Say what?" Juliet's voice was unnaturally high-pitched.

"That I'm hung up on Ken and doomed to die alone." I pulled into my parking space in the driveway and yanked up on the handle brake.

Juliet snorted. "You're definitely hung up on Ken, but you are not doomed to die alone. There's this guy in my Marketing class—"

A laugh sputtered out of me, followed by a stream of unexpected tears.

"Hey," Juliet prodded, hearing my quiet sobs, "you okay? I'm sorry. I'll lay off—"

"No, I'm fine." I sniffled and wiped my nose on the back of my arm. "I just…I just love you."

"Dawww. I just love you, too, bitch."

As I tucked my phone back into my purse and slammed my dented driver's side door, I realized that something felt off about my parents' house. Everything looked exactly the same. My mom's car was parked in front of the garage. The blinds were open, and the front door was shut. Birds sang, and ribbons of afternoon light streamed through the hundred-foot-tall pines. Yet my senses were on high-alert.

I shook off my paranoia, dismissing it as just a side effect of my overly emotional state, and let myself into the house.

My mom was leaning against the kitchen counter, sipping a celebratory *it's finally fucking Friday* beer. She still had on her Peach State Elementary T-shirt, covered in paint spatter and dried bits of clay, and her long red hair was pulled back in a messy bun with a pencil shoved through it.

"What are you doing here?" she asked, the corner of her mouth pulling up on one side.

"Uh, I live here." I plopped my bags down on the rickety kitchen island and plopped my bony ass down on a matching barstool.

My mom shook her head, trying to suppress a grin. "Not anymore you don't."

"Oh, really?" I smirked, flicking my eyes to her almost-full Corona. "How many of those have you had?"

"I'm serious," she said, not looking the slightest bit serious. She pulled her lips between her teeth, ineffectively trying to squelch her giddiness about something. "Go see for yourself." My mom cast her eyes up, in the direction of my bedroom.

"Okaaaay…" I left my bags on the table and walked backward out of the kitchen, not taking my eyes off my mom, who looked like she was about to erupt into hysterics at any moment.

She was the worst secret-keeper ever. She told me what she'd gotten me for Christmas every year, the end to every movie she'd ever seen, and what surprise she had planned for my birthday without fail. So, whatever was going on, the fact that she hadn't blurted it out yet let me know that it was pretty fucking serious.

Once I got to the stairs, I turned and took them two at a time, rounded the bend at the top, and flew down the hall to my open bedroom door.

Then, I lurched to a stop.

My dresser was gone.

My desk was gone.

My computer, my printer, all the clothes on the floor, my basket full of makeup, my books, my bed…

My whole life was just…gone.

I ran to the closet and threw open the door.

Empty.

I ran across the hall to my bathroom and pulled open the drawers.

Empty. Empty. Empty.

"Mom!"

I could hear her giggling downstairs, but she didn't reply.

"Mom! Where the fuck is my stuff? What did you do?"

"*I* didn't do anything!" she yelled in a guilty singsong tone.

Sprinting down the stairs, I slid into the kitchen, fuming. "Are you gonna tell me what the fuck is going on?"

My mom's fists were pulled up to her mouth, and her usually tired green eyes sparkled like emeralds. "It's just so romantic," she whispered, bouncing on her toes.

"What is, goddamn it?"

"Ken came and got your stuff this morning."

I spun on one heel to find my dad standing in the doorway between the kitchen and the living room. His expression wasn't nearly as excited as my mother's.

"He what?" I spat.

"He came by with a truck while you were at school. Said he'd borrowed it from his pop. We had a nice, long chat. Can't believe that boy moved your whole dresser by himself. That thing's solid cherry."

He said he was helping someone move today!

"Oh my God!" I swung my head from my dad to my mom and back again. "He just…he just took all my stuff without asking me? Who does that? Why would you let him do that?"

My mom bit her lip and grinned. My dad lifted one shoulder in a sad, resigned shrug.

"Go on." My mom shooed me with her hands toward the front door. "Get outta my house. You gotta call first if you want to come over now."

"This is bullshit!" I cried, slinging my backpack and purse over one shoulder. "You guys are all crazy!"

My parents sandwiched me in a hug before releasing me to my fate.

"I love you, baby!" my mom called out as I opened the front door.

"Love you, Scooter," my dad grumbled.

I huffed and glanced back at them from the doorway. My parents stood in the foyer, arm in arm, waving at me with glistening eyes. I didn't understand why they were so emotional when *I* was the one being kicked out.

"Love you, too," I sighed. Then, I slammed the door behind me like the pouty little brat that I was.

I sped over to Ken's house with my heart pounding, hands shaking, and thoughts racing.

He took my stuff.

That motherfucker took my fucking stuff!

I feel like I'm being sold into sexual slavery or something. How could my parents just sell me out like that? I finally date a guy with more mortgages than tattoos, and they're ready to pony up a dowry. What a couple of assholes!

And Ken. If he thinks he can just make me move in with him, then he doesn't know who the fuck he's dealing with.

I won't do it!

This is so not like him.

God, I miss him.

It's only been four days, but it feels like four months.

No, wait. Fuck him!

He can't just make me take him back. That's not how this works. I make the rules, goddamn it. And my rule is that you have to tell me you fucking love me before you force me to be your concubine.

When I pulled into the driveway of my favorite place on earth, I noticed that the garage door had been left up. Ken's little Eclipse convertible was parked on the left, and on the right was a big, open space where Chelsea used to park before she moved in with Bobby. I'd never parked in Ken's garage before—or any garage for that matter—but I figured, if that asshole could take my stuff, I could take a spot in his garage.

I smiled as I pulled in, feeling a tiny surge of badassery.

Boundaries schmoundaries, motherfucker. This is my garage now.

As I got out of the car and headed toward the door that led into the kitchen, I decided that barging in and yelling obscenities was probably the best way to go. So I flung open the door and stomped into the kitchen with my chin held high, ready to jam my finger so hard into that smug bastard's tie-covered chest that I poked his cold, dead—

"Ken!" I called out, swinging my head from left to right.

The TV was off in the living room. The lights were off too. But the blinds on the bay window were wide open, bathing everything in a pinkish-orange glow as the sun began to set behind the pines in the backyard.

"Ken?"

The sideways light danced and glittered across the edges of an assortment of stuff on Ken's breakfast table, which was usually stark and spotless. Papers and tiny objects were lined up neatly from one side to the other, and right in the middle was a glass vase filled with velvety red roses. Ken would never buy flowers—"A waste of money. They'll only die," he'd say—but I recognized those blooms. They were the same ones I'd admired every time I went to smoke out in the gazebo. The ones that matched the color of Ken's front door. He hadn't bought those flowers; he'd *grown* them.

I leaned forward and smelled one fat blossom before letting my eyes roam over the painstakingly perfect row of items on the table.

The key I'd left behind Monday morning sat, untouched, in the exact same spot where I'd laid it down. I traced it with two fingers, missing the weight of it on my keychain. Right next to it, Ken had placed his spare garage door opener. Tied with a red bow.

Damnit. I smirked. *I thought I'd stolen that parking spot.*

Next to the remote was a single piece of paper, folded into thirds and placed with precision. Looking over my shoulder to make sure that I was still alone, I took a deep breath and peeled open the parchment. I only scanned the first three sentences when my uncertainty was transmuted into absolute, effervescent excitement.

> *Congratulations, Mr. Easton. Your application to join the College of Business Administration's Accounting program has been accepted. We wish to welcome you to East Atlanta Technical College.*

I read those first few lines over and over again, a swell of pride filling my chest and making it ache. If nothing else came from our relationship, if I turned around and drove away and left things undone forever, the time I'd spent with Kenneth Easton would not have been in vain. He was going to be the best goddamn accountant the world had ever seen. He'd just needed a little push.

I clutched the letter to my chest, letting my eyes drift to the stack of papers at the end of the row. They were fanned out in a perfect arc, a blue pen placed vertically beside them.

I reluctantly set down the acceptance letter and picked up the top sheet in the stack.

United States Postal Service Change of Address Form.

Then, the next.

Department of Motor Vehicles Change of Address Form.

Then, the next.

Bank of America Change of Address Form.

"I would have filled them out for you, but you know how shitty my handwriting is."

I screamed and spun around, clutching the forms in my balled-up fist as Ken waltzed into the kitchen and leaned against the kitchen counter a few feet away. He was wearing gray sweatpants and a plain white T-shirt. His hair was tousled, damp from a shower, and he smelled like Irish Spring soap and home.

"You scared the shit out of me!" I yelled, swatting at him with the papers in my hand.

"Sorry." He smiled.

With that single smile, my heart forgave him for whatever he was apologizing for and whatever he was about to apologize for and whatever he would ever apologize for again.

But my brain hadn't caught up.

"What the fuck, Ken? You can't just steal my stuff and cut some flowers out of your yard and pick up some forms from the post office and think I'm gonna move in with you like nothing ever happened. That's not the point! None of this"—I waved the papers in the direction of the table—"is the fucking point!"

Ken's smile disappeared, and I hated that I'd made it go.

"I know." He looked at the ground, then the wall, then the ceiling—anywhere but at my accusatory face. Sticking his hand in his pocket, Ken pulled out a sheet of notebook paper, folded into a perfect rectangle. Unfolding it, he said, "You told me to write down what I wanted to say. So…I did." Ken's aqua eyes flicked to mine for just a moment and then fell back to the paper, now open in his hands. "I knew exactly what I wanted to say the whole time. I just…" Ken shook his head. "When I wrote it down, it made it seem so small. It's only three sentences."

Ken looked up at me with brave, terrified eyes.

"Nine words."

His chest expanded, nostrils flared.

"I can say nine words."

I was watching Ken fight one battle in a war he'd been waging his whole life. Seeing his struggle, seeing him trying to wrestle his feelings into words and force the words out of his mouth, was almost more than I could bear. I wanted to tell him to stop. That I didn't care if I ever heard him say it. But I realized that he was doing it for himself just as much as he was doing it for me, so I stood there and waited for him to emerge from battle victorious.

Handing me the piece of paper, Ken took a deep breath while I held mine.

Then, with his hands in his pockets and his eyes on the floor, Ken uttered the sweetest, most sincere nine words one person has ever said to another person.

"I love you. I miss you. Please come home."

My elation at hearing those nine little words was completely overshadowed by the pride I felt for Ken. A slow smile spread across my face, and overjoyed tears tickled my eyes as I watched the tension roll off his broad shoulders. Watched the relief dance into his features, lifting and brightening them, one by one. I blinked away my tears so that his adorably sheepish, self-satisfied smile would stop being so goddamn blurry.

Ken slid his hands out of his pockets and pulled me into his arms. He was hard and clean and warm and safe, and he pressed his lips to the top of my head as I cried dirty black tears all over his soft white shirt.

"I'm sorry I couldn't say it before," he murmured into my hair. "I wanted to. Every night when I called you, I told myself I would. I just…" Ken's voice trailed off, once again at a loss for words.

"I know, baby." I pulled away just enough to see his handsome face. "I know. I found out more about that today."

Ken's brows pulled together, and his posture stiffened. "There *is* something wrong."

"There was." I smiled. "But you fixed it. Just like you fix everything. You used all your strengths to make up for your one weakness. You fixed yourself." I pushed up onto my toes and planted a soft kiss on his worried lips. "And you fixed us."

Ken dropped his eyes to my shoulder as a deep crease slashed across his forehead. He seemed to be thinking about something, probably warring with himself to find the words he needed again. I wanted to ask him what was going on, but I decided to wait and let him tell me on his own.

He needed to tell me on his own.

"Brooke?" Ken eventually said, lifting his eyes to mine.

"Yeah?"

"Do you remember what you said when Amy broke up with Allen? About why she left?"

My relieved, pliable body froze solid in his embrace. My lungs burned, deciding that I needed to hear whatever was about to come out of Ken's mouth more than I needed oxygen.

"Uh-huh," I exhaled.

"You said she…wanted to get married." Ken pressed his forehead against mine and closed his eyes, probably to avoid having to make eye contact. "Do *you* want to get married?"

Thump, thump, thump, my heart pounded in my ears.

"Ken…"

Thump, thump, thump, my pulse throbbed in my throat.

"Are you…proposing?"

"No," he replied immediately.

The letdown almost caused my knees to buckle.

"But I will." Ken's voice was solid and resolute. He wasn't asking; he was telling.

"You will?" The pitch of my voice shot up at the end of that question almost as high as my rebounding spirits.

Ken nodded, his forehead pushing mine up and down along with it.

My chin quivered as I nodded along with him. It was everything I'd ever hoped for, but there was a nagging voice in the back of my skull telling me that Ken was offering more than he was capable of giving. I didn't want to live in a fantasy world anymore.

So, with a deep breath, I laid my hopes and dreams at his feet and asked him for the truth instead. "Ken, do *you* want to get married?"

He nodded again without hesitation. "If that will make you stay."

I smiled.

"If that will make you stay."

It wasn't romantic. It wasn't hearts and rainbows and fireworks. It was the simple, honest truth, and it was everything I'd been longing to hear. Well, almost…

"What about kids?"

"One kid."

An unexpected laugh burst out of me. Leaning away from Ken, I looked at him with one eye as I giggled and wiped a tear away from the other. "You're gonna give me a kid?"

"Just one, so you'd better make it a good one." With his hands on my waist, Ken walked me backward until the edge of the kitchen table hit the backs of my thighs.

"What if it's twins?" I laughed, clutching his shoulders for support. "They run in my family, you know."

Ken smirked, his hands moving from my waist to the button of my jeans. "Then, you're just gonna have to pick your favorite."

Zip.

I gasped as Ken's fingertips teased me over my panties, and his mouth found a tender spot just below my ear.

"Ken?" I breathed.

"Mmhmm…" he hummed against my neck.

"I love you."

Sliding his free hand up the back of my neck and into my shaved hair, Ken held my head as he placed a tender kiss on my parted mouth. "I love you, too."

Joyful tears streamed down my cheeks as I tried to kiss him back, but my lips simply wouldn't cooperate. I'd never realized how hard it was to make out with someone when you're both smiling like idiots.

I guess I'd never been in love enough to find out.

I want to tell you that Ken cleared the kitchen table with one swipe of his muscular forearm and took me right there in front of the open blinds. But he didn't. Instead, he led me through the living room where my easel and Eiffel Tower sketch had been placed in the corner, next to the fireplace; up the stairs where the series of Warhol-esque fruit paintings I'd done for art class in eleventh grade had been hung at perfect intervals; past Robin's old room, which now had my computer desk and bookshelf in it; and through the doorway of our new master bedroom.

The once-beige walls of Chelsea's old room were now a rich slate gray—my favorite color—and Ken had filled it with a blended collection of our furniture. His bed, my dresser, his nightstands, my curtains, his big-ass TV, my lamp. And, on every wall, my art.

Actions. Actions everywhere.

"I live here?" I whispered into my fingertips as Ken led me over to the bed.

"We live here," he corrected, smirking at me over his shoulder.

As my wide, misty eyes drank in every detail, every surprise cameo from my old life, Ken peeled off his T-shirt and sat on the edge of the mattress.

When my gaze swept over to him—chest bared, secrets bared, intentions bared—it was as if I was seeing him for the first time. I'd thought I loved Ken before, but what I'd fallen in love with were mere glimmers of the qualities he truly possessed. Now, they were on full display in high-definition. His strength. His selflessness. His grace. His love.

I'd kissed a prince, and somehow, he'd turned into an even better prince.

When I ran my hands through his damp hair, I didn't feel the urge to yank on it. When I kissed his upturned lips, I didn't nip or bite at all. And when I ran my hands up his biceps and down his shoulder blades, I kept my claws retracted. For the first time in our relationship, I had no frustrations to take out on Ken's body at all. I simply wanted to love him.

And, for once, he let me have my way.

I stood and undressed slowly, leaning in to steal a kiss or two between every article of clothing I removed. Ken's cerulean eyes watched me without a hint of challenge. His smirk was gone, replaced by heavy eyelids and a slightly parted mouth, which I kissed again as I stepped between his legs and stroked him over the fabric of his gray sweatpants.

I wanted to kiss him everywhere. For every time someone had wanted to tell him they loved him but didn't. I wanted to cover him with so much love that he never refused to accept it again.

I peppered kisses along his hard, stubbled jaw and over to his earlobe and smiled when I felt his cock jerk beneath my hand. As I reached into the waistband of his pants and gripped his shaft, Ken reached up and palmed my small breasts. When I ran my thumb over his slick tip, Ken ran his thumbs over my peaked, pierced nipples. As I kissed my way down his neck, Ken slid a flat hand down the center of my torso. And, as I traced my tongue along the valley of his sternum and over the ridges of his ab muscles, he slid two fingers over the barbell in my clit.

There was no power struggle. No taking or denying. No sadist or masochist. There was just *us*—two people who'd finally learned how to speak the same language.

I kissed my way up the length of his cock, bent at the waist and eager to please. But, before I could take him in my mouth, Ken grabbed my narrow hips and lifted me up onto the bed. I squealed, landing on my hands and knees beside him, as he reclined backward onto the mattress with a smug smile. My eyes followed the same trail my tongue had taken—from his perfect, pursed lips to his perfect, glistening cock. As I crawled over to him, intent on finishing what I'd started, Ken's hands grabbed my ass and guided me so that I was straddling that mouth I'd just been admiring.

I took him into my throat and moaned against his smooth flesh as he flicked and swirled his tongue across mine. My legs began to tremble as I worked him faster, trying not to collapse under the enormity of my feelings and the pleasure building between my thighs. It was too much, and I had nothing to hold on to. As my moans turned to whimpers and my trembles devolved into shakes, Ken listened to my screaming body and obliged.

Flipping me onto my stomach, he blanketed me with his heat and heaviness and humming, buzzing electricity. He grounded me like the live wire that I was, and when he filled me from behind, when I clenched around him and gripped his hands and cried out in ecstatic relief, I lit him up, too.

As soon as Ken cursed and collapsed on top of me, I smiled even bigger than Julia Roberts trying not to cry in Hugh Grant's bookstore. Because I wasn't a girl, standing in front of a boy, asking him to love her anymore. I was a girl, lying under a *man*, who loved her more than she'd ever thought possible.

From that moment on, a kind of peace settled over me that I'd never known was possible. Ken's promise to marry me felt like a security blanket, comforting my restless, wayward soul. I'd spent my whole life searching for my future. Aggressively. Obsessively. What would I do? Who would I be? Who would I marry? Where would I live? Every morning, I would wake up and resume my quest for adulthood, and every night, I would go to bed, discouraged and frustrated and exhausted from trying to claw my way out of the quicksand of adolescence. But, just as I'd begun to lose hope, Ken had reached in with both arms and dug me out. He'd dusted me off. And he'd whispered the answers I'd been searching for as we stood together, admiring our future.

We fell into a natural rhythm that weekend, finding our new normal. Ken did the dishes. I did the laundry. Ken did the yard work. I sat on the bench swing in the gazebo and smoked while I watched him do the yard work. Ken did the grocery shopping. I went with him but was not allowed to touch, look at, or even think about adding anything to the cart unless he had a coupon for it or it was on "a good sale."

On Monday morning, I woke to the sound of my alarm clock instead of the sensation of being burned alive, and when I curled up against Ken's back and told him I loved him, he squeezed my hand and said, "I love you, too."

I floated to school on a magic carpet woven from angel feathers and unicorn manes. I sailed through my classes on a fabric softener–scented breeze. And, as I skipped to the subway station that afternoon, eager to get back home to my betrothed, my phone damn near exploded in my purse.

Whistles and chimes and dings and *doodle-oodle-oodle-oo*s burst from my bag in all directions as I rode the escalator up to the train platform.

"Jesus fucking Christ," I muttered, digging in my purse until I finally grasped the source of the digital cacophony. The device vibrated violently in my hand as notification after notification flashed across the screen. One, two, three, four, six missed calls and four voicemails.

Flash, buzz, flash, buzz.

"What in the ever-loving fuck?"

I scrolled through the missed calls first, all from the same unknown number. Then, I listened to the voicemails that were flooding in as I waited for my train.

Tuesday, September 16, 1:03 a.m.: "What's up, BB? It's Zach. This is my cell in case you want to call me back. It was awesome, hanging out with you tonight. Come by anytime. Juliet's way less scary when you're around."

Tuesday, September 16, 8:38 p.m.: "Hey, BB. It's Zach. I just wanted to let you know that Drivin' N Cryin' are playing at the Georgia Theater this weekend, in case you want to go. My roommate's a bartender there, so I can get us free drinks. Hope you can make it."

Thursday, September 18, 5:22 p.m.: "Hey, BB. Sorry if I came on too strong last night. I blame the whiskey." Zach chuckled. "Listen, my buddy is having a soft launch for his new tapas restaurant tomorrow night, and I'd love for you to come with me. I'll be a perfect gentleman, I promise. Just let me know.

"***Sunday, September 21 12:38 p.m.***: "Hey, BB. It's Zach. Juliet told me you got back together with your boyfriend. I, uh…I kinda felt like we had a connection, but…I guess I was wrong. It's cool. Hope things work out for ya. See you around."

I stared at my phone.

I blinked at it.

I blinked again.

I put the tiny device back in my purse.

I stared at the train tracks in front of me.

I waited for actual thoughts to form.

Zach called?

Blink.

Zach. Called.

Blink.

Six times.

Blink, blink.

Zach called almost every day, and none of his calls went through.

Ken called every day, and all of his calls went through.

Blink.

Zach had been trying to ask me out.

My mouth fell open.

Oh my God! What if I had gotten those calls?

Some people would call it divine intervention; some would call it providence. All I know is that any doubts I'd had about guardian angels were smashed to bits with the realization that mine had been cockblocking Zach for an entire week. Like an overbearing mother, my angels had politely taken Zach's messages at the beep, but they hadn't let me have any of them until they were sure I was safely back on track with the guy they liked better.

"Motherfuckers." I laughed, shaking my head as my train approached.

The number on the front read *1111*.

Eleven eleven always showed me the way. And, that afternoon, my cockblocking angels sent it to carry me home.

EPILOGUE

May 2004

"Are you gonna pout for the rest of the trip?"

I stared out the chartered bus window at the rolling green hills and fat, fluffy sheep passing by. The sheep all had different-colored dots spray-painted on their butts. I wanted to smile and tap the glass with my finger and ask Ken what it meant. He would know. He actually listened when the tour guide talked.

But I was far too busy being a brat.

"I'll stop pouting when you stop being an unromantic asshole."

I actually said that. I called Ken an *unromantic asshole* while riding through Ireland on a trip that he'd paid for.

"Wow. Okay. So, because I don't want to get sand in everything I own, I'm an asshole?"

I kept staring out the window. "That was the most beautiful beach I've ever seen, and you wouldn't fucking hold my hand and walk on it with me because you didn't want to get sand in your shoes!"

"If I get sand in my shoes, then it'll get into my suitcase, and once that happens, it'll get into fucking everything. We can't just go do laundry, *Brooke*." He said my name like you would say the word *dumbass*.

I swung my head around to face him. "It's not just the fucking beach. You wouldn't stand on the top deck of the ferry boat and look at the castles with me because it was too windy."

"You weren't even supposed to be up there. The wind almost blew you off the deck!"

"And you wouldn't let me wear your jacket in London."

"I told you to bring a jacket. Why should I suffer because you don't listen?"

"And remember at Stonehenge? There were all those pretty yellow flowers growing by the ruins, and you wouldn't even pick one for me."

"Brooke, the ruins were fucking roped off."

"It was just a tiny little rope! No one was even looking!"

Ken huffed and turned to stare out the windows on the opposite side of the bus.

"We are surrounded by romance, and I feel like all you've done is find excuses not to share it with me. *It's too sandy. It's too windy. The sign says no. We better get back to the bus.* Wah, wah, wah." I tilted my head from side to side, mocking him in my best whiny voice. "Is it so much to ask for you to fucking kiss me in front of a castle? Jesus!"

Ken didn't reply. He'd shut me out, just like he always did when the topic of his romantic shortcomings came up. We'd been living together for nine blissful, uneventful months, but every once in a while, Ken's emotional deficiencies would cause me to erupt into a volcano of whiny bitchiness.

It didn't help that Allen and Amy had already gotten married, and Chelsea and Bobby's wedding was weeks away.

When Ken had said he was going to propose, I'd thought he meant soon. But when Christmas, Valentine's Day, and my college graduation came and went without a ring, I'd started to think maybe he was waiting for our Europe trip.

Yes! That has to be it! Ken is going to get down on one knee in front of Westminster Abbey! Ooh, or maybe he'll wait until we're at the top of the London Eye! Or he could steal me away to a quiet little meadow on the coast of Ireland during one of our walking tours, or maybe he'll do it on top of a mountain in Wales!

It was horrible. Every time we came upon some beautiful, scenic overlook or some magical, ancient cathedral, I'd turn to Ken and bat my eyelashes and tell him, *Do it! Do it here!* with my mind.

And then he would complain about leaving his sunglasses on the bus or the crowds or the drizzle and ruin the moment—every…single…time.

When we finally pulled up to the gates of Blarney Castle, I decided I needed to let it go. Kissing the Blarney Stone was on my bucket list, and I wasn't going to let anything ruin this experience, especially not my own unrealistic expectations.

He can't help it, I reminded myself as I followed Ken off the bus. *Stop trying to make him feel bad for something he can't help. He brought you on the trip of a lifetime, so at least try not to be a shithead, okay?*

Okay. I nodded to myself as our group followed the gravel path down to the castle. *Commencing Operation Don't Be a Shithead…now.*

I thought it was going to be hard to give up my pouting streak, but when the woods opened up and I found myself plunged into the most idyllic scene I could have ever imagined—*poof!*—there it went.

Blarney Castle wasn't some imposing medieval fortress, full of sad stories and old ghosts, like the other castles we'd seen. It was just a charming little stone tower, crumbling and fuzzy with moss, nestled into a grassy hill next to a glittering pond. It was the kind of place that made you want to craft a scepter out of a tree branch and play kings and queens inside its hollowed-out walls.

I grabbed Ken's arm and ran down the path, stopping abruptly every ten feet to take at least as many photos.

Run. Stop. Run. Stop. Ooh! Ahh! Ooh! Ahh! Click. Click. Click-click-click.

And, all the while, Ken followed, silent and patient, as I fangirled over a dead castle.

I glanced back at him a few times to make sure he was still there. To see if he was still mad at me for calling him an asshole. But he seemed fine. He smiled back. He looked around. And he reminded me that, if I wanted to kiss the Blarney Stone, I should probably do it before the bus left.

"Oh my God, the Blarney Stone!"

I'd been so wrapped up in the magic outside that I'd totally forgotten about the whole reason for coming. Grabbing Ken's hand, I dashed up the hill and into the castle, shocked to discover that it was just as sunny and grassy inside as it was outside. The roof was completely gone. Remnants of old rooms and staircases clung to the exterior walls, but the interior space was completely wide open to the spring sky.

Falling in line with the other tourists, we climbed up a tiny, twisty stone staircase, walked across a crumbling catwalk to another spiral staircase of doom, and emerged on top of the castle. The wind whipped through my auburn hair as I looked between the notches of the turret down at the pond and hills below. All that remained up there were the four exterior walls and a narrow stone ledge going around the perimeter. A ledge that we had to walk across to kiss the fabled Blarney Stone.

I can't believe you don't have to sign a waiver for this, I thought, trying not to look down at the gaping hole in the center of the castle as I advanced with slow, careful steps.

When I finally got to the fabled stone, I discovered that it was set into a wall.

That was separated from the walkway by a good three feet.

Of nothing.

Nothing but a ninety-foot drop to the lush green earth below.

Oh, and I would have to bend over backward and lean across the gap to kiss it while a nice old Irishman held me around the waist.

Because that makes sense.

"Why am I doing this again?" I grinned at the twinkly-eyed little leprechaun helping me get into position.

"For the gift of gab, las!" He beamed, wrapping his confident hands around my middle.

I laughed and pointed at Ken, who looked completely comfortable, standing on the edge of a derelict building almost a hundred feet above the ground. "Make sure he kisses it twice then."

As I arched my back and placed my lips on the same stone my Irish grandparents had kissed decades before, my heart swelled with gratitude for the handsome, quiet man who'd brought me there. The one who didn't want to get sand in his suitcase. The one who quietly went about making all my dreams come true without ever expressing any of his own.

I snapped off a dozen photos as Ken took his turn, graceful as ever, and laughed out loud when I caught him pressing his lips to the wall a second time.

Drunk on love, I clutched Ken's firm bicep for stability as we meandered back down the stairs of doom, careful not to die before I had a chance to thank him for the trip.

As soon as we exited the castle, Ken slipped my camera strap off my neck and said, "Wait here. I'm gonna get somebody to take our picture."

Aw, I thought. *Ken wants a picture of us together. That's kind of sweet.*

I watched as he approached a group of ladies clustered about twenty feet away. Their eyes lit up as he spoke to them—I assumed because he was so damn cute—and they beamed as they glanced from him to me and back again.

I just love this place. Everybody's so friendly.

Ken hustled back up the hill as I turned and faced the woman holding my camera. I held my arm out to wrap around Ken's waist, but he didn't slide into my side.

He knelt by my side instead.

Jeez, Ken. This lady's waiting. Do you really need to tie your shoe right—

I turned to figure out what the holdup was. Ken wasn't tying his shoe. Nor had his contact lens popped out. He wasn't picking a dandelion or doing any of the other hundred things that had run through my mind when he bent over in front of Blarney Castle that day.

Ken was down on one knee, holding a black velvet ring box, squinting up at me in the afternoon sun.

My hands flew to my gaping mouth as I floated above the earth, suspended in my disbelief that this could actually be happening.

It had taken nine words to get me to move in with him, but it only took eight to get me to agree to be his wife.

"I love you, Brooke. Will you marry me?"

I nodded vigorously, unable to take my hands away from my face, as Ken stood and opened the box.

Then, I cried.

There, smiling up at me, was my ring.

As Ken slipped it onto my shaking finger, I choked out parts of all of my questions, not really completing a single one.

"How did you…but it was gone…I went back the next day…somebody had bought it…"

Ken smirked, lifting his eyes from my hand to my confused, elated, dripping face. "They had a really good layaway plan. No interest for twelve months."

A laugh loud enough to scare off the birds burst out of me as I tried to wrap my head around what he'd just said.

"It was you?"

Ken nodded.

"But"—my mind flew back in time to the day Ken and Allen had come to see me at the mall—"Ken, we hadn't even kissed yet. I wasn't even your girlfriend."

Ken shrugged and dropped his eyes. "You liked it, and I liked you. I didn't know what I was doing, but I figured I had twelve months to figure it out."

"Interest free." I giggled.

"Interest free." Ken smiled, lifting his aqua eyes.

"Look at me, you two!" the woman holding my camera yelled, dotting her misty eyes with a tissue.

I wrapped my arms around my fiancé's waist, and we turned and smiled for our first picture as the future Mr. and Mrs. Easton. And, as if that moment wasn't magical enough, Ken did one last thing I'd completely given up on.

He kissed me in front of a castle.

June 2005

On the morning of my wedding, I stepped on the bathroom scale just like I did every morning—after peeing to make sure I was as light as possible—and the number that blinked up at me was almost more exciting than the fact that I was about to become Mrs. Brooke Bradley Easton.

Eighty-nine.

Eighty-fucking-nine.

The time between when Ken had asked me to marry him and when he actually did just so happened to coincide with the most stressful year of my entire life. I knew my parents couldn't afford a wedding, and I knew my fiancé would rather sing the national anthem on live TV than shell out thousands of dollars for a party, so I took it upon myself to plan and pay for the whole damn thing.

In order to raise the money, I'd exchanged my part-time retail job for a full-time gig, teaching a special education class for preschoolers with autism spectrum disorders. I did not have any training. I didn't even have a teaching degree. But I knew enough about autism from my psychology coursework that I was able to pass the state exams, and the county was so desperate for someone to fill the position that I got the job…

And immediately found out why no one else wanted it.

Every morning, I would get up and put on a full face of makeup, and every morning, I would cry it all off on my way to work, knowing that I was going to be hit, kicked, scratched, spat on, sneezed on, screamed at, resisted, run away from, and/or flat-out ignored for the next six hours. I was given nine beautiful, adorable, significantly developmentally delayed little boys and was told I needed to teach them to speak. I needed to teach them basic academic concepts. I needed to teach them to use scissors, write their names, eat with utensils, use the toilet, wash their own hands, initiate social interactions, and sit at a table for more than five minutes. And I'd had to do it all in spite of their aggression, their various perseverations and aversions, and my own complete lack of experience.

Then, after each exhausting, soul-sucking yet life-affirming day, I would fight rush-hour traffic all the way downtown to spend the rest of the day in class, working on my master's degree in school psychology.

And, as if that wasn't enough, I'd lost my last two living grandparents, the Irish ones, and an uncle I'd been very close to, all within a few months of the wedding.

My wedding dress was a size zero, and at my final fitting, they had to make it tighter. The forty-pound tulle ballgown bruised my jutting hip bones and clung desperately to my rib cage because those were the only things I had left to hold it up. But I was happy despite my appearance. I was happy in my relationship and happy with my grades and happy that all nine of my preschoolers had made tremendous progress by the end of the school year and happy that I was so skinny and happy that it was finally my wedding day. Sure, I was stressed out beyond belief and cried in my car every day and fainted from hunger sometimes and was constantly shivering and my hair was falling out and my feet would occasionally turn purple and go numb, but that was the price I paid for my success.

Totally worth it, I told myself. *Just look at all the goals I'm accomplishing!*

I was so sick. I was so sick, and nobody knew. Whenever the subject of my weight came up, I would write it off as stress. Whenever I had to eat in front of other people, I would. Then, I'd disappear as soon as I could to go throw it up. I'd never told Ken about my past hospitalization for anorexia. Because I was totally fine. I had everything under control.

Riiiiight.

I arrived at the wedding venue—the same old mansion with the gorgeous gardens that Amy and Allen had rented for their engagement party—with my bridesmaids by my side, my hair curled, my tiara on, and a skip in my step. It was going to be the best day of my life. I had planned everything to a T. Nothing could possibly go wrong.

Then, I stepped through the door.

The florist was a no-show.

The wedding cake looked like a pyramid instead of the Eiffel Tower.

It was beginning to rain, and our ceremony was supposed to be outside.

The wedding officiant was lost.

The DJ was having technical difficulties.

And my stoner parents were completely MIA.

When people weren't busy presenting me with new problems or asking for solutions to existing ones, I would run outside in my tulle ballgown to hide and hyperventilate until the urge to scream went away.

Sensing my impending panic attack, my sweet, sweet photographer—a plump, balding man in his forties who kept all of his camera equipment in the pockets of an army-green fishing vest—brought me a gift.

Peeking his rosy, round face out the side door where I was smoking, he said, "I know you're not supposed to see the groom before the wedding, but I thought it might be nice to snap a few photos of you two before the ceremony."

Then, he pushed the door open, revealing my future husband in a perfectly tailored three-piece suit—black with a white silk tie to match my dress.

Ken was coiffed, clean-shaven, and looked like a natural-born formalwear model. But better than that, he looked really, really happy. I beamed at him and lifted my arms in the air like a child wanting to be held. Ken closed the gap between us in two long strides, pulling me into his arms. I rested my cheek on his chest and felt all my stress and worry and self-punishing perfectionism roll off my shoulders and land in a puddle. I no longer cared if my flowers arrived or if the sound system worked or if my parents showed up or if the sky opened up or if the cake looked like we were going to Egypt on our honeymoon instead of Paris. I didn't give a single, solitary fuck about any of it. Because I was about to marry my very best friend.

"Hi," I said, probably getting blush all over his jacket.

"Hi." Ken wrapped his arms tighter around my shoulders.

I could hear the photographer's camera snapping off photos, but I didn't even bother to look up. I just stood there, in Ken's warm, buzzing bubble, and decided that everybody else could fuck right off.

"You look so handsome." I smiled, tilting my head back to see him better. I ran my fingertips along his smooth cheek.

Ken smirked down at me. "So do you."

"I look handsome?" I wrinkled my nose.

"Women can be handsome."

"Not when they're wearing a sparkly tulle ballgown and a tiara!" I pointed at the top of my head. "This updo took two hours!"

"You probably should have dressed like a pharaoh instead of a princess. Have you seen our cake?"

I snorted. "Oh my God. People keep asking me if we're going to Egypt on our honeymoon."

"Have you seen it in the last fifteen minutes?"

I eyed him suspiciously. "No…why?"

Ken's steely smile widened. "The little bride and groom slid off the top and completely fucked the icing up on one side."

I doubled over, as much as my corseted dress would allow, as a series of unladylike cackles tore out of me. "Oh my God! This place is haunted!" I shrieked. "I'm not going back in there!"

"Didn't you pay for the bar in advance?" Ken raised an eyebrow at me.

"You make an excellent point, sir." I straightened my tiara and took Ken's proffered elbow. "Lead the way."

By the time the ceremony started, I couldn't give two shits who was late or what was missing or where the fuck my flowers were. I was half-drunk and one hundred percent sure that I'd never made a better decision in my life.

When Ken and I locked eyes from opposite ends of the aisle, we smiled at each other like old pals. When we took turns reciting our vows—both sets written by me, of course—we tried not to laugh. When it was time to kiss, ours lasted a little too long to be appropriate. And, when the judge announced that we were husband and wife, Ken and I walked down the aisle to "All You Need Is Love" by The Beatles, just like they did in his new favorite Hugh Grant movie, *Love Actually*.

After dinner was served and the speeches were made and King Tut's tomb was sliced, the DJ turned the inside of the manor house into a nightclub, fully equipped with a disco ball, glow-in-the-dark accessories for all the guests, and a wall-rattling pop and hip-hop playlist that included a few '90s alternative jams just for us.

My dad put on a top hat and did the YMCA dance. Somebody got wasted and peed in a potted plant next to the dance floor. Juliet spilled her champagne down the front of my dress about an hour before the hem got caught on my high heel and ripped off. And Ken, Allen, and the Alexander brothers serenaded us—yes, Ken *sang* in front of real people—with some cheesy song from *Top Gun*.

Our wedding was a clusterfuck, a total shitshow, from start to finish, but as soon as we were together, Ken and I had the time of our lives. And isn't that what you want in a partner? Somebody who laughs when you burn dinner and orders take-out? Somebody who looks at a wrong turn on the interstate as an opportunity to listen to your favorite album a little longer? Somebody who loves you at your worst, knowing you're on your way to becoming your best?

That night, my husband carried me and my ripped, stained ballgown across the threshold of the house we shared…and into a magical wonderland filled with little votive candles and rose petals the color of our front door. He helped me out of my dress, which stood up on its own after I stepped out of it, and I helped him out of his suit.

Lying on his back as I climbed on top of his naked body, Ken returned my enthusiastic kisses. As I slid along his length, he lifted his hips to meet me. When I tugged on his sandy-brown hair, he gingerly removed the tiara from mine. While I bit his earlobe and nipped at his neck, Ken carefully plucked each bobby pin from my bun until my auburn curls tumbled all around us. Then, as he massaged my aching scalp, Ken pushed inside me with one slow, deep thrust.

"Mmmmmm…" I moaned in ecstasy, sucking on the middle finger of his free hand.

When I looked down at him, Ken met my gaze and arched an eyebrow at me. "How drunk are you?"

"Preh-y drunk," I mumbled around his finger.

He smirked, a wicked gleam in his eye. "Drunk enough for butt stuff?"

I stilled, mulling it over, and then nodded, Ken's hand in my mouth moving up and down along with my head. "Definilly drunk nuff."

February 2009

Ken and I were so poor for the next few years, living on his salary as movie theater manager and the pennies I got as an intern while we both finished college, but we never felt it. We had everything we needed—friends and family and our cute little house and cars that still ran despite the fact that Ken was too cheap to do any routine maintenance on them at all.

But, when I finally graduated, when I finally got my big-girl job, when I finally had money in my pocket and free time on my calendar…baby fever hit. And it hit *hard.*

Unfortunately, my husband was immune to that particular disease.

"Can I go off the pill now?"

"No."

"What about next month?"

"No."

"What about next year?"

"Um…no."

I had been begging and bargaining and pleading with Ken to let me have a baby for almost two years when my new best friend and colleague, Sara Snow, stepped in.

Sara and I got hired as school psychologists for the same school district at the same time. We met at the new-hire orientation, and it was love at first sight. She was the only person I'd ever met whose sense of humor was even *more* irreverent and off-color than mine. The things I only thought but didn't say out loud…she said 'em.

"Do you think I'll get fired for listing *drowning* as one of my intervention recommendations?" Sara looked so innocent with her big brown eyes, long black eyelashes, and cute little Afro that she wore, pulled up in a poofy bun on top of her head, but on the inside, she was pure evil.

I laughed into my pomegranate martini. "Do it. Nobody reads our reports anyway."

"Maybe I'll recommend *parental sterilization* while I'm at it. This kid's mom, BB"—Sara leaned across the table at our regular happy-hour spot, Bahama Breeze, and looked me dead in the eye—"she had a flesh-colored beard…just like Spencer Pratt."

I almost choked on my pink vodka. "She did not!"

"And she was wearing a shirt that said, *Chubby and Dangerous*."

"Shut up!" I coughed.

Sara smirked and leaned back in her booth. "I shit you not."

"Well, I had a parent tell me during a consultation today that her son isn't doing well in school because he's *a Taurus*."

"Ha! That's gonna be you one day." Sara tipped her half-empty martini glass at me. "I see you with, like, five kids, all named after different constellations, and you're going to send in notes to the school saying, *Please excuse Cassiopeia from school today. Her moon sign is in retrograde.*"

"That's ridiculous." I rolled my eyes. "The moon is never in retrograde."

Sara chuckled.

"Besides, I'll be lucky if Ken gives me one kid," I grumbled. "He's dragging his feet so hard, Sara. He wants to wait, like, five more years. And, when I do finally get pregnant, he's probably gonna want to name the thing something financial, like Cash or Benjamin or—"

"Dow Jones?" Sara smirked.

"Exactly." I shook my head in feigned sorrow. "I'm gonna have an only child named Dow Jones Industrial Average Easton. Pray for him."

"If it makes you feel any better, I tested a kid last week whose name was Anointed Love."

I snickered. "It does actually. What the hell does he go by?"

"I dunno." Sara shrugged. "I just called him Ted."

"Ted!" I cackled, drawing glares from the other diners.

"And, the week before, I tested a kid named Sevenn with two Ns."

I paused as I brought my glass to my lips. "Wait. Isn't that from a *Seinfeld* episode? Or *Married with Children*?"

"Both!" she cried, tossing the last few drops of her martini back. "Hey, have you been watching that new show, *Jon & Kate Plus 8*?"

"Dude, I'm obsessed."

"So, I've decided that Kate needs to divorce Jon and marry that guy from the Bengals, so they can rename the show *Kate Plus 8 Plus Ochocinco*."

I snickered, setting my empty glass on the table a little too hard. "Please tell me you're never having kids."

"Meh, you'll probably have enough for both of us."

"Not if Ken has anything to say about it." I rolled my eyes.

Sara's tipsy mouth twisted into an evil grin. I'd seen that grin. I loved that grin because it was usually followed by her giving me permission to do whatever bad thing I had already been thinking about doing.

Shaking her head at me like I was a silly little child, Sara said, "We don't ask. We tell."

April 2009

So, I quit smoking. I quit taking my birth control pills. And I quit fucking asking. I told Ken that, if he didn't want a kid, it was up to him to keep it from happening. I was done trying to prevent something I wanted so badly.

I was ready for Ken to put up a fight or at least go buy a lifetime supply of condoms at bulk rate prices, but he didn't. He accepted his fate with graceful resignation, and a few weeks later, I peed on a stick.

"Ken, is that two pink lines or one?"

"Two."

"But that second one is really faint."

"You just said *that second one.*"

"Maybe I should take another test. I mean, I haven't even missed my period yet."

"Then, why are you taking a test?"

"Because I've been getting headaches, and I kind of want to murder everyone all the time."

"Isn't that just PMS?"

"I DON'T KNOW! THAT'S WHY I'M TAKING THE TEST! Sorry. See? I told you. I'd better take another one."

"Look. The second line got darker."

"Oh my God. Ken…I'm pregnant."

"Congratulations."

That was it. *Congratulations.*

Fucker.

I went to the doctor the second I found out with a spring in my step and the sun shining on my glowing face. I was prepared for them to tell me that everything was perfect, that my baby was going to be the smartest, cutest, healthiest baby ever, *and* that, thanks to my knowledge of early childhood development, I was going to be the best mom ever. Then, they were going to pin a blue ribbon on my shirt and send me on my way.

They did not.

"Mrs. Easton," the doctor said, giving me a stern look over the top of my chart.

I worried the edge of my paper gown. "Yes?"

"Are you aware that you are fifteen pounds underweight for your height?"

"No," I lied.

Is that all? Damn.

He eyed me suspiciously. "Because of your weight, we are going to have to classify your pregnancy as high-risk."

High-risk?

"Honestly, you're lucky you were able to conceive at all."

What?

"I'm going to be frank, Mrs. Easton." The doctor set my chart on the counter and leveled me with a no-bullshit stare. "If you do not gain enough weight during this pregnancy and gain it consistently from nutrient-rich foods, your baby is at increased risk of being born preterm or having low birth weight, which, being a school psychologist, you should know could contribute to a variety of developmental delays and health problems."

Delays? Health problems? Because of me?

I walked back into the sunshine in a fog, holding a prescription for antinausea meds in one hand and my concave stomach in the other. My whole life, I'd been sure of one thing and one thing only—that I was going to be a great fucking mom. I'd known it as a little girl, giving bottles to my baby dolls. I'd known it as a teenager when I naturally found myself mothering all my wayward friends. I'd known it as I poured my heart and soul into my preschoolers, literally shedding blood, sweat, and tears to see them make progress. The idea of me being a good mom had never been challenged before, and I vowed, as I sat behind the wheel of my car, glaring up at my OB/GYN's office window, that it never would again.

I'll show you, motherfucker. I'm gonna grow a perfect baby. Just watch.

I was still just as obsessive about what I ate as I'd ever been, but now, I was counting milligrams of folate instead of calories. I was microwaving my lunchmeat to kill the listeria and abstaining from all caffeine and alcohol. I was making sure to get enough protein and calcium while cutting out processed foods and artificial dyes.

And, by my first ultrasound, they said I was on track to gain a healthy amount of weight and that my baby looked perfect.

Perfect. That word was everything I'd hoped to hear, but my joy and relief were overshadowed by anxiety and grief.

Not about the baby.

About the call I'd gotten two days before.

The call I'd been waiting for since the day I met Ronald "Knight" McKnight.

May 2009

I never saw Knight again after I moved in with Ken. He'd still called once in a while though. He'd said he was happy for me when I got married. He'd sounded sincere. He'd said he was still getting in a lot of bar fights, which didn't surprise me. He'd said he wouldn't live to see thirty.

He was right.

The news portrayed Ronald McKnight as a heroic veteran trying to break up a fight at a biker rally. They said he was shot during the altercation and died en route to the hospital. They showed a picture of him on the evening news, looking like an upstanding citizen in his military dress blues.

I didn't believe a word of it.

The Knight I knew wasn't a savior; he was a reckless, tattooed renegade with an explosive rage problem and a bad case of PTSD. He didn't break up fights. He started them. And, once he started them, I could see it taking a bullet to put him down.

But maybe that was just what I wanted to believe. Maybe it was easier for me to sleep at night, thinking Knight had brought his fate upon himself. Maybe the idea of him surviving two tours in Iraq just to be gunned down in the streets of the country he'd risked his life to serve was a tragedy I simply couldn't bear.

The pictures from my first ultrasound were still warm in my pocket as I walked into the Ivy and Sons funeral home. The place was packed wall-to-wall with greasy-looking bikers, the smell of cigarette smoke and gas fumes wafting from their leather cuts with every hug and back slap they gave one another. Girls with tattoos and torn black T-shirts wiped their heavily lined eyes as they watched a slide show on the far wall. Most of the pictures were of Knight on his chopper, Knight flipping off the camera, Knight petting one of his several rescued pit bulls *while* flipping off the camera. But one of them showed Knight posing with his arms around the necks of his club brothers, smiling.

I didn't recognize a single person in the photos—or in the room for that matter. No one from our high school had come, but why would they? Knight had pushed them all away, physically in most cases. His real dad was dead. His stepdad had a restraining order against him, and his mom…the last time I'd seen her, she had a pistol pointed at his face. Knight might not have found salvation or inner peace or even a reason to live, but as I looked around the room, it was obvious that he had finally found a family. And they'd loved him very much.

There was no formal service. No minister directing us in prayer. Just a gathering room full of bikers…

And one very open casket.

I noticed it as I turned to leave, over on the far side of the room. No one seemed to be paying any attention to it. Knight's MC buddies were all comforting each other and passing flasks around and reminiscing about old times. While Knight just lay there, being ignored at his own party.

I couldn't leave without at least saying hello.

Or, in this case, goodbye.

My pulse sped up with every step I took closer until it felt like it was going to pound its way right out of my chest. I'd spent almost half my life fearing Ronald McKnight, and suddenly, I was standing right next to him, trying to convince my body that it was safe.

I scanned his face, instinctively looking for those intense pale blue eyes, those laser-scope pupils that always burned right through my soul, but they were gone, snuffed out forever by two thin, veiny flaps of flesh. Without a whisper of pigment in his eyebrows, eyelashes, or slicked-back hair, Knight's leveling zombie eyes used to be the only pop of color on his otherwise pallid face. With them closed, his appearance was that of a man wearing a flaccid, flesh-toned rubber mask.

That was all he was, I guess. All any of us are. Just souls wearing masks.

But there was no one behind Knight's mask anymore. I could feel it. He was gone.

He's gone.

I'm safe.

He's gone.

I'm safe.

It was the mantra I used to repeat whenever I felt that sliver of fear slide down my spine. Whenever I felt those icy-blue eyes watching me from the shadows. But I would never feel that fear again.

I was free.

And so was Knight.

As my heart rate returned to normal, I realized that I had one hand in my jacket pocket, clutching the corner of my sonogram, and the other in my purse, clutching my can of pepper spray.

I pulled it out and stared at the leather pouch, tattered and worn, my thumb grazing the embossed letters. Unhooking it from my key ring, I took a deep breath and tucked it into the front of Knight's cut.

Patting the bulge beneath his leather vest, I whispered, "Bye, Knight," as my eyes welled with tears.

There was so much more I wanted to say, but my throat was too swollen with emotion to speak. So, I gave Knight one last look, committing every freckle and frown line to memory, and said it with my heart.

As I stepped outside, wishing like hell that I could drink or smoke or take something to make the pain in my chest go away, I caught the unmistakable scent of a menthol cigarette on the breeze. I inhaled deeply and followed my nose to a frail blonde woman sitting on the curb, smoking a skinny, six-inch-long Virginia Slim.

Candi.

My first instinct was to turn and run in the opposite direction, but the mother in me ached for the mother in her. Candi might not have been a good mom, but no one deserves to bury their only child. No one.

Sitting on the curb next to her, I opened my mouth to speak, but the only thing that came out was a sorrowful, "Hey."

Looking up, Candi's face was wet and wrinkled and makeup-free. I'd never even seen her without false eyelashes on before. She looked so old. So spent. Deep lines rimmed her thinning lips from years of smoking. Her crystalline-blue eyes were dull and bloodshot. And every muscle in her face sagged, as if she hadn't smiled in years.

"BB," she squeaked, her chin pulling in on itself. "Oh, BB." Throwing her skeletal arms around my slightly thicker body, she rested her forehead on my shoulder and sniffled. "I'm so happy you came."

Her redneck Southern accent, the one that she used to try to hide for her trophy-wife persona, was now on full display as well.

"Me, too." I patted her back with a stiff hand. "I'm so sorry."

Lifting her head, Candi looked me in the eyes. "I don't know nobody in there."

I smiled weakly. "Me either."

"I can't believe he's gone." She shook her head. "I always thought you were gonna be the mother of my grandchildren." Staring at a spot on the sidewalk, she added, "Now, I'll never have grandchildren."

I ran one hand over her bony back as I dragged my finger over the corner of the sonogram in my pocket. I didn't tell her about the baby. I just sat there and bore witness to her pain as the ash from her unsmoked cigarette fell onto my boot.

"Here," Candi said, suddenly stamping out her cigarette and reaching for something inside the neck of her black dress. "Ronnie woulda wanted you to have this." When her long acrylic nails emerged, they were pinching Knight's dog tags.

"Oh, Candi. No. You keep those."

"There's two of 'em," she said, unclasping the silver ball chain around her neck and sliding one off. "One for me"—she lifted her miserable eyes to mine as she held out her hand—"an' one for you."

I accepted the small metal plate stamped with Knight's identifying information hesitantly. I didn't feel right, taking it when I was married to someone else. But Candi was right. Knight would have wanted me to have it.

He would have wanted me to have the husband and the baby, too.

I swallowed my sobs as I hugged Candi goodbye, knowing I would never see her again. Then, I stood up, brushed myself off, and walked to my car, the end of one life and the beginning of another bouncing side by side in my pocket.

December 2009

My son was born seven months later after twenty-six hours of labor, two ineffective epidurals, and two worthless rounds of intravenous narcotics.

It turns out that some redheads are genetically resistant to painkillers.

Lucky me.

Ken was amazing through the whole process. He responded to all the orders I barked immediately, held one of my legs while I pushed, and watched me expel a little bald person out of my sliced-open vag hole like it was no big deal. He even cut the gnarly purple cord that came out with it.

When Ken handed the baby to me, I'd expected it to have its eyes closed like a little puppy but not this one. He stared me dead in the eye—*glared* was more like it—as if he were blaming me personally for what had just happened to him. I gave him my swollen boob as a peace offering. He accepted but refused to take his eyes off of mine the entire time he nursed.

"I hope you're amazing," I whispered down to my beautiful, healthy, oddly alert, and suspicious newborn, "because I am never doing that again."

Ken sat on the edge of the bed, and I watched him almost as intensely as our son watched me.

Would he cry? Would he be moved? Would he be freaked out? Would he be a good dad?

But all my worries were put to rest the moment the nurses came to take our son for his first bath.

Ken left with him and returned an hour later, pushing the hospital crib and talking a mile a minute. "They let me dry him off after his bath and change his diaper, and when you change his diaper, you have to remember to fold the front flap down because of his umbilical cord stump and—" Ken pulled out his phone and started showing me pictures he'd taken inside the nursery. "He's so long. Look at him when he was all stretched out. Twenty-one inches. And his head size is in the ninety-fifth percentile—"

"Yeah. I could tell while I was pushing it out." I smirked, but Ken ignored me and continued his energetic recap of everything I'd missed in the last hour.

God, he's talking so much.

And smiling.

This is weird. Why is he acting so weird?

And he's in half of these pictures. He actually had someone take pictures of him with the baby.

Oh my God, is Ken…excited?

Excited Ken was something I only got to see on the first day of football season every year and whenever he stumbled upon a Hugh Grant movie on TBS. But there he was, pacing around my hospital room, grinning and rambling about percentile ranks as I patiently waited for him to give me my baby back.

Ken wasn't *going* to be a great parent. He already was one.

I, on the other hand, had to work at it.

When I came home from the hospital, I looked like I was still five months pregnant. I was horrified by my postpartum body. All I wanted to do was chain myself to my treadmill and survive on a diet of hot water with lemon until the weight came off, but I couldn't. I'd chosen to breastfeed, which meant I had to eat. A lot. Then, I had to keep eating, even after the baby was weaned so that I would have enough energy to chase him around. Every meal—hell, every bite—was an excruciating battle between wanting to be a good mother and wanting to be thin.

But, I wanted to be a good mother more.

I started meditating to help myself stay focused on what was really important. I learned about gratitude. I learned that, instead of hating my body, I should be thankful for everything it had done for me. And during process of soul-searching, I also learned why I'd been so perfectionistic and self-harming in the first place; I had been born feeling incomplete.

I'd spent my whole life looking for something to fill that sense of emptiness—boys, drugs, alcohol, cigarettes, achievements, the quest for perfection, piercings, fast cars—but none of it had worked because the void wasn't existential. It wasn't emotional or imaginary. It was physical.

The emptiness was in my womb.

Ken never wanted to get married or have children, but he set his wants aside to take care of my needs. He opened his home to me when I was lost. He gave me a ring when I needed to feel secure. He showered me with support during though tough grad school years. And, no matter what color I dyed my hair or how sick I became, he always gave me his unconditional acceptance. Ken never once put any pressure on me to get healthy; he simply gave me the one thing I needed to do it myself.

My son.

Our happily ever after would have culminated there, but like his mother, Mini Ken had been born feeling incomplete as well. I could tell the moment I'd laid eyes on him that he was searching for answers. As he got older, he would roam the house, a determined scowl on his beautiful face, looking under beds and inside cabinets. Always searching. Never finding. I couldn't figure out what my smart, serious little boy was missing until he turned two and finally found the words to tell us.

"Mommydaddy," he said, his big blue eyes shifting from mine to Ken's, "when is my sister coming? Will she be here tomorrow?"

Mini Ken began asking about his mythical sister every day. He would go into our guest room and say, "Dis is my sister's room." He told us she had blonde hair and blue eyes. He said he would share his toys with her and push her on the swing. He even had the perfect name picked out for her—Frosting Spider-Man.

My heart went out to him. I knew firsthand what it felt like to miss someone you'd never met. I'd felt that way until the day he was born. If my little boy wanted a sister, I wanted to give him one.

Ken, of course, did not.

But, in true Ken form, he set his wants aside for ours.

That, and the fact that I promised him a vasectomy if everything went well.

April 2013

"What are you doing?" Ken squinted at me, leaning in the doorway of our master bathroom. "It's three in the morning."

I lowered my mascara wand and turned to face him, knocking my eyeshadow into the sink with my massive belly. "I think my water broke. Well, it's more of a trickle than a break, but I'm having some pretty serious—" I gripped the counter with both hands and hissed through my clenched teeth.

"Contractions?" Ken finished for me.

I nodded, my face twisted in pain.

"I'll call my mom to come over."

"No!" I took a deep breath, the viselike crushing pain at the base of my spine beginning to ease up. "Don't wake her up. Remember last time? We went to the hospital at six in the morning, and the baby wasn't born until eight at—" I winced and dropped the mascara, jamming my fingertips into my lower back for some counterpressure.

Ken raised a sleepy eyebrow at me. "Pack your shit. I'm calling my mom *and* the obstetrician."

Mrs. Easton arrived thirty minutes later, still in her pajamas. As she and Ken chatted in the living room, I tried to walk from one side of it to the other. I'd smile and comment on whatever they were talking about, take two steps, and double over in pain. Breathe, curse, wince, writhe, then stand back up, smile, and do it all over again.

"Uh," Mrs. Easton said, watching me in horror, "I think you need to get her to a hospital."

Ken helped me climb into the passenger seat of his SUV and then drove *past* the closet hospital to the better hospital. The one I'd already toured and filled out admission forms for. The one my doctor was supposed to meet me at as soon as we called him. The one that had my eighteen-page birth plan on file.

The one I was beginning to think I'd never see the inside of because my baby was about to be born in Ken's fucking Nissan Xterra.

They had an emergency parking area for those kinds of situations, but Ken didn't park there. He grabbed a spot in visitor parking, fucking sixty feet away from the door, and began unloading all the stuff he'd packed—my bag, his bag, the diaper bag, two regular pillows, my nursing pillow, my breast pump, a giant exercise ball, an extra copy of my birth plan in a clear plastic cover, cookies for the nurses…

"Ken!" I shouted, having only made it three feet away from the car before a massive contraction had me clinging to a concrete pillar for support. Pointing to the sliding glass doors ahead, I screamed, "Get a fucking wheelchair!"

Ken dashed off and returned seconds later with a wheelchair, an orderly, *and* a rolling cart for all our shit. I couldn't stand, but I didn't think I could sit either. So, I stood on the foot holders and gripped the armrests and rode into the hospital with my ass two feet off the seat.

When we got inside, the motherfuckers at the front desk made me sit/stand there while Ken filled out even…more… paperwork.

"I already…aaaaaaaaaaah…did that!" I screamed. Screamed. In the middle of the quiet hospital lobby, I screamed and writhed and then…the grunting started. Oh God. It was deep and guttural and sounded like I was taking the world's biggest shit. I was so embarrassed, but I couldn't stop the sounds coming out of my mouth. "My paperwork is on…uuuuuuuhhnggg…file! I need an…uuuuuuuhh-nnggg…epidural!"

I knew an epidural probably wouldn't work, but I was willing to try anything at that point.

"Ma'am, your doctor isn't here yet, but we have a midwife on staff who can deliver your—"

"Not a midwife. I need an anestheeeeeeeeeeeeeee-siologist!"

"Ma'am, I'm sorry, but there's no time. Your baby is coming right now."

My what is what?

And, with that, they wheeled me into a room, had me change into a giant paper gown—which was next to impossible with a head in my vagina—and then wheeled me into a delivery room where I was attacked by nurses.

I didn't see any of it. I couldn't have opened my eyes if I wanted to. The pain was so intense and unrelenting that all I could do was twist my face up, dig my fingertips into my thighs, and scream.

Oh, and grunt.

Luckily, the midwife was a fucking baby-birthing ninja angel, and twenty excruciating minutes later, she handed me an absolutely perfect baby girl with big blue eyes and long black eyelashes. This baby didn't glare at me the way her brother had. This one didn't have a care in the world. She blinked up at me a few times, then, satisfied with what she saw, little Frosting Spider-Man curled into my breast and nursed herself to sleep.

I smiled up at Ken, who looked pretty satisfied himself.

"Up high," he said, raising one hand in the air, a huge grin on his otherwise exhausted face.

I eyed my husband wearily, then gently slapped his hand, careful not to disturb the baby.

"No doctor. No epidural." He beamed. "This is gonna be the cheapest delivery ever!"

The End

Ken and BB's story continues in her bestselling, award-winning memoir, *44 Chapters About 4 Men*, available at http://a.co/dfJcjV2.

Read on for an excerpt…

Chapter 6: Enter the Evil Professor

August 29, 2013

Dear Journal,

There's a small chance that I might get disappeared soon, so I need you to know what happened in case the feds come snooping around.

I could write out the whole juicy story here, but I pretty much already did that in an email to my BFF, Sara, so I'm just going to copy and paste it in for the sake of time. And also, to prove that what I'm about to do was all *her* idea.

FROM: BB EASTON

TO: SARA SNOW

DATE: THURSDAY, AUGUST 29, 9:36 P.M.

SUBJECT: SHIT. JUST. GOT. REAL.

> *So…Ken read my fucking journal.*
>
> *I'm getting divorced.*
>
> *I'm getting poisoned or divorced.*
>
> *Just thought you should know.*

FROM: SARA SNOW

TO: BB EASTON

DATE: THURSDAY, AUGUST 29, 9:41 P.M.

SUBJECT: RE: SHIT. JUST. GOT. REAL.

No way. That doesn't sound like Ken. How do you know?

Sara Snow, PhD

Associate Professor, Department of Psychology, (name of university deleted)

FROM: BB EASTON

TO: SARA SNOW

DATE: THURSDAY, AUGUST 29, 9:47 P.M.

SUBJECT: RE: SHIT. JUST. GOT. REAL.

Dude, I know because, when I was coming downstairs a few nights ago after putting the kids to bed, I heard him slam my fucking laptop shut. That's how I know. By the time I got to the bottom of the stairs and rounded the corner into the living room, he was shoving my computer across the coffee table, looking guilty as shit.

He read my fucking journal, Sara. You have no idea what's in there. It's so, so graphic. After reading that shit, he could probably pick Knight's giant cock out of a lineup.

I haven't slept in, like, three days because I know, the second I close my eyes, Ken is going to go, "Shh, shh, shh," and smother me with a pillow.

Tell me what to do. Please!

FROM: SARA SNOW

TO: BB EASTON

DATE: THURSDAY, AUGUST 29, 10:01 P.M.

SUBJECT: RE: SHIT. JUST. GOT. REAL.

For starters, you should check your browser history. If whatever he read in your journal was that bad, then he probably used your computer to secure a safe house while he was at it. I'm going to save this email just in case you come up missing.

P.S. Why the hell didn't you password-protect your journal?

Sara Snow, PhD

Associate Professor, Department of Psychology, (name of university deleted)

FROM: BB EASTON

TO: SARA SNOW

DATE: THURSDAY, AUGUST 29, 10:13 P.M.

SUBJECT: RE: SHIT. JUST. GOT. REAL.

I know! I'm an idiot! I just honestly didn't think it was necessary. Ken never pays attention to anything I'm working on. I don't even think he knows that all the photos and paintings hanging in this house are mine. Plus, he's trying to watch all five seasons of The Wire and manage, like, four fantasy football leagues simultaneously right now. Who knew that fucker would pay enough attention to my covert typing to get suspicious?

I'm freaking out, Sara. It's like he's icing me or playing fucking mind games or something. Instead of dousing my computer with gasoline and piss, which would have been justified, he took me on a date. What the fuck is that?!?! Like, got a sitter, picked a restaurant, AND preordered movie tickets! I assumed he was going to serve me with papers at dinner since it was all so formal and out of character, but it was actually a really nice date. He didn't even make his usual complaint about the fact that he "could have purchased an entire vineyard" for the price of my one glass of Pinot G either.

Oh! OH! Then, after dinner, when I backed Ken into our bedroom so that I could say thanks by riding his lifeless body for a few minutes, he actually stopped me and asked if I wanted to try anything new. NEW! (As in, new to him, obviously. For a sex act to be new to me, it would require a stolen college mascot uniform, twelve yards of rappelling cable, a handful of gerbils, and thirty CCs of vampire blood.) And it was really good, Sara! The TV wasn't even on or anything!

And get this shit! The next day, Ken tells me that he's booked another sitter for next month so that we can go see David Koechner at The Punchline. Who is this man??? (Ken, not David Koechner. I know who he is, and he's fucking hilarious.)

Maybe he's going to off me at The Punchline? It is in a super-sketchy neighborhood…

FROM: SARA SNOW

TO: BB EASTON

DATE: THURSDAY, AUGUST 29, 10:35 P.M.

SUBJECT: RE: SHIT. JUST. GOT. REAL.

Ken's not icing you. He's responding to your intervention, B. Now that he has read your journal and knows how bored you are, he's making the appropriate adjustments. And the best part is that you didn't even have to talk about it. It's actually a beautiful design. I think you just discovered the holy fucking grail of marital behavior modification techniques!

Here's what you do. Now that you know he's reading your journal, you need to start planting really exaggerated stories in there so that you can milk this shit for all it's worth. Write specifically about whatever it is you want him to change, and make it as juicy as possible.

And I'M going to do a longitudinal study on the outcome so that I can go on Good Morning America and tell Robin Roberts how women across the country can save their marriages through Subliminal Spousal Bibliotherapy. (We'll call it SSB for short.) Bitch, you're going to get me tenure and an Audi R8 with this thing!

Sara Snow, PhD

Associate Professor, Department of Psychology, (name of university deleted)

FROM: BB EASTON

TO: SARA SNOW

DATE: THURSDAY, AUGUST 29, 10:48 P.M.

SUBJECT: RE: SHIT. JUST. GOT. REAL.

You.

Evil.

Fucking.

Genius.

I'm in. And I already have a list of target behaviors for progress monitoring:

1. *The initiation of hot, steamy, passionate hair-pulling sex*

2. *The giving of compliments*

3. *The bestowment of a nickname*

4. *And the procurement of a motherfucking heart tattoo with my name on it*

For data collection purposes, you can just set the baseline at zero in all four categories. Yes, zero—as in, Ken has never done any of those things. The way I see it, we have nowhere to go but up. I'll keep you abreast of my progress. (Pun intended!)

Also, you have to promise to tell George Stephanopoulos hi for me when you go on GMA. I've always liked him. I think it's because he reminds me of Michael J. Fox. Maybe don't tell him I said that. Or do?

Chapter 7: The Notorious K.E.N.

August 30, 2013

Dear Journal,

After consulting with the devil on my shoulder, I've decided to embark on a morally bankrupt psychological experiment with the hopes of transforming Ken into someone warm and affectionate whose love for me is so immense that he *needs* a tattoo of my name and/or likeness just so that he can better broadcast his feelings for me to the world. So, pack your bags and bring a flashlight, Journal, because from now on, you'll be hiding in a dark hole in the back of my hard drive under the title Baby Shower Diaper Cake Instructions.

Don't take it personally, Little Guy. It's for your own good. I need a place to take notes on Ken's progress without him catching wind of what I'm up to, and no man will ever come snooping around a file called Baby Shower Diaper Cake Instructions, located inside a folder called…wait for it…Cute Stuff I Found on Pinterest.

Oh, and don't get jealous, but in your old spot, I'm going to start planting a glossily exaggerated Lifetime movie version of you under the filename Super Private Journal That Ken Is Never, Never Allowed to Read Ever where I will plant completely fabricated stories about my ex-boyfriends, designed to inspire Ken to up his fucking game. And no, that filename isn't too obvious. Blatant reverse psychology is the only way to get shit done when you're dealing with a man—or a toddler.

Don't you read my journal again, Ken. Don't you do it. Oh…you'd better not.

It'll work. Trust me.

Aw, look at you, Journal. You're starting to feel bad for Ken, aren't you? That's adorable, but your sympathy is completely wasted on him. The man does not have feelings. I'm not entirely convinced that he even has nerve endings. I promise, you have absolutely nothing to worry about. Ken is a soulless gangsta, and he'll be just fine.

This playlist is a collection of songs that I either mentioned in the book, that I felt illustrated a feeling or a scene from the book, or that Ken made me add because he was trying to micromanage my playlist.

I am grateful to each and every one of the brilliant artists listed below. Their creativity fuels mine.

You can stream the playlist for free on Spotify at https://goo.gl/3uWecB.

Songs Added by BB

"26" by Paramore

"Alive with the Glory of Love" by Say Anything

"Bizarre Love Triangle" by Frente!

"Call It What You Want" by Taylor Swift

"Crazy" by Aerosmith

"Delicate" by Taylor Swift

"Drink About You" by Kate Nash

"El Scorcho" by Weezer

"Hands Open" by Snow Patrol

"IFFY" by Black Kids

"Jacked Up" by Weezer

"La La Lie" by Jack's Mannequin

"Swing Swing" by The All-American Rejects

"The Graveyard Near the House" by The Airborne Toxic Event

"This Charming Man" by Death Cab for Cutie

Songs Added by Ken

"Amber" by 311

"Cigarette Lighter Love Song" by Marvelous 3

"I Want You" by Third Eye Blind

"Please, Please, Please, Let Me Get What I Want" by The Smiths

"The Start of Something" by Voxtrot

Books by BB Easton

44 Chapters About 4 Men: A Memoir

THE 44 CHAPTERS SPIN-OFF SERIES

SKIN (Knight, Book 1)
SPEED (Harley, Book 2)
STAR (Hans, Book 3)
SUIT (Ken, Book 4)

FOR UPDATES ON NEW RELEASES, SALES, AND GIVEAWAYS, SIGN UP AT HTTP://EEPURL.COM/C4OCOH.

Ken, I think I've inflated your ego enough for one lifetime. Next!

Mom, you are the rock upon which I stand in order to touch the stars. If I am half as supportive of my children as you have always been of me, I'll be doing pretty damn well. Thank you for everything.

I want to thank **Ken's whole entire family** for knowing what I do, looking the other way while I do it, and selflessly agreeing to babysit so that Ken and I can fly all over the world in support of it. You might not be allowed to read my books or acknowledge that you know anything about them, but you still support me unconditionally, and for that, I am eternally grateful. Also, thank you for reluctantly letting me hug you now.

To **Larry and Miles**—I can't wait to tell the world what you've done for me. Thank you for opening the door to a future I never dared to dream for myself. You guys are my heroes.

To my Editors, **Jovana Shirley** and **Ellie McLove**—I am able to rest easy at night, knowing that my work is in your expert hands. I give you my heart, wrapped in newspaper, and you collaboratively turn it into a novel. Magicians, both of you. Thank you.

To my Beta Readers, **April C, Jamie Shaw, Sammie Lynn, Sara Snow, and Traci Finlay**—You girls are my ride or dies. I'd supervise an emergency body burial for any one of you badass bitches, no questions asked. Thank you!

Dr. Sara Snow, the scene with you at Bahama Breeze is only as funny as it is because I dug up actual emails from when we used to work together and stole all your jokes. I love your evil ass. Thank you for always inspiring me to be my best worst self.

Colleen Hoover, thank you for being born.

Tracey Frazier, you complete me. Literally. You finish my sentences. I love you and your beautiful face and your brilliant, fucked up books.

Staci Hart, Kandi Steiner, and Brittainy C. Cherry, thank you for expanding your CherrySteinHart trio into a quartet whenever I'm around. Getting to know you all better has been one of the highlights of my year.

To all my other author friends—In a society that teaches us to compete, compete, compete, you ladies choose to share instead. You share with me your time, your advice, your encouragement, your resources, and often, your platforms to help me succeed in an oversaturated market where so very few do. Thank you for letting this pink-haired, foul-mouthed, new kid sit with you. I love you!

To the girls (and boys) of #TeamBB—Thank you for the gorgeous Instagram teasers, the Facebook posts, the gifts, and the relentless pimping you've showered me with over the years. It is because of you, telling your friends and your book clubs and your sisters and your husbands to read my books, that I've been able to pursue this dream at all. I'm humbled by your support and proud to call you all friends. And a special shout out to my #TeamBB admins, **Kellie Richardson, Sunny Borek, and Sonya Paul**—If any of y'all ever need a kidney, I'm your girl.

And to **you**—If you are still reading this, thank you for stepping out of your comfort zone and taking a chance on a weird book series that's not quite romance and not quite memoir and mostly nonfiction but definitely fictionalized. I hope you enjoyed the ride. I hope it made you laugh. I hope it made you look at your partner and think, *Maybe this asshole isn't so bad after all.* I hope it made you look at your teen years and think, *Damn. I guess it coulda been worse.* And I hope it makes you look at your future and think, *If BB could survive all that, maybe I'm gonna be okay, too.* Because you are. I promise.

BB Easton lives in the suburbs of Atlanta, Georgia, with her long-suffering husband, Ken, and two adorable children. She recently quit her job as a school psychologist to write stories about her punk rock past and deviant sexual history full-time. Ken is suuuper excited about it.

If that sounds like the kind of person you want to go around being friends with, then by all means, feel free to drop her a line. Just don't be surprised if you get a reply at four a.m. with an inexplicable Shia LaBeouf meme or a text that was clearly meant for someone else. BB is what doctors call *chronically sleep-deprived*, or as Ken pronounces it, "depraved."

You can find her:

On email: authorbbeaston@gmail.com

On her website: www.authorbbeaston.com

On Facebook:
www.facebook.com/bbeaston

On Instagram:
www.instagram.com/author.bb.easton

On Twitter: www.twitter.com/bb_easton

On Pinterest:
www.pinterest.com/artbyeaston

On Goodreads: https://goo.gl/4hiwiR

On Spotify:
https://open.spotify.com/user/bbeaston

Selling signed books and original art on Etsy: www.etsy.com/shop/artbyeaston

Giving stuff away in her #TeamBB Facebook group:
www.facebook.com/groups/BBEaston

And giving away a free ebook from one of her author friends each month in her newsletter: http://eepurl.com/c4OCOH